Flee from Evil

CONNIE ALMONY

Dedication

To my three sisters, Jody Kilmer, Kelley Burcham, and Jan Wisooker. Your love and encouragement have strengthened me. Your wisdom has enlightened me. Your care has protected me ... And your personalities have given me plenty of fodder from which to paint colorful characters!!!

Thank you, Jesus!

And we know that in all things God works for the good of those who love Him, who have been called according to His purpose. (Romans 8:28)

Note on Autism:

The character in this novel who has been diagnosed with the developmental disorder known as autism is in no way meant to represent the characteristics of all those who struggle with the effects of this disorder or the family members who care for them. This disorder takes many forms and the challenges are all unique to those dealing with it. The character, Tibo, was inspired by only one young man who has blessed me greatly. I praise God for the opportunity to know him as I do, and hope others will see him for his gifts as well.

Table of Contents

Prologue

Dear Diary,

I can't sleep. I had one of those dreams tonight. I don't know why I call them dreams when they really are nightmares, but they carry a truth I don't want to believe, while preparing me to deal with what's to come. And even now, I'm left with a weird mixture of fear … and awe.

It's been over a year since the last one, three days after my fourteenth birthday. The one I now know was telling me Daddy would die, preparing me for the grief, and reminding me to focus on eternity in spite of my temporary loss. I'd written about it in my journal the next morning (at least three notebooks ago), but I can't seem to find it now. I think I lost that book in the move from Philadelphia.

And yet, I need to remember …

In the first dream, my entire family—Mom, Dad, my little brother, Tibo, and I—walked through a lush garden on a beautiful day. The sweet smell of honeysuckle saturated the air, birds sang in the trees, and a soft breeze tickled my skin. It was amazing how a dream could stir every sense the way this one did. Mom and Dad swung Tibo by his arms. He giggled so hard I thought he'd turn blue. Tibo's body never seems to warn him of its limits like other kid's bodies do—one of the many dysfunctions that come with his version of autism.

The wind picked up, whipping through our clothes and hair. The fluffy white clouds grew dark and full then lightning split the sky.

I looked to Daddy. He squeezed my shoulder, and gave me the it's okay *smile. The one he'd wear while handing me tissues as a little girl having a tear-fest over a lost stuffed animal or a fight with my best friend. Somehow, no matter how bad things were, that smile made everything right. I knew, at least, my Daddy loved*

1

me.

Just as my pulse slowed with the gesture, the wind grew fierce and the black clouds formed into scaly, dragon-like creatures that swooped down and around us with extensive oscillating wings, lifting us off our feet, and setting us back to earth. After my toes touched the ground, I scanned the garden for my dad, only to spy him in the taloned grip of one of the creatures as it flew toward the sun.

My heart took off again as my mother clutched Tibo in a fit of hysterics. But Daddy gave me the smile once more. A tinge of melancholy laced his voice as he called out. "We'll be together again soon, Sweetheart. Until then, lean on your heavenly Father."

The clouds broke open, and amidst the brilliant beams of the sun's rays pouring to the earth, all four creatures erupted into a glistening white reflected against the silver scales that covered their bodies, radiating a majestic beauty. Somehow, I knew my father was in good hands.

I think about his words, to lean on God, every day. I need to remind myself each morning since I no longer have an earthly father to support me. But what did he mean that he'd see me soon?

Was tonight's dream the answer to that question?

Once again the vision placed us in the garden—only Mom, Tibo and me, this time. My little brother spun in circles, as he always does, only in this dream the spinning seemed to possess a purposefulness they'd never had before. Again, the sky turned dark, and the clouds formed creatures. Again, I was lifted with the wind, but rather than being settled back to earth, I found myself in the arms of a beast. A stretching distance yawned between myself and my family.

Where was this creature taking me?

As the ominous form carried me through the sky, darkness and light flashed around me as though the two fought a heated battle against each other. Were they fighting for me? Were the creatures my enemy ... or my protection?

What is God trying to tell me now? I'm afraid to ask. Am I going to die? Will I see my Daddy soon as he'd promised in the other dream?

I feel peace in the possibility. But my only concern, if this is truly the case, is who will care for Mom and Tibo when I'm gone?

Sophie

Chapter One

Cassandra strode through the parking lot, her kids, Sophie and Tibo, in tow. "I can't believe you still go to this church, Mom."

Mom lifted her brow. "You mean the redneck church?"

"I didn't say that." Cassandra's ten-year-old son turned in a circle—one of his many autism perseverations. She pulled him along.

Mom tucked her purse under her arm. "But that's what your fancy friends at that Country Club used to call it."

Cassandra ground her teeth. "They weren't my friends, Mom. They were patrons. I waitressed there, and that was a long time ago."

Mom waved her hand. "Didn't you hang out with a few?"

Cassandra shrugged to stave off the shiver her body ached to do. She didn't want to go there. Too many bad memories. Tibo took another circle. Sophie, his fifteen-year-old sister, prodded him straight this time.

"You know Jesus was a redneck."

Would her mother ever understand that Cassandra's choice to get a college degree had nothing to do with placing herself above her family, as Mom always seemed to suggest. She just loved the study of things, and knew God chose each to follow different paths with different goals, all for the same glory.

Mom's chin hitched higher. "That's okay. Since Pastor Vince started here, we've become very diverse. His goal was to make us look more like the body of Christ. You know, different parts with different functions, all working in the same body."

Huh? Did Mom just pick those words from her brain.

4

Cassandra might just like the new associate pastor.

"But even so, we've kind of adopted the term, redneck. It was first used for field workers with sunburned backs, so we take it to mean hard-working and down-to-earth. At least that's what Pastor Vince always says. You'll love Pastor Vince. I think he's leading the sermon this morning."

Cassandra sighed. The words *you'll love Pastor Vince* seemed her mother's mantra these days.

"He's cute. He's single."

"Mom—"

"And he's refined. Well educated. Just your type."

So maybe he didn't look like a Duck Dynasty knock-off. "And a former drug dealer as I recall you mentioning."

"Yes, a forgiven sinner."

Or a man capitalizing on his wastrel youth.

"Mom, I'm not looking to replace Tim." There'd never be another Tim. He had everything the world could offer in terms of physical possessions and still willing to give it all away. That's why his parents had always kept a tight rein on his earnings at their pharmaceuticals company. Why had Tim let them control his life? Cassandra guessed he'd hoped they'd come to know Jesus one day like he had in college.

Finally reaching the front steps of the church, Cassandra and her mom shook hands with the greeters.

Patting Mom's arm, Cassandra said, "I'll take Tibo to Children's Church." She released a breath. "And explain everything."

Mom pointed. "Down that hall, first door on the right. I already gave the teacher the heads up about Tibo. He'll be fine."

Cassandra wasn't convinced. She wished she'd interviewed the woman before they came, but with the move from the large home she'd lived in with her husband of almost 16 years, back to her home town of Water's Edge, Maryland, she'd been a bit preoccupied.

She squeezed her son's hand, and peered at the blond hair and profile so much like her late husband's. "Your Daddy loved you so much."

If only she could be certain Tibo understood.

"Much," he repeated, as he usually did the last word of her sentences.

After introducing herself to the Children's Church leader, and enduring the look of fear at the word *autism*, Cassandra assured the woman her son was docile and wouldn't cause any trouble. Hadn't her mother already explained this? More questions followed. Cassandra answered each, and gave the teacher her cell number, promising to keep it on despite the rule of no phones on during the service.

Exiting the room on a sigh, she glanced at her watch then stopped at the closed sanctuary door. The minister's voice murmured from the other side. Not the familiar rasp of the senior pastor, Pastor John, whom she'd grown accustomed to as a child attending Water's Edge Community Church. Something about the tone gave her gooseflesh. Smooth and silky—like a scam artist's voice, selling a bill of goods she didn't need to buy. Boy, she was predisposed not to like this guy. Was it because her mother wanted to fix them up?

A greeter wished her a good morning as he opened the door. If only Mom didn't have to sit near the front—probably to ogle the minister she'd been raving about for years now.

Cassandra accepted the Bible from the gentleman in the back, and walked down the center aisle as the pastor's voice praised his Creator. Too embarrassed at coming in late, she focused on straightening her pencil skirt and finding her family in the second-row pew.

But that voice …

So familiar, it drew out memories she'd hidden deep—dark memories.

This time more than gooseflesh erupted from her skin. Her knees threatened to buckle. She didn't want to confirm her fears, but she had to. She pulled her gaze from the carpeted floor, up the steps of the altar, ascending from the loafers, crisp jeans, tidy polo, dark goatee … into the eyes of …

Satan!

~*~

Whoa! That was worse than the knife that nearly killed him so many years ago. Vince knew the congregation noticed too. They shifted in their seats waiting for him to continue what had formerly been an unblemished sermon.

The woman looked up and stole his sanity.

Cass ...

Man, she still looked good. Those auburn curls cascading down her shoulders. But it was more than that. Her green eyes blazed as she caught sight of him in the pulpit. He thought she might take the rest of the aisle and hammer him dead.

Instead, she froze. Jaw clenched. Hands balled. She stepped back like she was going to flee the enemy, until a young girl called out to her.

"Mom," the dark-haired teen whispered forcefully. "We're right here."

Cass thawed. Vince could almost see the icicles breaking off her shoulders and hitting the ground. She managed a weak smile, but her eyes were filled with something else. Probably the memories he'd given her. Memories he wished he could cherish, but he'd ruined them. Instead, they held themes of betrayal and hurt.

I am forgiven. He had to say that to himself in a way he could believe it. He shuffled through his sermon notes and saw those words scribbled on the sides. When had he written them?

A peace washed over him, but the cloud still hung over his head. *Even though I walk through the valley of the shadow of death ...*

He sensed he was headed to that valley again. A different path this time, but shadow and death lurked all the same.

Vince finally mustered speech. "You are forgiven." He scanned the faces of the parishioners. Some enraptured by his supposed oratory gift, others seemingly incredulous that he'd faltered. He'd never done that before.

His gaze hit on Cass, and he couldn't drag it away. "You are forgiven," he repeated. Her jaw tensed and her nostrils flared. Vince swept his attention over her head and around the congregation again. "You are set free."

Crazy. Seeing Cass at that moment reminded him of how free he really was. Far from the man he'd been before. He no longer bore the same chains. Though he could see Cass still saw him in light of those. He couldn't tell her. Not today. Because if the congregation knew she was part of his past, after the spectacle he'd just made of himself, they'd also know she was part of *that* past—the one he'd admitted to when he first became a pastor here. He couldn't do that to her. She was different from all the rest. The one who truly loved him. Maybe not him for him, but she loved him because that's the person she was. He glanced toward her to confirm the ire in her eyes. Was she still that person?

The service ended. Vince took his place at the exit, greeting the grateful congregants.

"Pastor Vince." Eleanor Drummond grasped his hand with a shake that could rival a linebacker's. "Never seen you flounder like that before." She didn't mince words. Just stared those chocolate brown eyes into his, as if to read his thoughts.

He gave a weary chuckle. "It happens to the best of us." His eyes wavered, but he refrained from scanning for Cass, as he continued to wonder why her husband hadn't attended with her. "Lost my place. Guess God needs to keep me humble." He squeezed her hand and tilted his smile the way that always weakened the ladies. "Happens to the best of us," he repeated, his mind whirling with torturous memories.

"Pastor Vince." Kat Lewis, sporting contrasting blond and brown tresses, pinched the edges of his hair. "Gettin' a little long, don't ya think?"

"I have an appointment with you this week." He winked.

Her husband reached out his tattoo-laden arm to shake. "You flirtin' with my wife, Pastor." His growl ended with a note at humor, but left Vince shaken just the same.

"Of course not, Billy."

Kat smacked her husband on the sleeve of his church-going Harley T-shirt—the one less faded and without holes. "You know I only have eyes for you."

Billy fished his fingers through his motorcycle-blown hair. "Then maybe you should stop touchin' the pastor's neck."

"That's my job you big dope."

Should the church do a Bible study on love and respect in marriage? Vince smiled as he looked between the two parishioners. He couldn't find a couple more in love than this one. Their love just looked a little different sometimes.

"Wonderful sermon." Greta Hessing practically worshiped him. Great. He could use an ally. "This is my daughter, Cassandra."

"Cass …" *Breathe.*

Her eyes burned into his.

He sucked in some air. "Cassandra, nice to meet you." He gave a curt, but friendly nod.

Cassandra's nod was not so friendly. She gathered a young boy and the teenage girl to her, and trundled them out the door.

Mrs. Hessing's brows knit as she stared after her daughter. She turned back to Vince. "I'm sorry. I've taught her better than that." She put her hand to her chest. "I guess things are still hard for her since her husband's death a year ago."

He schooled the shock from appearing on his face. Cass had already suffered too much with the early loss of her father. He'd been told she'd married well that fall, and always hoped her husband was a man who'd care for her as she'd deserved. Vince certainly hadn't been that man. And now, more grief.

Vince nodded. "Yes, very hard, Mrs. Hessing." *Search for platitudes.* "Just keep praying. God will get her through."

Ugh! He hated platitudes—even if they were true—but he couldn't reach his heart right now. Must be somewhere nailed to the blue carpet, under his feet.

~*~

9

How dare he?

Cassandra's teeth hurt from clenching so hard through that entire service. She now knew what it was like to turn to stone. It had been her only defense as the memories assaulted her, tearing at her weakened flesh.

How dare he act like he didn't even know her? Although, in a way, she was glad he did. She didn't need to explain her past relationship with him to her mom.

How dare he become a pastor? What a joke. Vince Steegle a pastor. A beloved pastor at that. Her mother practically worshiped the grass he trod. *Pastor Vince, this* and *Pastor Vince, that.* Cassandra had had no idea her mother's icon of righteousness was Satan incarnate. Last she knew, he'd aspired to politics.

Cassandra pushed her kids through the parking lot. Sophie almost tripped as she stepped over a curb. Tibo did his requisite twirl and followed behind.

"Tibo, hurry up." She waved at him like they were crossing a busy intersection.

He caught up.

She rushed them over to the used Lincoln Aviator Tim's parents had bought her five years before his crash in the Lexus. They sat silently in the car, waiting for Mom, but the woman took her time moseying from person to person, greeting them as if she had nowhere better to go. She didn't, but Cassandra needed to be free of this place—now.

"Mom, why did you rush us out of there?" Sophie's voice wobbled from the back seat. Cassandra knew she hesitated to ask. Always so keen to Cassandra's emotions. So mature for someone so young, having helped to care for her special-needs brother, and transition to life without a father … or his family's money. Not to mention all the accusations she'd endured from her paternal grandparents. They never said them to her face, but it was apparent in everything they did. They'd never accepted her little Sophie as their own.

10

~*~

Sophie's mom just turned the ignition, practically squealing wheels out of the church parking lot. She never even answered the question Sophie had asked, not even the one in Grandma's eyes when she finally got into the front seat of the car.

What was that about?

Mom had been on edge from the moment she entered the sanctuary, and now her knuckles were white against the pink of her fingers gripping the steering wheel. She must have had a run-in with the children's church leader over Tibo.

Sophie glanced to the seat beside her where her little brother smiled at the vehicles passing by. "Fire." He pointed to an emergency engine.

Sighing, Sophie pulled her hair behind her ears then stared at the Midnight Blue nail polish chipping from the edges of her thumb. She didn't even know why she painted her nails. It wasn't like there were any interested boys around she could look good for.

Mom's eyes darted to Grandma then back on the road. Her jaw hardened as if working tighter against the questions she refused to answer. Could Tibo's teacher have been that bad?

If only Tibo could talk like other ten-year-old boys. If only he could understand even simple directions. If only he could read, tie his shoes, pull his own covers up on a frigid night. He'd shiver to death before thinking to do that.

If only the world could see him for all he was rather than what he wasn't.

If only …

Another sigh escaped. It had been Tibo who sat on the arm of the chair and played with her hair as Sophie had sobbed her heart out after they'd found out her Daddy had died. Mom had been too busy retching in the bathroom to comfort her. Tibo's soft fingers had tugged so gently on the strands it felt like a caress. He'd searched her eyes, his brows scrunched, as if trying to figure

11

out where the tears had come from on her face. "Pway." His single word meant so much. Reminding her that God was with them. Peace and love seemed to pour from him into her, making her believe everything would be all right.

How could he do that? Only Tibo had such a gift.

The car's tires crunched over the gravel before Sophie had realized they were home. Mom was out of the car even before the engine stopped rattling, Grandma close behind. "What is wrong with you?"

Mom kept walking as though she could outrun Grandma's determined strides.

Sophie unclipped Tibo's seatbelt as his name drifted from their conversation. Grandma never wanted to talk about Tibo's "issues" in front of him. Did she know how far her voice carried?

Tibo's eyes communicated thanks before he opened the car door. Good thing that latch wasn't as tough as Dad's Lexus's used to be.

Sophie's mind flashed to the image of the Lexus mangled by the side of the road as they'd passed it that night. Mom screeched her breaks, got out of the car, and took off running toward the crash scene. A firefighter blocked her flailing body as she screamed Dad's name then fell to the asphalt and cried.

Sophie had turned numb. She'd stayed in the car to make sure Tibo was safe. Just like she did today.

Now, they stepped up the front, wooden steps that creaked with loose boards, and entered the small house—now her home.

"Why don't you tell me, then?" Grandma's voice carried through the halls. Mom's was low and controlled.

Sophie tugged Tibo's gentle fingers, and led him back out. "Let's go for a walk."

Tibo smiled as only he could, obediently following.

They strolled down the street, noting the water to the right, where the Chesapeake Bay emptied into inlets all around Water's Edge, Maryland.

So beautiful here. But something hung in the air like a

dark, city smog. Sophie sensed it as they drove from Philadelphia. So thick, so heavy. It seemed to weigh on her mother even more than her father's death.

Sophie knew her mother could weather anything in time because she relied heavily on her faith. With Dad's help, she'd even overcome bouts of panic attacks years ago.

But today, something changed. Could that something crush her?

Chapter Two

Hands held her forcefully to him. His mouth closed onto hers as she tried to scream. It didn't matter. There was no one to hear.

He laughed as she struggled to free herself from his grip. He tore at her blouse and unbuttoned her jeans. She screamed again, only to receive the same torment as before.

He fell against her in the grass, his weight pinning her as she called out.

Only crickets answered.

"Please ..." as if this monster would heed her polite request. *"Don't do this."*

He laughed again as he thrust his weight to subdue her thrashing.

"Why?" Did it really matter?

"Because I can."

Cassandra broke from the sheets that bound her, and clasped them to her breast as though they could protect her. Her heart pounded against the fist at her sternum that held the bedclothes like a shield. Her hand almost moved with the hard beat against bone.

She labored for air and swung her gaze around the darkened room. Not her home. Where was she?

Mom's. Cassandra's childhood bedroom. Her pulse slowed, but the breath labored on.

As her eyes adjusted to the light, she took in the same furniture, the same walls—the colors she woke to the morning after ...

The pictures! They were different. She peered at the comforter over her legs. Different too. She bunched it under her arms and trod down the hall to the living room. Also different. Thank goodness her mother had redecorated after her father's death that fall. Maybe Mom wanted to escape memories as well.

Cassandra dragged the bedspread across the living room and stubbed her toe with a clatter. Tibo's cars had been lined up straight out from the wall. Rather than curse the pain the toy pick-up had caused her pinky toe, she grinned at the thought of her sweet little boy and his kooky obsession making straight lines with his belongings.

The vision of her small son's smile made her muscles release. Her memory traveled to the words of his newest speech therapist who was certain she could improve his language. That was what they all said having heard him mutter what seemed to be full, grammatically mature and contextually appropriate sentences under his breath, only to never be repeated no matter how many times a person asked him to. More was going on in her son's mind than he was able to display. She knew it. But how to unlock that information was the question no one had the answer to.

After rubbing the appendage that took the hit from the small vehicle, she stretched her comforter over the couch, and doubled back to the blow-up mattress where her son slumbered. Leaning in, she pressed her lips to his warm temple. He stretched and curled again, pulling the sheet from his shoulder. Cassandra lifted the cover to his chin as he cooed in his sleep.

Peace. It seemed to pour from him and into her. So unlike what she'd seen from other children with autism. She thanked God for that one reprieve, but wondered—as always—if it would last.

Taking Tibo's gift of calm, She headed back to the living room, snuggled into the brown, microfiber couch, balled into a fetal position under the plush comforter, and sighed.

She thought back to what woke her. Why those dreams tonight? She hadn't had one in almost eight years. Tim had comforted her through them before, until one day they were no more.

But now, she no longer had Tim to hold her. Only memories of Tim. And memories of … things she didn't want to remember.

She'd slept in that bedroom a week now, since they moved back. So, why the nightmares tonight?

Images of Vince Steegle slid through her mind, tainting both past and present. Some held hints of hopes she'd had of a future with him, which only proved to be a lie. She needed to shake free, but knew she couldn't as long as that man was so near.

Could she live here with her mother? She had no other choice. Despite her in-laws vast wealth, there was none available to her. Not for her, nor the children who had called their son Daddy.

There was nowhere to go. No jobs that would allow her the care of a high-maintenance, special-needs child and the bills that came with his therapies. There seemed no options but to live with her mom who could help her watch over Tibo, and give her a place to live at no cost. She glanced at the once diamond ring setting, now sporting a piece of glass fashioned to look like the stone her husband had given her. The means with which she'd paid the remainder of her bills before leaving Philadelphia.

Could her family home be the respite she'd hoped to have for her and her kids? Not if it meant enduring the mention of her mother's pastor … unless Cassandra told her mother what he really was.

No. She couldn't do that. She couldn't even speak the words.

Cassandra closed her eyes on a breath and prayed, "Father why have you exchanged good for evil?"

We know that all things work for the good of those who love Him.

Could she believe that? Cassandra knew Tim would.

But after years of finally learning to love her best friend, Tim was now dead.

~*~

16

Vince swung the pitching wedge and connected with the ball. It lofted to the edge of the circle he'd cut into the field beside the church. He'd have to make his little green larger the next time he brought his mower to the grounds. Couldn't seem to hit anything today.

"Rough morning?" John sauntered up behind him, and thrust his hands into his navy pants.

Vince nodded.

"Good thing you have this little patch of heaven to help you think." That's what Vince had called this field next to Water's Edge Community. His own back yard wasn't much more than a postage stamp, so he couldn't practice chipping there. It was nice to clear his mind this way after a long day. Only this day had just begun.

Vince swatted at another ball in the line. Shank.

John groaned. "She must have been important to you. Don't think I've ever seen you flub a shot like that before." Evidently, Vince's reaction to the latecomer yesterday hadn't escaped John's notice.

Vince pulled another ball with his club.

"Do you wanna talk about it?"

Vince shook his head.

"It might help to unload your burdens."

Vince drew in a breath and leaned on the club. After several heartbeats, he met John's fatherly gaze. "I know, John. I don't think I can right now." He wasn't sure what he thought or felt. What could he say? He didn't even want to tell the story since it was only partly his. Telling it would reveal things Cass wouldn't want known. Could he talk to anyone about it?

"I take it you hurt her pretty bad."

Vince's shoulders slumped. He almost dropped the club in the grass.

"I'm sorry, Vince. I didn't mean to lay more guilt on your shoulders. I just want you to know you can come to me. I won't judge. I know you've been forgiven alrea—"

17

"Not by Cass." Vince gasped at his own use of her name. He hadn't meant to say it. He hadn't meant to reveal it, even though it was obvious John already knew. But to confirm it with his own lips felt like sacrilege.

"She's Greta Hessing's daughter. I've known Cassandra since she was a little girl."

That stilled Vince. It hadn't even dawned on him that this had been Cassandra's church before it had been his. Now he knew he couldn't tell John. He felt like an extra heel having hurt a member of the man's flock.

"She's a very sweet and caring person."

More knives turned into his flesh at how he'd victimized someone so good, so vulnerable.

"Her faith has always been strong, even in the hardest of circumstances." John jangled the change in his pocket. "She'll forgive you eventually."

Vince's head rocked back and forth. His guilt was too thick to penetrate. He pushed out the breath that seemed to strangle him. "I don't think I could if I were her."

John dropped a hand on Vince's shoulder. "Let's just thank God she's better than you." He pushed up a little smile that lightened the air around them.

"She is that." Vince swallowed hard.

John squeezed Vince's shoulder, leaving him with that fatherly strength before turning back to the building. Vince always loved how John not only knew what to say, but also knew when not to say anything at all. He'd leave Vince in the field to work out his frustration with the golf ball then hash it out later in prayer to his Creator. And if he needed to talk, Vince knew John would listen. Though this was not a story Cass's childhood pastor should hear.

So for now, the golf balls would know his self-inflicted wrath.

~*~

"I thought I told you to stack the manure bags in the garden center."

Kevin Perkins' gaze slid from the paint cans to his supervisor who was full of the stuff himself. "I was just—"

"Don't mouth me. And no excuses." The squat man's left eye twitched when he got excited. "It's growing season, and we need the garden section stocked."

Growing season. Kevin peered at the little man's patch of facial hair. For some reason it made him think of a *growing* fungus. Kevin squeezed his fists tight. He'd like to rip out that weed.

"Excuse me." A red-haired lady interrupted. "Is there someone who can help me choose paints?"

Kevin shifted to leave.

Squat man's voice cracked. "Sure. Kevin'll help you."

Kevin's eyes burned like fire. If only they had projectile capability. He plastered a you-know-this-is-a-fake-smile on his face, but it dropped as he got a better look at the woman in front of him—Cassandra Hessing. The girl who thought she was too good for everyone in high school. Too self-righteous with all that religion. But not too self-righteous when it came to dating rich boys.

His gaze dropped to the rock on her finger. That's right, she married into that pharmaceuticals family. Mega-wealth. Figures. Kevin had heard the guy died. Probably leaving her dripping in dough.

He waited for her to recognize him. Didn't know why. Not like she ever paid attention to him then. His eyes roamed down the buttons of her blouse and up again. He'd thought about her night and day for at least three years after graduation.

Cassandra's lashes lifted as he caught her eye. A flicker passed through them. "Did you—?"

"I don't know why you have to start painting right away. It's like you've been on fire all day." The older lady next to Cassandra, stared as if waiting for a response.

"Grandma, please …" The tone of the teen girl with them seemed to placate the woman.

A young blond boy palmed every last paint can Kevin had just stacked. "No touch." He kept repeating the phrase with every contact.

Better not knock them over.

Cassandra tugged him away like she was protecting the boy from Kevin's heated glare. "He has autism." Her words came out as if to accuse Kevin of stabbing the kid. So much for happy reunions.

The diamond ring flashed from the florescent lights above as she pulled a curl from her eyes. Her daughter didn't seem to have inherited much of the curls and none of the red. Coal black. But her blue eyes grabbed him in just the same way Cassandra's did.

Cassandra shifted. "Can you help us or not?"

Kevin's attention dropped to the ring again before scanning the high priced outfit and fancy shoes. Reminded him of his ex-wife. Is that what you call the deceased? An ex? Except that woman didn't come with the hefty bank account. She was better at unloading it. Kevin had taken care of that little fault.

"Sure, what can I do for you?" He made his smile more genuine this time. He could help Cassandra all right—right out of her inheritance. It was the reason Kevin worked the retail establishment. He'd roam the aisles, assisting customers and suggest they hire a professional for their home improvement needs. Oh yes, and he just happened to be that professional. Brilliant, if he did say so himself. A great way to case a house for valuables. He could only imagine the valuables Cassandra possessed.

~*~

Aisles and aisles of paint. Aisles and aisles of lumber. Sophie tugged and redirected Tibo as he twirled and touched things, grinning like the feel of the cold metal cans and shelves brought him relief of some kind.

Grandma had abandoned them long ago to look into the

garden section.

Mom charged through rows with the orange-vested guy who'd gone from talking her through paints to promising to give her a reasonable quote for the addition he'd build on the back of Grandma's house. Sophie didn't think they'd do that until after Mom finally found a job. But Grandma said she'd foot the bill, and the guy agreed to a payment plan. Mom was hooked.

Something about him gave her the creeps. One minute, Mom was getting all defensive about Tibo. The next he was charming her into a contracting job.

Sophie shuddered.

Finally, they got in the line with a basket full of paints and brushes. But just as the lady in front of them finished paying …

"Oh, I forgot the tape."

"Mom." Too late, Mom was down the aisle, beyond hearing. The lady behind Sophie harrumphed.

The cashier—who was hotter than Juan Pablo, the way his blond hair curled around his ear and his T-shirt stretched over his biceps—took the paint brush and whispered, "Don't worry, I'll take it slow." His wink made her go all silly inside. Searching over the brush, his strong fingers pried off the price sticker, secretly flicking it to the floor under the counter. Giving Sophie a knowing look, he said, "I'll have to get a price check on this item."

The woman behind sighed so hard Sophie felt the breath in her hair.

The cashier switched his numbered sign to blink, and gave the brush to another orange-vested employee. "Can you get me a price on this?"

He and Sophie shared a smile as he scanned the other items—carefully. They rang up on the display.

Out of breath, Mom rushed back to the line carrying a roll of blue tape. "Got it."

Hot dude scanned it as his friend handed him a new brush.

"Fifty-eight dollars and eighty three cents, total."

Mom released a lungful of air while pulling out her credit

card. Sophie knew every penny counted right now, which is why she didn't understand the need to repaint the bedroom or add another room, even if Grandma said she'd help with the cost. Sophie could continue to share a bed with Grandma, and Tibo liked his blow-up mattress.

Mom pushed the cart away from the cashier.

Sophie turned. "See ya round." Where did that come from? She waved to the guy even.

His smile was intoxicating. "Name's Sky."

Sky. "I'm Sophie." Down-boy, heart!

Chapter Three

The furniture had been pushed to the center of the room. Drop cloths were strewn over the carpet. A step ladder was placed here and there. Cassandra scanned the bedroom. She was almost ready to open the paint cans.

First, she needed to put the hairbrushes, make-up, and curling iron into drawers. She opened a top one and cleared the junk into it … except the silver music box her grandmother had given her when she was a little girl, complete with a pile of lint balls sticking out of the top. Another one of Tibo's idiosyncrasies—collecting lint in any container with a hinged lid.

Cassandra picked up the music box, and read the verse again on the bottom—Jeremiah 33:3. Good one. This needed to be handled with care. She opened her lingerie drawer, and tucked it deep under her unmentionables, smiling thinking of the word her grandmother would have used for her undergarments.

Sophie entered the bedroom in an old T-shirt and cut-off shorts, long, dark hair wrapped in a bun with a bandanna framing her hairline.

She held out the paint can. Sea-foam green. "Are we starting with this one?"

Cassandra planned to alternate colors on each wall. She didn't just want it to look different in the day time. The contrasting colors would stand out even in the dim light of dawn—her most vulnerable time, when the nightmares seemed most vivid. This way she could wake up and allow her mind to move away from the memories rather than confirm them.

Mom peeked in. "You know that Kevin guy is only going to scuff your walls when he tromps through with his equipment to build the addition."

Cassandra ignored her. She needed this done now. Otherwise she'd have to explain her continual trips to the couch for restful sleep.

"Grandma." Sophie pointed a playful, reprimand her way. Her daughter was her biggest defender since her daddy died. Cassandra couldn't believe how much of Tim's character shown in her.

"Where's Tibo?" This was Cassandra's constant question since Tibo had learned to walk. Her quiet son would drift in and out of rooms as though only an apparition. It sometimes jolted her the way he'd appear out of nowhere, and worse, sometimes *dis*appear.

"He's in the living room watching that *Lots of Trucks* video," she rolled her eyes, "again." Mom shook her head, and strode down the hall.

"So are you going to texturize it like you did my room back in Philly?" Sophie bounced as she waited for Cassandra to pour the paint. She always looked forward to creative projects.

"Not today, but I might add to it later."

"I loved the way my old bedroom walls looked like joyful clouds surrounded me." Sophie sloshed the paint roller through the pan.

Cassandra had loved it too. "Your dad painted those."

Sophie stilled. "He did?"

"Yeah. He was actually quite the artist."

Sophie rolled the paint along the wall. "I never knew that."

Cassandra dipped a brush into the liquid to prep the trim. "He never had much time to be creative when he worked for your grandparents." She closed her eyes at the wonder of the memory. "But he had so much fun painting that room for you." She chuckled. "It's probably why you see the joy in those clouds. That's how he felt when he painted them."

Sophie's smile grew as she stretched the roller up and down the wall. "We need to make joyful clouds in here."

"Hm. Too much to do."

24

Mom showed up in the doorway again, holding Cassandra's ringing cell. "I think it's that Kevin guy. It says 'unavailable.'" He was the only call she got regularly that said that.

Cassandra grabbed it from her. "Hello?"

"Mrs. Whitaker. I thought I'd stop by today and look at the house for the addition."

"Oh. Hang on." She peeked at her mom. "What time is that hair appointment?"

"Two o'clock."

"And don't forget. You promised to drop me and Tibo off at the pool."

"Yes, Sophie, you'll get there. But remember to be ready to come home by five. Tibo's new behavior therapist is coming for a home visit tonight."

Sophie nodded.

Cassandra spoke into the phone. "Sorry, Kevin. I don't think there'll be any time today. Can we try tomorrow?"

"I'll have to call you back as soon as I get my schedule from the store."

"Okay."

She clicked off and handed the cell to her mother.

Mom sighed. "I can't wait till all this upheaval fades." She disappeared down the hall, grumbling all the way.

Sophie and Cassandra caught gazes and laughed. Cassandra turned serious. "Don't forget to watch Tibo at the pool. He still can't swim, and you know how he sometimes drifts off when you're not looking."

"Don't worry, Mom." Though her daughter said it flippantly, Cassandra knew she took her role as big sister to Tibo very seriously. He would never come to harm in Sophie's care. She hoped.

~*~

Sophie showed her membership card to the lifeguard at

25

the entrance. Finally, a chance for some fun, though she'd have to keep an eye on Tibo in the shallow end of the pool.

"Potty."

Not this *now*! "Tibo, I told you to do that before we left."

He gave her the puppy-dog eyes that always made her melt. "Potty."

She glanced between the restroom signs. One silhouette in a dress. The other in pants. Sophie had no choice but to take this growing boy into the ladies dressing room so he wouldn't pee in the pool.

She stood at the entrance, shook out the towel from her bag, and wrapped it around her little brother's eyes making him look like the Disney *Aladdin*. She didn't want to freak out any of the less-than-modest dressers who pranced around as though the world should appreciate their naked perfection. Otherwise, he'd just stand inside the middle of the men's room waiting for directions that never came, unless Sophie accompanied him there.

Yeah, that'd work.

Sophie blew the hair from her face. Times like these, she missed her dad for Tibo's sake and not just her own.

After nudging her blindfolded brother to a stall, she stepped inside, locked the door, and unwrapped his head. "Go potty," she said and waited for the waterfall sound to stop, while praying silently no one would see them leaving the stall together.

No luck. An elderly woman shot her a pointed glare. "Boys that age don't belong in the women's dressing room."

Sophie barely made eye contact. "He has autism."

The woman scanned him up and down. "So."

"He can't speak or understand enough to—"

She harrumphed and tromped away.

Sophie heard more voices so she wrapped the towel over his eyes, and nudged him toward the door.

Just as they crossed the threshold …

"You playing hide and seek?"

There he was. The hotter-than-Juan-Pablo home improvement cashier—Sky—sans orange vest. In fact, as testified by Sophie's pounding pulse, he was sans shirt as well.

His lips tilted as he awaited her answer. Oh yeah, he'd asked a question.

"Uh …" She glanced toward the dressing room. "He had to go to the bathroom, and—"

His eyebrows jumped. "You took him into the ladies' room?"

Now she felt like a complete dork. "He has autism. He needs help in the bathroom."

Sky's expression fell. "Oh." He pivoted to the sound of a car roaring beyond the chain-link fence, and seemed to tense.

The sound startled her as well. Sophie took Tibo's hand, tugging him to the grassy area. "Well, it was nice seeing you again."

"Hey wait." He strode up beside her. "Your name's Sophie, right?"

Her breath caught.

The red sports car peeled out of the parking lot, making Sophie jolt. Man, this guy's proximity wound her tight.

Sky chuckled as his eyes followed the flashy vehicle to the exit. "Some dudes need to show off." He turned his gaze back to her. "What's your brother's name?"

"Tibo." They entered the grassy area.

"Nice to meet you, Tibo." Sky touched Tibo's shoulder.

Tibo stopped and peered up at him.

Sky smiled.

"Ask him to high-five."

Sky did and Tibo slapped his hand with a proud giggle, before launching into twirls.

"Is he doing that because I high-fived him?"

"No. That's a perseveration."

"A persever-what?"

"Something kids with autism do over and over again to calm themselves."

"Oh." Sky seemed mesmerized by the action. "What would happen if he didn't do it? Would he get upset?"

27

"Some kids might have a meltdown. Tibo'd probably just be extra anxious."

Sky shook his head. "Doesn't that make him dizzy?"

Sophie tugged at Tibo to continue forward. "Only if he goes in the wrong direction."

Sky pointed to a lounge chair. "Why don't you put your stuff with mine? It's right near the edge of the pool so you can keep an eye on it."

Sophie's mouth dropped opened. Was this guy wanting to hang out with her? Scanning the property, she must have spotted at least ten other girls who filled out their shapely bathing suits better than she did her girlie pink one, and yet Sky was here with her.

"What do you say?"

Her pulse took off, and her cheeks warmed to a thousand degrees. "Um, sure."

That began the most wonderful three hours she'd ever spent at a public pool. Sky showed Tibo and her, every nook and cranny of fun. He ran through the sprinklers and sprays with Tibo. He gave Tibo rides on his shoulders in the deep end, caught him at the bottom of the slide, and even made sand castles in the volleyball area.

She'd have been jealous of her little brother if it weren't for the flirtatious smiles and genuine questions Sky asked to get to know her better. It was definitely unfamiliar territory. Most guys she knew monopolized the conversation with rambling stories of their sporting achievements. She almost felt naked from unveiling so much of herself—her favorite music, favorite subject in school, favorite books and movies. He seemed to be fascinated by everything she said.

There was the one awkward moment when she told him about her father's death, but he seemed to recover better than most—by splashing her.

They discovered they'd be going to the same high school in the fall, only he would be two grades ahead of her.

Sky leaned against the edge of the pool, tilting his

beautifully tanned face to the sun. "Have you started driving yet?"

"Oh, no. I've got another year before I get my license." Did that make her seem like a little girl?

He opened his eyes and captured her gaze. "So. You can still learn in an empty parking lot somewhere, like at the school. My uncle taught me from the time I was fourteen."

"Really?" She could stare at him all day.

"Yeah. I'm a real good driver." He pushed some water at her with a grin. "I could even teach you sometime."

"I'm not ready for that." She checked on her brother making a whirlpool in the shallow end.

Sky's dimple twitched. "Are you ready for this?" He grabbed her arms and dropped into the deep water, pulling her under and close to him. She fell into his chest, face inches from his, heart pounding. His brown eyes locked with hers, a smile lifting his full lips as bubbles escaped between them, and their hair floated toward the top.

She needed to breathe—for more reasons than one—so pushed to the surface. "Are you trying to kill me?" She asked the guy who was shaking his wet, golden curls at her.

The dimple deepened on one cheek. "Nope. Just having a little fun."

Chapter Four

Cassandra's muscles released as the warm water drizzled over her hair and into the shampoo bowl at Kat's hair salon.

"I have a rinse that would really make your hair glow."

Between the energy in Kat's voice and the word *glow*, Cassandra imagined a neon sign on her head. "No, that's okay." Plus if the rinse cost even a dollar more, she needed to conserve it.

"So you said your husband is a mechanic?" When would Cassandra even have the money to get the needed repairs on her car done?

Her mother peeked from the side of the magazine she was reading. "Billy's the best. And reasonable too."

Kat turned off the water and let the hose drop into the hole at the edge of the sink. "No, the best would be his father, Lew. But Lew won't work for Billy. He's a driver for a delivery company, now."

Cassandra loved the feel of Kat scrubbing at her temples. Even the jangle of her bracelets sounded like wind chimes. "Why won't he work for Billy?" Something about this woman felt so open. Maybe it was the profession. People often said hairdressers—and bartenders—were like therapists. Cassandra felt she could ask almost anything. Maybe even tell her … well, not tell her *everything*.

Kat rinsed her hair again. "They fought a lot when Billy was a kid, and Lew wasn't around much otherwise. He was a dirt-track race car driver, and traveled a bunch. Billy's been tryin' to patch things between them, but Lew can't see that. Lew thinks it's just cuz Billy wants him to help with the car-care ministry." She chuckled mirthlessly. "Lew won't have anything to do with church-folk."

If Cassandra's car only needed what that ministry provided, minor maintenance work, she wouldn't feel so bone dry when it came to finances.

"Kat, what do you know about job openings?" Mom seemed to read her mind.

A muffled jangle accompanied the hairdresser's toweling of Cassandra's hair. "What kind of work experience do you have?"

Cassandra sighed. She hadn't worked outside the home since she'd waitressed at the country club sixteen years ago. Sophie was born her first year of marriage and Tim agreed for her to stay home.

"She developed a special-needs program at the church she used to go to."

Kat's fingers stilled.

"Mom, that's not work. I volunteered, hoping to provide something for Tibo."

"It was a beautiful program, and attracted lots of new families who wouldn't have come to the church if it hadn't been there."

Cassandra loved her Mom. Seeing only the best in Cassandra's small accomplishments. Even if she was also blind to the faults of pastors. "Mom—"

Kat lifted the seat back from the sink. "You should talk to Pastor Vince."

A throbbing began in Cassandra's head. Was the hairdresser a Vince groupie too?

"He's been trying to start a special needs ministry for a couple months."

This didn't sound like the self-centered man she knew. "Why?"

Kat scanned the hair salon as if looking for someone. "I think it's because of Isabella."

Of course—a woman.

"Isabella is one of my hair dressers. She's a single mom

31

and her son has autism too." She wrapped the small towel around Cassandra's neck. "She came to our church once, but her son caused such a ruckus in Children's worship she swore she'd never come back."

That's what caused the fear in the teacher's eye when she'd mentioned Tibo's issues.

"It really bothered Pastor Vince, because he feels those who are hurting are the ones who need the church the most." Kat led Cassandra to her station. "So he researched the proportion of families with special needs children in the area, and realized the church sees a smaller percentage than the public schools. He says the church should see more, not less." Her voice became animated. She obviously loved the pastor as much as Cassandra's mom. Noticing Kat's intense gaze pointed at her through the station mirror, Cassandra suppressed the eye-roll.

"He said when Jesus told the weary and burdened to come to Him, that means the church should have more weary and burdened."

Boy, Vince still knew how to charm the ladies. Appeal to their vanity and their sense of compassion. If only she could gag out loud.

The bell on the door jangled.

"Pastor Vince." Kat's smile split her face. "We were just talking about you."

At least he had the sense to look concerned, his gaze questioning Cassandra's reflection. What did he think she'd divulge?

"Oh yeah?" He had a small tremor in his voice.

"Did you know Cassandra, here, started a special needs program at her church in Philadelphia?"

His blue eyes darkened hinting at intense interest.

"And." She patted Cassandra's shoulder. "She's looking for a job."

He stilled.

~*~

Cass looking for a job and him needing someone to design this program. Vince peered at the hefty diamond ring and the fancy shoes resting on the little bar at the end of the chair. Something didn't set right. He'd heard she'd married rich. Very rich. Had her husband not left her provided for? Or were her tastes too high class now she always needed more?

No. Not Cass. It was instinct for Vince to think that way given his upbringing on the high end. And even among those he knew from the drug trade. Those who had, wanted more. Like it would fill the chasm in their souls that only deepened with the pursuit of things.

"I'm not interested in developing a special needs ministry." Cass didn't even look at him.

Her mom gasped, eyes incredulous. "What are you saying? You need the money and you'd be perfect for it."

"Your pastor," her eyes met his for one painful second in the mirror, "does not need to be saddled with an employee just because I need a job."

He sat in the station next to where Kat trimmed those luscious auburn curls. Vince's mind traveled to the memory of the feel of them running through his fingers. He shook out of it, and softened his voice. "I do really need to hire someone." He thought about the boy with her in church, obviously special needs himself. "You could work from home."

"Sorry, I'm late." Isabella's Hispanic accent cracked with emotion as she flew in through the back entrance. "Sean had a tantrum at the school, and I needed to calm him."

Vince's heart plunged at the stress on the young woman's face. He could see in Cassandra's eyes—so did hers. Would Isabella ever find peace? She dropped her purse at the station where Vince sat, then closed herself into the bathroom, sobs murmuring through the salon.

Vince glared at the door then back at Cass. He whispered, "She needs you."

Cass's eyes flashed as she mouthed, "That's not fair."

Kat's brows drew together at the gesture.

Leaning back in the salon chair, Vince contemplated his one last argument. He knew this would seal the deal. "Unfortunately, if you took the job, you'd have to visit other church services on Sundays to see what their programs are like. I hope that won't be a problem." He knew it was the excuse she needed. "Your mom could bring your kids to our church while you check the others out."

Cass's look reminded him of his old best friend, Drew's, when they played chess. She released a long-suffering breath. "How about we meet at your office to discuss the possibility?"

He nodded. *Check.* But something about the tone of her voice and the tension in her jaw told him it was anything but check-mate.

~*~

Archibald Lewis pressed the gas of the big boxy delivery truck, feeling it labor just to make the speed limit. Was he dragging an elephant on its back, by its ear? The slow pace of the ride was maddening. The only worse thing about this job was the cutesy brown shorts they made him wear. It reminded him of the Easter suit his mother bought him when he was five. He tugged at the buttoned-up collar, and wondered again whether or not he should accept Billy's offer to work at the garage.

Bah! He couldn't be an employee of his own boy.

Lew, as his friends called him, fished the thermos from his pack while cruising the interstate, unscrewed the nozzle and took a gulp of soda mixed with scotch. He needed something to calm the ole ticker that wanted to speed as much as he did—like the old days at the dirt-track.

A car horn blared. He swore. Probably shouldn't drift into another lane while someone's passing him. With a belch he replaced the thermos in his bag.

First delivery. He rolled his eyes. Billy's church. The one his son talked about all day long. The one that brought him to Jeezuss! The boy was practically a preacher himself. It got so bad Lew contemplated stuffing toilet paper in his ears whenever his son visited. Was Lew so awful Billy needed to knit-pick about every last fault? He was only human. Knowing what Billy thought of him, he didn't need an answer to that question.

Lew pulled off the exit, down the local roads of Water's Edge and entered the Community Church parking lot.

After fishing around the back for the heavy box, he tromped up the steps and into the building.

"Oh yes! My new computer is here." The black woman grabbed the box right out of his arms.

"Whoa, there, woman."

She arched a brow.

"You need to sign the doo-hicky first."

She slid the box onto a table and scribbled on the little window.

Lew released a long breath.

The woman jerked back and bunched her eyebrows. "You know we have lots of services here for people." She watched the pen loop her name. "Grief groups, Marriage Prep." Her eyeballs seized him with an unholy glare. "A.A."

Lew shifted. "I don't need no groups."

Billy's pastor—John, was it?—slapped him on the shoulder. "Hey, Lew, I see you brought Yolanda's computer." His silver-haired head nodded at her to leave.

She gave one last hard look at Lew and harrumphed as she strolled away with her new toy.

"You just made her day."

"I can tell."

John gave a good-natured chuckle. "Stop by and see us on a Sunday sometime."

"No thanks, preacher. All that organ music and holy people …" He looked down the hall at the woman with the box.

"Yep. I guess you'd be disappointed here then, Lew. We sold the organ ten years ago to pay for the band equipment, and nothin' but sinners warming the pews since the day we opened our doors."

Lew's eyes followed the secretary. "Yeah, I bet."

John seemed amused. "Don't mind her. She's a sinner too."

"Does she know that?"

John's eyebrows jumped. "You bet she does. It's the reason she speaks her mind. She'd rather prevent others from seeing the destruction she saw in her younger years. She's just not real good at ..." John twisted his mouth this way then that, " ... *softening* her concern."

The pastor turned to follow the Yolanda woman and called over his shoulder. "Tell Billy I said hi."

"Sure." If he even saw him.

Chapter Five

Cassandra hitched her briefcase under her arm pit, straightened her black, pencil skirt and smoothed a curl from her face before entering the church office. This moment felt somewhere between critical job interview and being fed to a ravenous wolf.

"May I help you?" The thirty-ish woman peeked up from under her desk, a large opened box with plastic wrap and styrofoam sticking out in all directions, beside her. Her expression held more question than necessary.

"I'm here to interview for the job of Special Needs Ministry Coordinator." Cassandra kept the business in her voice, though she stacked emotional armor around herself as she followed the woman's gaze to a crooked window that peered into an office. Inside it, Vince sat at a large desk, piles of paper lining the edges, talking on the phone.

She gestured to a hard plastic chair. "Have a seat. He'll be right out." She grunted and ducked to the floor again, apparently hooking cables to the computer equipment.

Cassandra did as she was instructed, breathing a sigh while she still had the chance, and peeked again at the misshapen frame around Vince's office window.

The secretary lifted from her position, straightened out her clothes then dropped into her chair, pushing buttons on several devices. A smile stretched across her dark-skinned face as she appraised the obviously new equipment booting up. Glancing at Cassandra, her smile transformed into a smirk. "You're probably wondering why the window to his office looks outta whack."

"Yes." Maybe small-talk would calm her nerves.

"Pastor Vince cut that into the wall himself after studying a Youtube video on how to install windows." Her wary eyes told Cassandra what she thought of the idea. "He said if church members were going to build houses and make repairs for the poor, he needed to learn how to be handy with a hammer and nail." She chuckled. "Truth is, we all wish he'd give up and just rake leaves or something. He spends more time in the emergency room for injuries on sites than he does actually helping."

Cassandra looked through the window again, wondering if they were talking about the same man. "Then why does he do it?"

The woman grimaced. "He has this romantic notion about people who build things. Like they're all Jesus, the carpenter. And he feels he should be more like them."

Vince? He was a bigger con-artist now than ever. How long could he keep up that charade? And what did he stand to benefit?

"Why a window into the office?"

The woman sobered. "I'm sure you've heard about his history?" She glanced around. "With women?"

Boy had she.

"He felt it best that since everyone knows about his past, that his behavior is above reproach and transparent. No chance for rumors. He never counsels anyone unless there is someone out here who can see him, and the blinds to the office are open."

It sounded like a fishbowl. "What about the person being counseled?"

"They can sit on the other side where they won't be visible in case they become upset."

Vince's constant chatter stopped, and he returned his phone to the cradle. Cassandra couldn't take her eyes off the man behind the window as he opened a drawer of his desk and grasped something from it. He dropped his head back into the large office chair and closed his eyes, holding the object in both hands as if it brought him life. Finally, his eyes opened, and he placed the object back into the drawer.

He stood, causing Cassandra's heart to pound. Why was

38

she here? This idea was pure stupidity. Did she really think she could face this man again and tell him what she thought of his scam?

The office door swung open and he rushed out. "Yolanda, did the home for the mentally challenged ever call?"

"No, Pastor Vince."

He rubbed at the black goatee that now graced what once had been a smooth, always tanned, jawline.

Cassandra swallowed the lump in her throat. How could she even speak to this man?

"They said they were going to send us someone to help with janitorial work." His eyebrows knotted, his breaths seemed shallow.

"I know that, Pastor Vince." Her voice was soft as though to calm the man's agitated demeanor. Yolanda lifted her hand in Cassandra's direction. "Your ten-o'clock is early."

He stiffened. "Cass—um, Mrs. Whitaker, why don't you come into my office?"

Cassandra's facial muscles jerked as her gaze dropped from his face to her shoes. She stood, entered the office, pulling the chair in front of the desk back a few inches to afford less of a view to the woman outside the window.

Her muscles seized at the click of the door shutting. Trapped.

A dramatic pause followed the sound before Vince finally moved behind the desk and found his seat. He didn't say anything. It was almost as if he thought she should be the first to speak.

She couldn't.

"Cass—"

"Don't call me that." The name felt like tiny bits of broken glass slicing through the inside of her veins.

He drew in a breath. "Cassandra—"

~*~

"It's Mrs. Whitaker to you."

This was a bad idea. Vince didn't know why he'd gone along with it. But he couldn't pass up the opportunity while Kat's eyes were on him at the hair salon, and after hearing Isabella sobbing in the bathroom. He knew something needed to be done. Why had God sent Cass to be his savior? Maybe because she'd been his savior, of sorts, before.

"Mrs. Whitaker."

Could green eyes harden like steel? Apparently.

"Let's just clear the air, here, *Pastor* Vince."

"I'd like to." He didn't dare look at her. The heat of her anger seared through him.

"I'm not here because of you."

"I didn't think that."

"Or because you made a plea for that poor girl."

"I—"

She held up her hand. "I'm here because I need a job," she sucked in a breath, "and an excuse not to go to your church on Sundays."

He resisted the little smile that tugged on his lips. He knew that would work. "Yes, I am well aware how much you loathe me and need to be out of my presence."

"Loathe you? Do you think this is a joke?"

He finally lifted his gaze to meet hers. It traveled along her designer suit that seemed to see a few years use, with frayed edges and slightly worn spots, then met her eyes again. "This is not a joke to me either, Mrs. Whitaker." His lips almost stumbled over the too-distant name. "I really need someone to design this program, and you appear to be the one most qualified."

She pulled a stack of papers out of her brief case and plopped it on his desk. "Then, this is how it's going to be." She located a page with a list of addresses. "These are the churches with special needs programs in the Baltimore-Washington area, currently. I will be visiting each on Sundays for the next several weeks to observe how they work. I will interview church leaders and members with special needs children, and will report on my findings once I've finished."

Vince's left brow rose involuntarily. Who was interviewing whom? Maybe it was best to let her have her way. Clearly, she knew her stuff.

"I will also be conducting a needs assessment with leaders of the surrounding community—"

"I've already done that."

Cassandra stilled, the look in her eyes reminding him of moments together when she shared her passion for helping others. Her hope, way back then, had been to be involved in program development for those in need. He remembered her chatting on and on about how important a needs assessment was in order to make sure the program met the desired goal without duplicating services. Her idealism seeped into the cracks he'd laid open to her, breaking through the veneer of his self-absorption. Did Cassandra remember those conversations too?

"Uh, well. Good. I guess I won't need to do that." Her lashes lifted as her eyes hardened. "I'll need to see what you've done to be certain it is adequate for our purposes."

"Of course." He fished through a drawer and handed her a copy.

She stood, gathered her purse and briefcase, leaving her notes on his desk. She pointed a finger at him. "You stay away from me, and maybe we can make this work."

Vince swallowed.

"I don't know how you've hypnotized my mother." She looked around. "Not to mention the rest of this congregation, but it won't work on me. If I could, I'd tell my mother what you are."

He only stared. Usually good with words, none came now. None were adequate.

"But you know I won't do that, don't you?"

"Cass—" His jaw hardened at the flame in her eyes. "You can tell her whatever you think she should hear."

She pivoted. The air in the room swirled with the force of the opening door.

Yolanda stared after Cassandra as she strode out of the

office. "Well I guess you didn't hire her."

Vince's forefinger ran the edge of his goatee. "Actually, I think I just did."

~*~

Cassandra shook so hard her keys rattled when she attempted to open the car door. She flinched at the screech of tires as a sports car with tinted windows burned rubber against the asphalt in the parking lot. Was the driver showing off, or escaping from someone? After a meeting with Vince Steegle, she suspected nefarious intentions around every corner. She'd have to learn to calm herself. After all, she'd be working for the man. The thought almost brought convulsions. She dropped into her seat, dragged her briefcase across her chest to the passenger seat and closed the door before leaning her head on the steering wheel.

One. Two. Three breaths.

She must be desperate.

The pages of the needs assessment crinkled as she dragged them from her bag and flipped through them. Her eyes burned as they scanned the pages listing statistics from schools, interviews with medical professionals, and concerns from church personnel in the area. Had Vince really done all this? He'd summarized literature on special needs programs, and written a thorough argument for including a ministry at Water's Edge Community. No wonder the church agreed to pay the part-time salary she'd be collecting.

All this at the hands of the man who'd pretended to be interested in her dreams and plans, her idealism, making her feel important, wanted, loved … only to use her in the end. Had he really been absorbing her constant chatter on the shores of the inlet as they laid in the sun, listening to the water lap the sand? She flipped the pages again and shook her head. The report looked exactly like something she'd produce if she had the means. How did he know how to do this?

Surely, they taught it in his divinity courses. She shook off the intimacy of the alternative. Why did she feel so exposed? Something about that man always made her that way. Only before, she'd also felt protected by him. Now, she knew it only made her more vulnerable to his selfish desires.

She'd never let that happen again.

Cassandra folded the report in half, then quarters, and stuffed it deep into her bag. She'd have to insert her key into the ignition with wavering fingers. She cranked the reluctant SUV engine. It sputtered as it rolled backwards, out of the space. "Hold on girl. I'll get you to a doctor soon." Kat's husband, Billy, owned a garage. When would Cassandra have the funds to do all of what needed fixing? Just a few more weeks—her first paycheck from Vince—and she might chance a meeting with the repair man.

The car hummed for a few seconds, giving Cassandra hope, before lapsing into its usual clunking. She calmed before realizing the worst. If Cassandra spent her Sundays checking out other churches without her kids, Mom would be taking them to Water's Edge. Oh, no no! This would not work. Why hadn't she thought of that before? Probably because her pulse pounded in her ears every time the subject came up. Typical Vince. She could never think straight in his presence. He wormed his way into her brain and made it impossible to see clearly.

But what harm could he do her kids?

Plenty. Even though she couldn't come up with a method at the moment. Still, that man could wrap Attila the Hun around his pinky.

The car coughed. Cassandra's shoulders sagged. She had few choices these days. She'd work this job, collect a paycheck … and prepare to deprogram her kids after the brainwashing they'd receive at the instigation of Vince Steegle.

~*~

Vince headed toward the men's room down the hall, his mind still burning from the meeting with Cass. He couldn't clear the image of her hatred. It played over and over again as though

43

on unlimited battery life. He needed to consult with someone about this new business arrangement with a woman who couldn't stand him, but knowing John's long-time relationship with the family, he also knew it couldn't be the senior pastor.

Could Billy Lewis advise him? He was an elder at the church, and Vince's best friend. Vince shook his head. He knew what Billy would say.

A large man with dark hair, glasses, and olive skin, stood stock-still inside the glass front doors.

Vince approached. "Can I help you?"

The man twisted an envelope in his grip. "I lookeen for Passa Vince."

Vince stepped closer. "I'm Pastor Vince."

The man's eyes lit with the grin. He thrust the wrinkled envelope forward.

Vince took it. He hesitated before lifting the flap to look inside.

The man nodded for him to proceed.

Vince unfolded the letter and read:

Pastor Vince,

I am the janitor you asked for. I will work very hard for you. I will make you proud, and I love the Bible.

Amit

"So, Amit, you love the Bible, huh?"

The man revealed his crooked teeth with an emphatic nod of the head. "Spessily Pwovers. I wearn quick."

Amit must have been dropped off by the home for mentally challenged adults Vince had contacted. "That's great, Amit. We love the Bible, here, too." He flipped the envelope back and forth, as well as the page to see if any letterhead could be found. Nothing. Didn't they usually send a staff member from the home to help acclimate the residents to the position? Vince shrugged. "Okay, Amit, let me show you the janitorial closet." Vince gestured for the man to follow.

He jerked forward. "De fear of de Lord is de beginnin' of knowledge, but fools despise woosdom an' discpwin.'"

Vince nodded as he strode the corridor. "Very good."

"If sinnaws entice 'ou, do not give in to dem."

"Wow. You've got a great memory." Vince figured it was his savant skill. Well, if anyone lost a Bible, they could always grab Amit. It made him think of the end of that Denzel Washington movie.

Vince opened the small closet, noting all the chemical detergents scattered on the top shelves and cleaning devices littering the floor. Rags, sponges, and scouring pads were piled into a large bin. It's clear, since looking to transition to The Home residents, church staff had not taken much pride filling in the position. Would this simple man know what to use for what?

Amit gasped. "Oh no!" He pulled the bleach bottle from next to the ammonia bottle. "No mix. Could die!" He grabbed a few more cleansers and placed them on different levels of the shelves.

Vince backed against the wall to make room for his task. Amit pulled some sponges from the box and placed them next to the bathroom cleaners. The dust cloths were piled by the spray wax and the toilet brushes by the toilet cleaner.

Amit clapped his hands, surveyed the new system, and sighed. "Aw bettaw." He turned to Vince and startled. "'Ou still here?"

Vince nodded.

Amit wiggled his fingers as if to make him go away.

Vince uncrossed his arms.

"I awganize. Later, I show 'ou."

Vince started to turn.

"Den 'ou tell me what nex."

"Okay Amit."

Vince wasn't sure what to think, but figured he'd let the

guy go, and see what happened. What harm could he do? He glanced to the heavens. "God, I'm giving this over to You."

Entering his office, Vince took in the faint scent of Cass's cologne still lingering in the air. Or was that his imagination? Her presence dogged him everywhere he went since that day she showed up in church. The chair in front of his desk seemed to vibrate from her energy.

He'd had this crazy fantasy that he'd explain his actions, beg forgiveness, and she'd accept it. He shook his head at the uselessness of the thought. She could never forgive him. He wouldn't if he were her.

Vince sat at his desk, fired off a few emails, polished this week's sermon, and glanced at his watch. An hour had passed, and Amit hadn't come looking for him. How long did it take the man to organize a closet? He'd better check on him.

When he'd entered the supply room, the place looked sparse. Nothing tossed here or there, but placed by the way each item was to be used. It even smelled better.

Vince ran a finger along a shelf and rubbed it with his thumb. No dust. The floor didn't even have that gritty crunch it usually had when he walked inside.

But where was the man? Had he disappeared from whence he came?

Yolanda appeared at the door. "Who's—? What happened in here?"

"We finally got someone from The Home. He organized."

Her gaze ran the length of the space. "That must be the guy singin' in the ladies' room."

"His name is Amit."

"Well he can come to my house any day." Her eyebrows see-sawed. "Just don't let him join the choir." Yolanda pivoted and headed toward the office.

Vince stood outside the ladies' room door propped open with a wringing bucket, and listened to the boisterous voice echo from the tile in song. "Anyone in there?"

"Juss me, Passa Vince."

Vince entered and followed the singing to the far corner stall where shiny black shoes peeked out on the floor through the opened door. Amit, on hands and knees, scrubbed the base of the toilet with a small brush.

Vince stood over him, hands on hips.

Amit peeked back then stopped as if caught. "Oh! Uh-oh. I fawgot to tell 'ou." He pointed to the crevices where blackened grout had been replaced by clean surfaces. "Verwy bad. I stawt here."

Vince just watched.

"Lazy men aw soon poor. Hawd workaws get wich."

"Yes, that's true." Vince couldn't remember the terms of payment he'd promised The Home.

"Goss Word."

Vince smiled.

Amit wiggled his fingers for Vince to leave. "Hard work means posperwity. Oney a fool idles away hiss time."

"Okay, Amit. I'll get back to work then."

Chapter Six

Vince didn't like that twinkle in Billy Lewis's eye when he looked up from the counter in the office of his auto-repair garage.

The fu-man-chu bent up. "What brings you here, today, Vince?" There was a definite lilt in his voice, as if he'd expected the visit.

"Oil change." Vince didn't look to see the incredulity likely stretched across his best friend's face.

Billy checked his watch. "It hasn't been a year yet."

"You told me to bring it every three months or three-thousand miles."

Billy tapped at the keyboard in front of him. "I've been telling you that for ten years now, and you still go six, at least. What gives?"

Obviously, Billy already knew. Vince just couldn't say the words, so instead he dropped his attention to the grime-covered floor. "You ever clean this place?"

Billy strolled around the counter and laid a beefy forearm across Vince's shoulder. "Come on, Vince. Fess up."

Vince chewed his lip. "Look, I finally make it in for regular car maintenance and you give me grief."

"Fine, let's get your car on the rack. Give me the keys, and I'll have it ready for you in a half hour."

Vince slapped the fob into the man's hand, and Billy drove the Elantra into the shop. "I got it from here. Have a seat in the waiting room."

Vince didn't move from the concrete floor of the bay as Billy stepped out of the car. Billy shook his head. "It's the woman isn't it?"

"What woman?"

Billy squinted. "Just cuz I don't got your high-priced education doesn't mean I'm stupid."

Vince glared back. "Enough with the 'dumb-redneck-pride' junk and help me out, here."

Here it comes. "What do ya mean 'dumb red-neck pride?'" Billy looked about to pounce.

"That's where you get all offended 'cause I insulted your intelligence, then puffed up because you know you have more common sense than the book-learnin' dude."

"I don't do that."

"You do it all the time, Billy."

"Do not."

"Come on, Billy. Can't you see I'm having a hard time?"

Billy's head shook. "That's what I've been saying. You're the one denying it."

"Fine. You're smarter than I am. Okay?"

Billy's chest lifted. "Nah. Just got more common sense."

Vince sagged his shoulders.

"Sorry, man." Billy rolled his hands in a move-along gesture. "Empty up. You obviously need something."

"I'm not sure I can put words to it." Vince leaned against a greasy work table, only to get his tan Dockers smudged.

"How about the full-on truth."

"You can't say anything to Kat."

Billy stilled and stared. Vince almost snapped his fingers in front of the man's eyes to see if he was still awake.

Finally he spoke. "Do you seriously believe you can keep anything from that woman? She's like an x-ray machine on steroids. Don't even try to hide information from her. Once she sniffs blood, she hones in for the kill. You know how she hates secrets. Even her own." He grimaced. "Not to mention mine."

"That's because she thinks everyone is as non-judgmental as she is." Vince sighed. "Which is why I need to talk to *you*. I'll shield myself from her later."

Billy grimaced. "Good luck." The facial hair bent. "So tell

49

me 'bout the red-head."

"Auburn."

"Fine. Auuuuuburn," he elaborated in a stuffy accent.

Vince rubbed his goatee.

Billy pulled a rag from his back pocket and handed it to Vince. "Got grease on your face."

Great. "I knew her from the country club." He wiped at his cheek.

Billy pointed to the other side of his face. "Figured that. She had a sort of uppity air."

Vince shook his head. "That's only 'cause she hates me. She was a waitress there."

"Wow, Vince. I didn't think it was possible for a female to hate you."

"Oh, it's possible. She's the president of the 'Hate Vince' Fan club."

"What'd'ya do to her."

"She's the one I told you about before."

Billy whistled. "Oooooh. That one."

"Yeah."

Billy took back the rag from Vince and wiped his fingers as if removing Vince's stain from them. "Sorry to hear that, man."

"I don't know what to do about it. She's Greta Hessing's daughter."

"Well, maybe she won't come back to church, and you won't have to do anything."

Vince rolled a stray bolt on the floor with the toe of his loafer. "Except that I sort of hired her to develop the special needs program." He winced.

Billy had that staring look again, complete with open mouth.

This time Vince did snap his fingers. "Billy?"

"You what?"

"I hired her to coordinate the special needs program." Vince's voice came out like a little-boy confession.

"Why, on God's green earth, would you do such a thing."

"Your wife made me."

"You're blaming this on Kat?"

Vince waved his hands in the air. "We were at the shop. Kat found out she needed a job and had the right experience. She sort of cornered me. Gave me those eyes she does when you know she won't let something go."

Billy expelled a burst of air. "Yeah, I know that look. Sorry, man. So what are you going to do?"

"Well, I finagled it so she could work from home. She came to me with a plan that wouldn't require us getting together much."

"Glad I wasn't a fly on *that* wall."

"Tell me about it. I barely breathed."

"So she's really going to be the coordinator?"

"Yep." The word came from the side of his mouth.

"What were we saying about common sense?"

Vince glared.

Billy slapped a palm on Vince's shoulder. "I'm prayin' for you pastor." He shook his weary head. "Yer gonna need it."

~*~

Vince grasped the hand of the last congregant in the line after service. He blew an exhausted sigh and headed toward the offices. Lately, his job seemed more wearying than ever. The same faces came in and out of the doors. No new souls saved. No additional lives recovered. No cries of joy in heaven for the newly found. What a let down from his first two years. Pastor John believed his sermons had increased the membership one-hundred percent, which prompted the building of additional space in the sanctuary.

Amit stood in front of him as if to block his steps. He looked awful dapper in his suit and tie. Vince hadn't expected the man to come to services when he started working on the janitorial staff. He just wanted to provide a job to someone from The Home. It was part of his plan to help those with special needs.

"For de revelation awaits un appointed time; it speaks of de end and will not pwoove false." Amit's eyelids fluttered. "Dough it lingers, wait fo' it; it will certainwy come and will not deway."

Vince smiled at the man, then realized he'd quoted from Habakkuk rather than his usual Proverbs. Had he finally moved onto another book?

As if to answer the question Vince hadn't voiced, Amit said, "Wet your eyes wook stwait ahead, fix your gaze duwectly before ou—Pwovers 4:25."

"Yes, Amit. You're learning those well." Vince was amazed at how he could memorize so much scripture word-for-word. It was kind of funny how the simple man had mostly chosen Proverbs to quote—the book of wisdom. He probably didn't even know what the words meant. Still, Vince wished his parishioners took as much time to learn scripture as Amit did.

Amit tugged at the lapels of his crisply ironed navy suit jacket displaying a proud smile, and walked away.

Fix your gaze directly before you. The words fluttered in Vince's mind for some reason. *Wait for the appointed time.* A shiver rippled through him. He shook his head and walked on through the hallway.

Is this all there is, Lord? His heart cried out. Was his usefulness waning? Would he only preach to the choir now? He wanted to do more. He'd spent years at his old haunt, The Dock Bar and Grill, hoping to recover an old friend from his former lawless life. But though they tolerated him—and his profession—it came more in the form of teasing than it did movement toward any real faith of their own. Vince knew these things took time, but somehow—today—it felt meaningless. Like it wasn't enough.

His thoughts ran to Cass again, and her lack of presence in the pews. Her mom was there with Cass's kids, which only made the pew seem more empty. The hole in his chest grew wider, knowing she'd never forgive him. There was nothing he could do to cleanse what he'd done to her. He'd betrayed her in the worst possible way. Led her to believe in him—in them—only for her to discover it hadn't been real. Or at least that's what he'd tried to tell himself back then. It had only been a game. One that had left him less in control of his feelings than before it had started. What he'd done to her that night was unforgivable.

Vince's steps shuffled along the carpeted floor, his hands stuffed in his pockets. A couple volunteers from classrooms greeted him on their way out. He smiled, nodded and whispered goodbyes, but his heart lay in his shoes.

"Pastor Vince."

He began to hate the sound of his name and title as people called to him, wanting him to lead them here, guide them there. Pray for them. Heal them. Didn't they know he was just a man? Didn't they know he needed guiding, prayer, and healing too?

"Pastor Vince." Greta Hessing's voice. Cass's mom.

He turned. Mrs. Hessing dragged Cass's son along as the teen girl followed closely behind. Mrs. Hessing stopped short and tilted her head. "Are you okay?"

He forced a smile all the way through his eyes. A skill his father had taught him. "'Course I am. What's up?" He needed to be strong for his congregation so they would know God was working in his life.

"I just wanted to introduce my grandkids to you." She wrapped an arm around the dark-haired teen. "This is Sophie." And patted the blond boy's head. "This is Tibo."

"Tibo?" He lowered to one knee in order to be eye-level with the boy. "That's an intriguing name."

"Name." The boy smiled.

Mrs. Hessing sighed. "It's short for Tim-Bob." She grimaced. "His real name is Timothy Robert, Jr. His father always liked that football player, so he thought it would be fun to call him by the same name, though they spell it differently."

"Well, Tibo, do you like my church?"

Tibo's brows furrowed as his eyes reached deep into Vince's soul. Vince didn't know how to respond to the wordless boy. Cass's son.

"Ask him to high-five," Sophie said.

"High-five, Tibo?" Vince held his palm in the air.

Tibo slapped it, a proud smile gracing his features.

"Thank you." Vince mouthed to Sophie as he stood. "And how old are you?"

"Fifteen."

That old? A shot ran through him. He didn't dare ask her birth date. He looked at Sophie's dark hair, then Tibo's sandy blond. Neither donned the red curls of their mother. Suddenly, Vince wanted to know what Tim, Sr. looked like. But he couldn't ask. "Have you gone to our youth services yet? They're really cool."

"She's a little shy, Pastor Vince."

"Grandma." Sophie peered up from behind her long bangs.

"We're still trying to get her accustomed to all the changes."

"She might find the service more energetic and the sermons easier to follow than my ramblings."

Mrs. Hessing chuckled. "Oh believe me, Sophie follows. She could probably write a few herself. She's a bit on the mature side."

"Grandma." Sophie's plea was more emphatic this time. Something about the girl's expression was familiar. More than Cass's features. Like something he'd seen a thousand times before.

"Is that so? Well, then you really need to go to youth services. You can mentor some of our other students."

Sophie harrumphed. "Yeah, like that would make me a lot of friends."

He patted her shoulder. "I guess you're right. Maybe you should just get to know them first."

~*~

"Is it really true you were a drug dealer?"

"Sophie!" Grandma had that exasperated tone, but Sophie wanted to know.

54

Pastor Vince only laughed. "It's okay. It's not a big secret." His eyes got all serious. "Yes. It's true. Not a time I'm particularly proud of."

She checked the guy out, from his wavy black hair to his leather loafers. "You don't look like a drug dealer."

His blue eyes sparkled. "What's one supposed to look like?"

Tibo twirled and twirled beside them.

Sophie shrugged. "I don't know. Just not like you."

The man sucked in a big breath. "My supplier used to think that was an advantage." His expression got heavy. "That I could move in richer circles because of it. People who could afford more of what I had to offer."

"That didn't happen?" Something tugged at Sophie's heart.

The pastor shook his head. "Oh, I sold to them all right. But I don't think I'd say I traveled in their circles any more. Once I became their dealer, I became less and less a friend."

She wanted to know more. "My father used to be a collector of testimonies."

Pastor's eyebrows shot up. "A what?"

Grandma corralled Tibo. "Tim always had a story about people he met who came to know Jesus in extraordinary ways. He loved to share these stories to inspire people. We called him 'The Collector of Testimonies.'"

"Is that so?"

Sophie studied the funny smile encircled in a black goatee. "Yes, what's yours?"

"Sophie!"

Pastor Vince held up a palm. "That's okay, Mrs. Hessing." He turned to Sophie. "So you plan to carry on the title?"

Something about that idea felt warm like melted chocolate in her mouth. "I guess."

"I bet you have a picture of your dad in your wallet."

Where'd that come from? "I do."

"I'd love to see it. You obviously loved him very much."

Sophie reached into her bag, and pulled out her wallet. "This is a picture of the two of us when I was three." It felt strange showing it to him. No one had ever asked to see it before. People mostly avoided the topic of her dead father if they could. Little did they know how much she loved to talk about him.

His eyes narrowed as he glanced between the picture and her, as if to find a resemblance. Only there wasn't much of one. Sophie had more of Mom's physical qualities than Dad's, but her mom said she made up for it in having so much of his personality and character. That always made her smile.

"You haven't said whether or not you'd tell me your testimony."

He sighed as he handed her the wallet. "Mine is a very long story, with lots of layers. Rich man. Poor man. Prison. Pastor."

"Will you tell me some time?" She'd give anything to know more.

His blue eyes reached into her as his smile shortened. "I think I will." He turned slightly. "If your mom will let me."

Did she hear him right? "What about my mom?"

He rubbed his neck and shook his head. "She might not like the pastor filling your head with his sordid past."

"I hope Cassandra hasn't been too standoffish with you." Grandma's voice held the reprimand Sophie knew was for her mother. "Don't mind her. She just thinks I'm trying to fix you two up 'cause you're both single. I know better than to do that with her. It usually sends her running in the other direction." Grandma pulled Tibo into a hug. "She's just a bit uptight right now, worrying how she'll provide for the kids."

Pastor Vince's head tilted, eyes filled with questions he didn't ask. Sophie could almost feel the concern ooze from him. Was he like that with all his parishioners? She could understand why so many loved him.

"Come on, Sophie. We better get going and let the pastor get back to work."

Chapter Seven

Cassandra organized the forms on her mother's dining room table. She sat before spreadsheets listing churches with special needs programs, numbers of students, types of services, sizes of congregations, median incomes, and locations. She stared at the stacks of literature each church had sent her when she called to request information. They were categorized based on method — those that used buddy systems to include the children in the regular youth services, and those that placed special needs students in a separate classroom.

She looked at Tibo running his favorite truck along the carpet, leaving a trail as the fibers changed directions. He loved "drawing roads" that way.

Would he be better off in a separate room with kids more like him, or included with the other students? And what about the non-special-needs children? Shouldn't they be more exposed to the ways of the developmentally challenged? Cassandra was never sure how to answer that question. Sometimes, it seemed nice for Tibo to relate with children most like him.

She sighed, and Tibo's gaze rose to hers. His brown eyes seemed to sink into the delicate folds of her heart. "Pway."

Did he know what she was thinking, or was that word just another perseveration? It didn't matter, it was exactly what she needed to do.

After following Tibo's suggestion, she opened her eyes from that moment with God to find her son's gentle smile facing her way. He went back to drawing roads. "Dugga-dugga-dugga. Beep-beep-beep."

"Mom, I can't find my bathing suit." Sophie always began

her sentences before she even entered the room.

Cassandra scanned Sophie's fitted T-shirt and hipster shorts. When had she become a woman? Pride and fear mingled in Cassandra's chest at the thought. Her little girl was beautiful and there wasn't a thing she could do about it. "The pink one is still hanging in the bathroom."

"Not that one, Mom. The royal blue."

Cassandra's pulse skipped. "You mean the one with the plunging neckline that I now regret buying?"

Sophie shifted. "Mom."

When did her title first take on two syllables?

"Is this change in swim wear because you saw that boy from the home improvement store at the pool last week?"

Sophie huffed, but didn't answer.

Cassandra waved her hand in the air. "I think it's in the laundry basket in my room."

"I still can't believe Sky goes to our pool." Sophie's eyes lit with excitement. "What are the odds of that? I'm going to ask him to church if I see him."

"And you need that bathing suit to do it?"

Her smile grew mischievous. "It's all for the cause."

Cassandra smirked back. "Oh, don't think I don't know what's going on in your head. I was your age once." And that's exactly what worried her. She shot a glance to the heavens with an added prayer for protection for her daughter as she negotiated the teen years.

Mom came out of the kitchen in her bathing suit cover-up. "You sure you can't come with us to the pool."

Cassandra sighed. "I'm sure. I have to make some notes on these programs, call a couple more churches, research on the internet, and that guy who's going to build the addition is coming at eleven."

"Okay, dear."

"Just please keep a good eye on Tibo in the water."

"I won't let him out of my sight. Besides, you know Sophie'll shadow his every move."

"Well, she'll have her eye on something else at that pool, it seems." Cassandra's heart ached. "And I want her to be able to think of something besides caring for her brother for once. She needs a little fun."

"I know, honey. You need a little fun too, you know." Mom folded a towel, and stuffed it in a bag. "I'll take care of the kids today. Don't worry."

"I know you will." Cassandra stared at the mosaic of forms in front of her. "I need to figure out which type of program will work best for this congregation." She shook her head. "I just can't believe I'm doing this for Vince Steegle."

Her mother's brows furrowed.

"I mean Pastor Vince."

"I don't know what you have against him. He's a wonderful man, and preaches some of the best sermons I've ever heard."

"A little too smooth if you ask me." Cassandra didn't mean for her voice to be so hard. "I don't trust anyone that smooth."

"Cassandra …" Her mother seemed to war with what to say … or ask.

Please don't put the bread crumbs I've dropped together, Mom. I can't bear for you to find out.

Mom's features softened. "He's a very good man. So what if he has a terrible past. It's what made him value his present—his salvation. And he's real good to your kids too."

Cassandra jolted. The last thing she needed was for Vince Steegle to become closer with more members of her family. She stared at the burgeoning young woman entering the room, now dressed in her adult-like bathing suit with those dark wavy locks and piercing blue eyes. Cassandra's chest pounded an erratic beat.

Next thing Mom would say was that Vince Steegle would be a wonderful father. Little did she know his usual method of fatherhood, back when she knew him, was to pay for the ending of his child's life.

"He knelt to speak with Tibo, and even got a high-five

from him. He's promised to tell Sophie his testimony."

The gasp came out before Cassandra could suppress it. Her mother stared.

"Sophie doesn't need to be immersed in his decadent history."

"She wants to be a 'collector of testimonies.'" Mom glared. "Like her dad."

Cassandra gathered her hair in a sloppy bun. "Well, maybe she should start a little smaller."

~*~

Kevin pulled his Dodge truck up in front of the ranch-style home. Cassandra's mom's house. Why hadn't Cassandra bought herself a fancy mansion in the more expensive neighborhoods surrounding Annapolis, with all that Whitaker pharmaceutical money? Every time someone sneezed they had to pay the Whitakers to cure it. She must have moved here for the retarded kid, so he could be with his grandma.

The door opened as soon as he knocked. "You're here. Great. I'll show you the room." Cassandra's hair poured out of her funny-looking bun, spraying all around her face. Even frazzled she was hot.

Expensive. That's what Kevin needed to remind himself. All she cared about was a guy's bottom line. So, he didn't have the cash her usual boyfriends had. But that was about to change. And he'd be long gone before she realized her own worth had decreased in the process.

His gaze rolled down the back of her as she led him through the hall, noticing the way her black, stretchy pants clung to her legs. What would it be like to … ? He shook his head. *Focus Perkins.* The money. That was what he was here for. But—

"The addition will start right about here." She pointed to the wall. "And attach to this bedroom." Then she gestured to an open door.

Kevin nodded. *Whatever you say, lady.*

"Something simple.Windows on each side." Cassandra turned and put her palms on her hips. "You can do it for the price we talked about, right?"

"Sure." It didn't matter the cost, he'd drain her wallet anyhow. Not sure which way to choose. What was her greatest vulnerability? Scanning the bedroom, he stopped at the pictures next to her bed. Her little family. How cute. His lip curled. Hmmmm. Ideas were beginning to form, but maybe those were too complicated. He'd look around for a simple hit-n-run method first, but if that wasn't possible, he knew what his hail-mary pass would be.

"So when can you begin?"

"I'll have the supplies here on Wednesday morning. I can start soon after that."

~*~

Waterlogged. That's how Sophie felt watching Tibo bounce and splash in the shallow end of the pool. The chlorinated soup swirled around her with the movement of the crowd dancing within it, swaying Sophie like a strawberry-banana smoothie whipping in a blender. She could feel the heat of the sun, baking her nose and shoulders as she tried to maintain her footing.

Where was Sky? He said he was off work today, and planned to be here. Could she really count on the promise of a guy she barely knew?

Sophie scanned the patches of grass surrounding the concrete walkway. Old ladies stuffed into bathing suits that should be illegal in their lack of fabric, kids chasing after friends with water guns. Mothers screaming across the water to one child dunking another. All this interrupted by short, shrill whistles from the lifeguard warning a swimmer on the brink.

"What ya lookin' for, Soph?" Sky's voice had a rumble that rained warmth down her back. She turned, only to get lost in those golden brown eyes that almost matched his tan. His blond hair seemed kissed by the sun.

"Hi Sky." Sophie resisted the urge to note the poetry of that phrase.

He sat at the edge of the pool then lowered himself into the water next to her, biceps bulging as he did. Did it suddenly get colder? She shivered.

His eyes seemed to travel the length of her, caressing her in a way she kind of liked. "You're not even wet, yet."

She pointed to her brother, twirling in the water. "I'm watching Tibo."

His smile made her bones noodley. "You can do that wet." A wave of water erupted as he pushed it with his large hands.

Bracing herself against the cold, she screamed.

He laughed.

"Okay, you're asking for it." She scooped a handful of water and let him have it.

He wrapped his strong arm around her waist and plunged her beneath the waves.

"Aaaaa—blub-blub-blub," was all Sophie could say until she straightened out of the deep, tugged at the front of her bathing suit to make sure all parts were covered, and sucked in a big breath.

"You look good wet." His full lips nudged up on one side. "I like the new bathing suit."

Smoothing strands of hair from her face, she made a check for Tibo.

Sky nodded to the side. "He's right there. Still circling."

The thought of all those circles made Sophie dizzy. Oh wait, it was Sky who did that to her.

Sky swooshed through the water toward her brother. "Hey, little man." Tibo's grin was uncontainable as Sky lifted him and twirled him around, making giant, circular waves.

Sophie's breath caught as she feared Sky would throw him into the deep. But he didn't. He seemed to sense that Tibo didn't possess the same survival instinct as normal kids, and would more likely sink than swim. Instead, Sky pulled him up and down, plunging him, but keeping his face above the surface all the time.

Sophie knew she beamed watching this guy, corded muscles rippling his back, as he played with her autistic brother. But she couldn't help it. Likely, her expression resembled Happy—or Dopey—in the Disney version of Snow White as her heart swelled, and her gaze trailed his every move.

Could there be a more perfect man?

Sky turned and caught her staring. His smile lengthened as he gave Tibo one last splash and muss of the hair. "Gotta play with your sister now, big guy." He held up his hand for a high-five, and Tibo obliged before bouncing a few times then went back to twirling.

"So." Water glistened from his thick eyelashes. "You gonna take me up on the driving lessons or not?"

Did she hear right? "I thought you were kidding when you offered the other day."

"No." He lifted a shoulder. "I think it'll be fun."

"Or you have a death wish."

"That too. But let's start with fun. Do you think your mom'll be cool with it?"

"As long as we stay in the school parking lot, she'll be fine." The image of her mother rushing out to meet one of Tibo's therapists, then another of her leaning over all that special needs information stacked on the table, passed through mind. "She'll probably be relieved she doesn't have to do it herself."

"Great. I'll pick you up on Sunday morning."

Sophie pressed her lips together, wondering if this was the right time to suggest it.

"What's wrong?"

"I have to go to church on Sunday." Why did she make it sound like a chore?

"Won't your mom let you take one Sunday off," he lifted a shoulder, " … to do something for yourself?"

"Actually," She felt a little timid now. "I like going to church. I don't wanna miss."

His brows drew together, and his mouth pursed into a funny smile. "Are you serious?"

Sophie nodded. She'd have loved to explain the church activities she and her dad had been involved in. Doing God's work in the homeless shelters. Playing baseball with kids in the slums after helping them clean up trash from the street. Her mom had been there too, but these were the moments she cherished most with her father.

Gone forever.

"We can go after. Just tell me when to pick you up."

"Why don't you come with us?" There. The words were out.

The funny smile and brow crunching were back. She waited as he took his time considering the idea. What conversation played in his head? "Should I go? Shouldn't I go? Should I go? Shouldn't I go?" Which one would win? She almost tapped her toe under the water.

"Okay."

"Okay?" Was he serious?

Sky chuckled. "Yes. Okay. Just tell me what time, and I'll be there."

Chapter Eight

"Hurry up and finish, dear."

Sophie eyed Grandma, then the eight legged, crustacean—as her former Earth Science teacher called it—staring lifelessly from the table. How does someone hurry eating crabs? She wasn't sure she understood Marylanders who worked so hard for tiny bits of meat. Steak and potatoes. That's what they ate back home in PA. She missed that. Here, there was no A-1 sauce in sight.

Grandma grabbed the crab carcass. "Let me show you again." She pulled the legs out, snapped, hammered, pried, and gathered the sparse protein into a little pile. "There."

This was the seventh shelled creature Grandma picked out for her, and Sophie's stomach still growled. If it wasn't for the salty seasoning she'd have surrendered long ago, and filled up on hush puppies. Now *those* made sense. "Why are we hurrying anyway? Do you have a big date or something?"

"Oh, pooh," Grandma slapped her hand.

Mom fished more corn chips to Tibo from the gluten-free stash she always carried in her purse, in case restaurants didn't provide an alternative. "Yeah. Why are we rushing?"

Grandma's gaze seemed to follow a boat motoring up to the pier alongside The Dock Bar and Grill. "Well, the clientele gets a little rough after dinner hours."

"What do you mean rough?" Mom speared Grandma with that glare that brought shivers to Sophie's spine.

Grandma cleared her throat. "Seedy. Drunken. Not-quite-law-abiding." She nodded toward the guys tying up the boat, and Sophie suddenly wondered what was in those back packs they carried.

65

"Criminals?" Mom's eyes went wide.

"Shh." Grandma waved her hand. "Not so loud."

"Mom, you brought us to a haven for the underworld?" she whispered with force. "Why would you do that?"

Grandma wiped her mouth with the paper crab-eating bib, folded it, and placed it on the table. "They have the best crabs in town."

The front door opened and Pastor Vince entered. Mom's jaw hardened. "More riff-raff. What's your pastor doing here?"

What did Mom have against the guy? He was always nice to Sophie.

"Pastor Vince comes often. He became friends with a lot of folk here when he dealt drugs." The words sounded funny coming from Grandma's mouth. Like it was an okay part of his life.

Sophie still couldn't believe the man had been a dealer. He looked so tidy, upper-crusty too.

Grandma nodded to the pastor. "See the guy he's talking to at the table? He shared a jail cell with Vince."

The pastor passed to the bar.

"And that guy owns a pawn shop around the corner. Most people think it's a fence for stolen goods."

Mom's mouth hung. "This is your pastor?"

A lot different from Pastor Johnson back in Philly. But Sophie kind of liked the guy. She thought about what her father would've said. "Isn't that what Jesus would do, Mom? Hang out with tax collectors and sinners."

Mom threw her bib on the plate. "You mean the IRS is here too? Sheesh! What a dump."

Sophie rolled her eyes. "You know what I mean."

Mom's smile felt like love as she patted Sophie's hand. "Yes, I do. And you're right about Jesus. It's just that pastor I question."

~*~

66

Vince felt her presence even before he saw her. She'd always had that power over him—one he thought he could control when he made that bet with Drew—his once best friend—so many years ago. He'd conquer Cassandra, The Pure. He'd reasoned it would be like fighting fire with fire, taking control of his growing feelings—the ones that made men weak—according to his father, at least.

She was like a magnet, drawing his gaze, but he fought it while he grasped the hand of his former cell mate, Chen, who'd done time for burglarizing homes. Vince felt her stare, and knew the hurried speech of her mother filled in his connection to the guy. He almost shook his head with the realization it was another black mark against him. He looked to the ceiling reminding himself he'd been washed of those.

Really? What did it matter anyway? She'd hate him forever for what he did. Why should he care that she'd found out about his jail time?

He slapped a handshake with Eddie at the bar.

"S'up, man." Eddie glanced at the family preparing to leave before his eyebrow twitched.

Cass stood and blew a curl from her face. Something about the gesture pulled at a memory of her serving his table at the country club. He'd smiled at her as she cleared the table, and she'd done a double-take. He'd chuckled at the incredulous expression on her face as she turned away and hoofed it to the kitchen.

His father had almost stopped the conversation with his business partner to congratulate him on his ability to fluster the female help. Dear ole Dad saw that as Vince's greatest asset—charming the ladies to get them to do whatever he wanted. That's the other reason the bet with Drew had appealed to him. It seemed a slam-dunk. Easy money.

Cass brushed at her skirt, straightened, and took her son into the Ladies' Room.

"Hey Vince." Eddie cocked a brow. "Chick's hot, but she's gone now." He snapped his fingers. "I was talking to you."

Vince smiled. "Just cause I'm a pastor now, doesn't mean I can't appreciate the finer things in life."

"She was fine. That's for sure." He waved over Vince's head. "Hey, Lew, over here."

Vince turned to see Archibald Lewis, Billy's father. Thoughts of all the petitions Billy and Kat said on that man's behalf at prayer meetings filled his mind as the man stared daggers into Vince's skull.

"Not sittin' with the preacher." He smoothed back his thinning black hair. "Lilly-whites always give me the creeps."

Eddie patted the stool on the other side. "You won't be sittin' with the preacher. You'll be sittin' with me," he jabbed a thumb to the side, "and Vince."

Vince raised his palms in surrender. "I promise I won't ply you with Bible verses."

The man rolled his eyes so hard his head moved the circle with them. He thumped his thick fingers on the bar. "Scotch." The bartender complied. Lew looked down his nose. "What you drinkin' preacher?"

Vince held up the glass and patted his middle. "Diet Coke. Gotta watch the waistline."

"Hmph."

"C'mon Lew, the guy's cool." Eddie gave Vince a once-over. "Even if his hands are too soft."

"Hey, I've got callouses now. Look." Vince flipped his hands to display his most prized possessions.

"Whoa. Where'd you get those?"

Vince smiled with pride. "Church projects. Repairing houses."

"Widows and orphans, huh?"

"Something like that."

Lew downed his shot. "Yeah, you guys always look so good." He leered. "Saving cats from trees, and helping old ladies cross streets in public." His cheek twitched. "Probl'y beat yer kids in the basement."

Vince almost choked on his soda. "Sorry to disappoint

you, Lew, but I don't have any kids."

Eddie gulped his beer. "I wish someone'd come out and help *my* ole lady. Not exactly a widow, since she never married, but she's been real sick lately. Can hardly get outta bed."

Vince fished a pen out of his pocket and slid a cocktail napkin over to him. "Put her name and number on here, and I'll make sure she gets a meal."

Eddie's lip curled. "You serious? Someone'll bring her food? My brother doesn't even do that, and he lives with her."

"I tell you what, I'll take the dish to her myself."

Eddie scribbled on the napkin as if to challenge Vince to follow through.

Lew grumbled beside him. "Do you all ever actually work for a living? Billy's been trying to sucker me into volunteering for his car-care ministry."

"Yep. We'd love to have you." Vince tried to make eye contact, but the man's gaze ran the length of the bar. "He says you're a whiz with engines. You can fix them, build them, and race them." Billy was so proud of his father's ability he even showed videos of his old dirt-track events.

Lew nodded to the bartender for a refill. He tipped it back and slammed the empty shot glass on the bar. "Long time ago." He watched dregs of amber liquid puddle at the bottom. "Reflexes slow with age."

Or too much drink.

Vince held that thought to himself. "You don't need good reflexes to fix cars."

Lew's expression soured. "Especially for old ladies and poor people."

"Is that beneath you?" Vince hadn't realized the challenge in his voice until he saw the reaction in the man's eyes.

"Beneath me?" He slipped off the stool and hovered his wiry frame over Vince, breath thick with Scotch between them. "Let's not talk levels here, Country Club. I knew your set." Spit flung as he slurred. "I knew yer dad, too."

Those last words bit. Couldn't be a star endorsement on

his resume.

"Don't act like yer gonna swoop in and give me God."
Lew thumbed his chest. "I know what I'm worth, and I don't need
you to tell me."

Vince's gaze traveled the stubbled chin, down the stained
T-shirt and dirty jeans, wondering what kind of worth the man
had calculated for himself.

God saw so much more.

Lew glared as if noting the perusal and coming up
wanting.

"Vrooooooom!" Cass's young son bolted from the
bathroom, and headed straight toward Vince. He wove around
one table, then another. Did the boy recognize him from church?

Cass's eyes went wide as she took after him."Tibo," She
called with a look of mortification on her face.

Vince readied himself to catch the boy until ...

"Umpf!"

~*~

Crazy kid.

Lew wrapped his arms around the boy to make sure they
both didn't land on the beer-soaked floor.

"Tibo!" The woman turned a pleading look to Lew. "I'm so
sorry. He has autism. He doesn't always do what he's supposed
to."

Tibo peeked up from Lew's grasp and let out a roiling
giggle. Something about it swirled around Lew making him want
to join in the joke. "That's okay. Kid just wants to drive fast, that's
all." Lew could understand.

"Mrs. Whitaker, this is Billy Lewis's dad, Lew." Preacher
boy barely made eye contact with the lady as he introduced them.

She jutted out her hand. "Please, call me Cassandra."

You'd have thought the preacher'd been stuck by a sword
the way he looked when she used her first name. Did the guy not
like her being familiar with the likes of him?

70

"Kat tells me you're really good fixing cars."

He grunted. What was he supposed to say—*oh, yes, I'm the best?*

Tibo pulled on Lew's T-shirt, like he wanted the man to join him in a race around the bar. Lew resisted the urge.

"Tibo, leave the man alone."

Lew held up his hand. "That's okay. He's not bothering me." Something about the kid made him want to crack a smile—just a little. He glanced between Vince and Cassandra, and realized they'd never really looked at each other. He suspected a soap opera there.

"Well, I was just leavin'." Lew tousled the boy's hair. "See ya round, kid."

Cassandra pulled on her son and turned. "Us too. Nice meeting you, Lew."

"Yep."

She never said a word to the man staring after her as she walked out the door.

Chapter Nine

Sophie gripped the fabric of her skirt as Sky parked his Honda Civic in front of Water's Edge High School. She peeked sideways at the guy looking very dressed up in his polo and dress pants. It felt too quiet in the car. "You look nice today."

He chuckled. "Never thought I'd need these clothes again. My uncle bought them for a funeral we had to go to."

Should she ask who died? "Your uncle?"

"He's my guardian."

So many questions ran through Sophie's mind as her eyes got caught up in his. He seemed to dare her to ask and warn her of the repercussions at the same time. She waited.

Finally, he dropped his gaze to the arm rest between them. "Social Services took me from my mom when I was ten." The words came out as if he were speaking of someone else. "I spent some time with a foster family." A wistful smile spread as he stared at the bottom of the steering wheel. "They were real nice. Eventually, I was placed with my uncle ..."

Was he disappointed?

"... since he's family."

What could she say to that? "I'm sorry," was all she could think of as several other questions swirled in her head, like *where is your mother now?* And *is your father in the picture at all?*

His laugh rumbled in his chest. "I think I was the only guy not wearing jeans there."

She guessed this was not the time to ask. "There were some people dressed up. But yeah, the church is kind of casual."

Sky popped the latch. "Let's get started." He jogged around and opened her door before she knew what hit her. "It's

72

your turn to drive."

Sophie's mouth dropped open. "Already?"

"Of course. Did you think I was going to demonstrate from the driver's seat?"

Sophie gave herself a mental slap as she stepped from the vehicle, palms clammy, and swapped places with Sky. She stared at the buttons, knobs and levers all around the steering column. "What do I do?" Could she hear his words over the pulse in her ears?

"Your mother really hasn't taken you driving at all?"

She suddenly felt defensive for her mom who was super busy all the time. "She's been kind of distracted."

"Okay. First, you turn the key in the ignition while you gently pump the gas." His instructive tone made her feel safe, like he knew what he was doing.

She cranked the starter, and flinched at the car's hard rev. Sky's slow grin calmed her. Sophie exhaled as the Honda's roar settled into a hum.

"Now, put your foot on the brake, and shift into gear."

Sophie loved the way he went step-by-step without making her feel like an idiot. She followed his instruction, moving the car forward in fits and starts.

He took the motion well. "Just make that—" jerk "—left turn—" he grabbed the dash "—around the gym. Lighter on the pedals, there."

She turned the wheel, and the car lurched to the left.

"Whoa! Not so much. Take it easy." He grimaced. "We're in no hurry to get to the other side of the school." Except his crooked smile seemed to block all transmission from her brain.

He sucked in a breath and blew it from his full lips.

"At least there's no one here I can hit."

"Yep. We got that goin' for us."

He led her through the parking lot in one direction three times, then the other direction four. Little by little it became more second nature. Sophie's breathing calmed, and her grip relaxed on the wheel.

Sky pointed to the school's front entrance. "Now park over there."

She eased the car up against—Wham!—the curb.

His brows jumped as he grabbed his seat.

"Oh! Oh! I'm sorry, Sky. I didn't hurt anything did I?"

He winced. "That's okay." The words were not convincing. "I think my tires can handle it." He mumbled, "And hopefully the alignment is still good."

Sophie froze. She couldn't unstick her fingers from the wheel to shift backwards.

"Back up and straighten out a bit." His baritone soothed her.

She complied.

Sky hopped out of the car, before she could ask what was next, and popped his trunk. After rustling around, he pulled out two traffic cones, placed them next to the curb, and stuck up-ended brooms in each. He had a dangerous spark in his eye as he turned to look in through the windshield.

Sophie shook her head. "Oh, no. I'm not ready to parallel park. You just saw what I did to the curb."

He jogged to the opened window, leaning his elbows on the door, his cologne meandering after him as a gentle breeze touched the blond curls at his collar. "You can do it, Soph. I know you can. So what if I need new tires after." He tugged at the sleeve of her blouse, leaving a warm imprint on her arm where his fingers had brushed.

Back in the car, Sky gave her directions about shifting, turning, gassing, braking. She followed as best she could, bumping into the broomsticks over and over, Sky claiming she nailed his Aunt Shirley's car the first time, Grandma Gertrude's another, and a few cousins in between. When he groaned over the death of his pet warthog, named Oinker, Sophie laughed so hard she ran over the cone and almost up the curb.

"Whoa!"

Sophie braked and parked.

"Man, when you take em' down, you don't mess around."

His wide eyes softened. "Now one last time. But keep it slow."

After Sky set the broom back in the cone, Sophie pulled up next to it, shifted to reverse, then rotated the steering wheel all the way to the left as she inched into the spot. Reversing the wheel, she let up on the brake, easing some more. She stopped and grasped the gear shift.

Sky's hand covered hers. "Not yet. Back up a little more."

Sophie's brows knotted. Not just because of the warmth of Sky's palm across the back of her hand, but because she wondered why it felt so rough, bumpy. Not like callouses, but sores. She flinched.

He pulled his hand back and fisted it between his knees, staring out his window. "Go ahead." Words tight.

The air in the vehicle seemed to harden as Sophie peeked at the guy next to her. She backed up, shifted into drive, and pulled up to the front broom.

"I did it!" The accomplishment bubbled up inside.

Sky nodded curtly. "Yes, you did."

The bubbles popped. What just happened? "Thank you, Sky. You're a great teacher."

He nodded again. "I better get you back home now."

She unfastened her seatbelt and pulled the door latch. "Yeah. Sure."

They traded places, and rode to Sophie's house in absolute silence.

~*~

Vince poked the doorbell at Cecelia Crenshaw's house — Eddie's mom. Yolanda stood next to him carrying a cooler and a casserole dish. The button fell from the encasement and dangled precariously. Had it even sounded inside the house?

He scanned the front — shingles missing, lawn and garden overgrown, trash piled high.

"I can see your friend takes good care of his Mama." Yolanda's tone did not register appreciation for the man.

Vince decided to knock on the screen door this time. It rattled as if made of foil.

The door swung open. A large dude in a muscle shirt eyed them up and down. "We don't want any."

"We're friends of Eddie's." Vince slung the words as if to race the closing door.

It halted. Then slowly peeled back revealing muscle-shirt guy again, a question mark on his face as he scanned the two intruders. "You can't be serious. Eddie's got *tidy* friends?"

Why did Vince suddenly feel overdressed in his Dockers and polo? And why did it feel as though the word *tidy* somehow translated into *prissy*?

Yolanda pushed through the entrance. "We brought your Mama food." She lifted the coolers and bags she carried while staring the man down. "Show me the kitchen."

Muscle Shirt let go of the door, lifting a brow at the woman, even if he did let her have her way. Yolanda marched in as if she were the President's personal chef, preparing for a state visit.

Vince followed past the weight bench strewn with T-shirts, stepped over balled up socks and scattered sneakers to find the woman already opening and shutting cabinets as she looked for cooking utensils. He placed his bags on the counters.

Yolanda pivoted to Muscle Shirt, pointing to the dish-filled sink. "You ever clean these?"

He shrugged. "Dishwasher's broken."

She glared. "The *faucet* work?" Vince could tell she fought hard to hold back a Z-snap.

The guy sneered as he pivoted toward the living room.

Yolanda turned to Vince. "Go meet with the woman. I'll take care of this place."

The rabble of a daytime reality show grew in volume as Muscle Shirt flopped on the couch and sunk into its cushions.

Vince took the short hall to find the lady he'd heard had been bed-ridden with pneumonia. He knocked on the door frame. "Mrs. Crenshaw?"

The middle-aged woman, propped up on pillows, turned from the soap opera in front of her. "Who are you?"

"My name's Vince Steegle. Edd—"

"You that pastor he said would visit? I didn't believe him."

Vince smirked. "That's okay. I don't think Eddie did either."

She eyed him suspiciously. "You gonna heal me with a prayer, Preacher?"

He chuckled and shook his head. "I'm not that kind of minister."

Her lips twisted into a sardonic grin. "Then what good are you?"

"I brought food." He shoved his hands in his pockets. "Well, actually, Yolanda brought it. She's heating some soup for you now, and she's got a couple of casseroles to tide you over the next week."

Her eyebrows rose.

"Would you like us to serve you here, or can I escort you to the kitchen for lunch."

"*Escort* me?" Her forehead creased. "You got Prince Charming out there too?"

Vince guffawed thinking of the woman preparing the meal. "No. More like Oscar the Grouch." He reached out his hand in a gallant gesture, giving Cecelia Crenshaw his most charming smile. "Your chariot awaits."

She eyed him sideways. Then front-ways. Then tilted her head before pulling the sheets from her pajama-clad legs. She expelled a croupy cough that sounded like she might relieve herself of her previous meal. If she'd even had one.

"Have you seen a doctor?"

Cecelia grasped his hand and leaned into him as she stood from the bed. "Emergency room two days ago. I got a few weeks of antibiotics that make my stomach queasy."

He led her down the hall, now saturated in the aroma of home-made bone-broth chicken soup—Yolanda's supposed cure-all for anything—and fresh biscuits.

Cecelia sucked a breath through her nose, eyes closing as her smile stretched. They opened as Vince pulled a chair from under the table for her to sit on. Yolanda placed a steaming bowl in front of her.

"Can I pray for you?" He sat next to her.

She nodded.

Rolling his eyes, Muscle Shirt strode in and bent over the soup.

Yolanda slapped his fingers when he reached for the ladle. "That's for your mama." Her glare sent him out of the kitchen like a puppy faced with a rolled up newspaper.

Suppressing a chuckle, Vince began, "Dear Heavenly Father," His fingers swallowed up the sick woman's small ones, "We pray you will bring healing to Cecelia."

She ground out another string of phlegm-filled noise.

Vince flinched at its violence. "Clear her lungs. Strengthen her body. Make her whole." His thoughts turned more to the spiritual than the physical.

She pulled a hand from his grasp to cover her mouth for another torrent.

Vince peeked out of one eye. She grimaced back.

"Fill her with your Holy Spirit. Make her well, Lord." He drew in the scent of the broth. "We also ask You to bless this food to its intended use. In Your Son, Jesus' name. Amen."

Her amen was punctuated by another clearing.

Vince glanced to Yolanda washing the dishes that filled the sink from who knows how many days worth of meals. She nodded and smiled.

Chapter Ten

"I like this place." Cassandra slid into the seat across the table from Kat and pulled out a chair for Tibo. Sophie dropped down next to her on the other side.

Cassandra sipped her latte. "I've never seen a Christian bookstore, or any bookstore for that matter, like this one."

Kat's bracelets clacked together as she pushed her freshly permed locks from her well-tanned face. "Ten years ago it was a plain-ole Christian retailer—a few Jesus-centered gifty-thingies here and there." She waved her bangled arm toward some shelves. "But when e-readers and online shopping took over, the owners prayed hard and came up with a more interactive, people-centered gathering place."

Cassandra's gaze ran over the floor-to-ceiling selection of Christian books, classics to hot releases, clusters of seating for Bible studies and small groups, and an open computer-search area where an employee helped customers find new items both in paperback and available for immediate download. Right then, the cashier was giving a tutorial to an elderly woman on how to use her new iPad app.

"Mom, can we come on Café Night?" Sophie's blue eyes sparked with enthusiasm. "The kids at youth group say some of the local musicians are really good."

"Sure, Sophie." Cassandra fished a few toy cars from her purse and drove them across the table to her son. He took them and scurried toward the carpeted area near a couch.

"I'm gonna check out the music section." Sophie headed to a shelf with earphones.

Kat twirled a new curl while bouncing her leg over a knee.

"I hear you met Billy's pop, Lew."

Cassandra chuckled. "How'd you hear about that?"

"Well, sort of from the man himself." She tugged the curl straight. "Actually, he came by for a free haircut and started asking me a bunch of questions about autism. I asked him why he wanted to know, and he told me about meeting Tibo at The Dock."

"Poor man. He stood to leave and Tibo barreled into him."

"Lew didn't seem to mind. He said Tibo'd been acting like a race car—Lew's lingo." Kat smirked. "If he could become a car himself, I think it would be his dying wish."

Cassandra's gaze turned toward her son driving a small vehicle up the side of a chair leg. "I guess he and Tibo share that passion."

"Lew even cracked a smile while talking about him …" Kat blinked, "I think."

"Tibo does that to people." Cassandra looked into her cup. "At least those not put off by his disability."

Kat sighed. "If only Lew didn't drink so much, he might actually be good with kids. He worries me every time I think about him driving one of those big delivery trucks. He's gonna kill himself, or someone else, one of these days."

Cassandra thought about the shots he threw back at the bar. "Is he an alcoholic?"

Kat nodded. "Probably where Billy got his tendencies from."

Cassandra almost gasped at the woman's openness. "Is Billy—?"

Kat's eyes narrowed. "Worse. Or he *was* worse." Kat pulled in a long sip of java as she re-crossed her legs. "Billy had a drug problem some years ago. All kinds of lovely stuff. It took him three tries at rehab, lots of prayers from customers at his shop who suspected, and one bold man continually inviting him to church, before he gave it all to the Lord and surrendered his addiction. That's how we came to Water's Edge Community."

Suddenly, Cassandra felt grateful for the short time she

had with a husband who'd sought to follow God the whole time she'd known him. "That must have been awful."

Kat leaned forward. "You don't know the half of it. Before he finally got help, he almost lost his business. Billy's work had become sloppy, the income was going to his drugs, and he'd begun to hang out with a bunch of low-lifes," she dropped her voice and looked around, "who found him opportunities to make easy cash to support his habit." She shook her head. "Our world was sinking and there didn't seem to be a way to stop it. Eventually, I had to protect myself and our daughter, and kicked him out. I told him to clean up before he showed his face again."

It was weird to hear this side of the man who held the respect of each church member for his hard work in various ministries. She'd already learned about his car-care ministry and how he oversaw the housing repair projects parishioners engaged in on a regular basis. Obviously, his wife was proud of him too.

"So he got help after that?"

Kat's laugh lacked humor. "Billy's a good man." She grimaced. "Billy-on-drugs was not. Both of us, and our daughter, Shelby, wanted the good man back. So he got help."

Cassandra stared into her cup and meditated on the warmth emanating from it into her palms.

"What are you thinking?" The woman had the most probing gold in her eyes sometimes. They let you know she would not leave something unsaid if she'd planned to hear it.

Cassandra's gaze met them. "I'm thinking how you barely know me, and yet feel free to open your life to me."

Kat's smile tilted. "Some people call that my curse." She shrugged and peeled off a layer of the cinnamon roll in her hand. "I hate lies. I prefer to live by truth." Her gaze traveled around the book shop. "I also feel it's important to let people see our brokenness, to let them know we've been there too. That's where Jesus meets us. Our story can give others hope." Her shoulder lifted again. "If they see how we got through it, maybe they'll have strength to overcome something as well."

Cassandra nodded. Billy's story gave *her* strength, like the many testimonies Tim had shared with her over the years. Yes, Jesus met us in our brokenness. Maybe that's why she felt so close to Him. She glanced to the little boy who melted hearts with a simple smile, feeling the depth of her inadequacy in caring for him as he needed. She could only trust that God had a plan.

Cassandra leaned back in her seat. "I didn't realize you had a daughter."

"She's away at college, doing a summer internship." The bracelets jangled as she waved her arm. "Anyway, I worry what it will take to make Lew see the light. That man's got a tougher shell than most."

"Maybe he needs something to soften it."

"Hmph."

Cassandra's mind meandered into thoughts of her own in-laws. She knew what it was like to have concerns on that front, though hers were completely different. Still, Tim had never given her a moment of grief. Too bad she hadn't learned to appreciate the man enough until it was too late.

Kat's eyes moved back and forth as if reading Cassandra's thoughts. "What are you thinking about?" There was that question again.

Cassandra better learn to school her expressions in front of the woman. Otherwise, Kat might probe things Cassandra hadn't planned to reveal. "My husband."

"Tim?" Obviously, Mom had filled Kat in on her entire history—what she knew of it.

Cassandra turned her cup back and forth and nodded.

"What was he like?" Though Kat didn't shy away from the hard subjects, she whispered the words as if requesting permission to ask. There was a safety in it.

Cassandra's eyes stung less than usual, but the pain was still there. "Perfect." She met Kat's gaze. "And yet God took him from me anyway." She hadn't meant to sound so ungrateful, but maybe she was.

Kat patted her hand. "He's hard to figure out sometimes, isn't He?"

"Yes," was all she croaked out.

"Yet willing to die for us."

Cassandra nodded. A change of subject would be good. "So you stayed with Billy after all that."

Her friend's expression suggested she understood, and was willing to move once again to her own former troubles. "When he accepted the help, I couldn't leave him." She shrugged. "I love him."

Sophie bounded up and dropped three CD cases in front of Cassandra. "Can I have an advance on my allowance? I'd really like to get these."

Cassandra sifted through them—David Crowder, Third Day and NEEDTOBREATHE. Her favorites. Sure Sophie could have an advance. "Okay, honey."

Sophie looked between the ladies. "Did I hear you talking about love?" Her eyebrows jumped.

They both smiled back.

Sophie swiveled toward Kat and dropped her chin in her palms. "How did you know you were in love with your husband?" Her favorite topic these days.

Kat leaned back and stirred her coffee round and round with the little red stick. "Hmm. Let me think." Her sandaled foot bounced. "We'd known each other since elementary school. He pulled my hair in third grade when I sat in front of him in homeroom."

Cassandra giggled. "Sounds like love to me."

Kat's smile was wistful. "I always thought he was a big pest until one day in middle school this little shadow appeared right here on his face." She tapped the dip between her lower lip and chin then sighed. "Peach fuzz—powerful stuff. My heart was never the same. I'd never seen a more manly hunk—from my eighth-grade estimation—in my entire life."

Sophie joined the chuckles and turned to Cassandra. "How about you, Mom?"

Uh-oh.

"When did you know you were in love with Dad?"

Cassandra stilled. She couldn't answer. Both Kat and Sophie stared as if wondering what took her so long. She looked again to the little boy on the carpet whose features so reflected his father's, his attention planted on her as though waiting for the answer himself. How could she tell them it was only after years of marriage that she realized she loved her husband?

"Mom?" Sophie held out her palms. "Did he do something grand to win you over?"

Did he ever! And still she resisted his love.

Sophie turned to Kat. "He was always doing special things for us."

Cassandra melted at the thought.

"So, Mom. What was it?"

Cassandra released the captured breath. "I think it was the combination of a lot of things that won me over. We knew each other for years before I finally realized how much I loved him."

The way Kat's brows drew together unnerved Cassandra. Like she saw more than she should.

"Awww. No big moment?" Sophie seemed disappointed.

"Sometimes the best love comes in being there for the every-day kinds of things." Tim had certainly done that for her— when she needed him the most. "And you know your father."

Sophie's smile spread across her face. "Yeah, he was the best."

Cassandra swallowed hard. Yes, he was. She'd never find someone like Tim again.

~*~

Lew shifted up his '69 Camaro and swerved left around the puttering station wagon filled with screaming brats. Straight line, free of cars, in the fast lane of the interstate. Some woman in an SUV, talking illegally on her cell phone, swayed in front of him. Lew sighed and jammed his brake pedal.

Speed. He just wanted a little rush and couldn't wait to get to the old dirt road that made his heart beat again.

Alive.

It had taken him ten years to restore this baby. One paycheck at a time, and livin' on Ramen Noodles, but it was worth it. He smoothed his fingers along the dash, letting the roar of the engine flow through his arm, rumbling into his backbone.

Sweet music.

He swung across three lanes and exited the Hagerstown off-ramp. Almost there.

He pulled onto the local road. And cursed! A wide-load flatbed crept along the two-lane route, like if it made one false move, half the double-wide home would tumble off. He inched left to watch for vehicles in the on-coming lane. A line of them. His fingers tapped the wheel. When would this beast finally turn off? He inched over again. Two sedans, a big space, then a bunch of other cars. He could fit.

The sedans passed. One. Two. He swerved out, saw his chance and gunned into the emptiness. A dually truck came barreling toward him as the wide-load faded to the right. Lew could make it. A smile crept up his lips as he punched the clutch and shifted higher. A horn blared. He squeezed the gas pedal for more juice and swung in front of the wide-load, the dually passing to the left. Lew's pulse thrummed in his neck like the beat of a hard-driving classic-rock tune.

Yes!

Lew scanned the tree-lined drive for the hidden entrance. He'd discovered this road two years ago on his way to a dirt-track race event in Hagerstown. A god-send. It wouldn't be too long before somebody developed this property and made his "road of salvation" a yuppie townhome haven.

There it was. Taking the turn at full speed, his back wheels skidded sideways along the pavement. The car consumed the dirt path ahead as he entered. Lew loved the feel of gravel under his tires. Controlled chaos. Not having as much grip, it took a skilled driver to subdue. And Lew was its master.

Once.

The dirt path through the overhanging trees stretched in

front of him. *Thread the needle.* Curving to the left, the wheels sluiced in the dirt. A tree closed into view. Lew maneuvered the steering wheel. The tires gripped.

He cleared the tree.

The control of the road washed over him as he skidded right and barely missed another trunk. Now to the straightaway. The long stretch of path that led to the pit—the gaping chasm of earth left by the abandoned quarry. Probably the reason it had never been developed.

Lew's mind ran over the shifting, turning, *feeling* he'd need to evade that pit at high speed. Otherwise he'd jettison into ...

Death.

Something about that word intrigued Lew. Invited him. What would it be like to fly off that precipice, floating over the crevice of earth? Weightless, as his classic Camara arced forward, then plummeted to the jagged rock below. Lew imagined an instant of elation as his stomach rose from the lack of gravity. Adrenaline pumping through his veins, then ...

Nothing.

Why did that appeal so much to him right now? Almost like a drug he couldn't take, dangled in front of him, calling him, teasing him.

Then visions of Billy crashed into his mind. The smile draped by that fu-man-chu that looked like a chocolate milk mustache had dripped to his chin on either side. He'd slap Lew on the back and tell him how much he appreciated his help at the garage. Could Lew really believe his son loved him after a lifetime of neglect? All those prayers that he'd change one day.

Lew ground his teeth. He'd never live up to Billy's hopes. The kid would always want Lew to be something more, ever since he'd gone through rehab ten years ago and got religion.

The trees whizzed by as the end of the road zoomed forward. He could see the far edge of the quarry and the tiny trees that dotted the ridge. How far would the Camaro fly before it made its downward trajectory? Lew's heart raced faster than the tires spun. Just a few seconds more and he wouldn't need to measure up to anyone's standards again.

The little blond boy came to mind—Tibo was it?—and the feel of his delicate arms around Lew. If only he could roll back the years with his own son. He'd change things. Would his boy have looked at him like little Tibo did?

You can't change the past.

Lew's chest constricted. He gulped air, shifted higher, squeezed the gas. More power, more speed. He wanted to bridge the gap as far as he could. One last moment of glory.

Boy, that kid's deep brown eyes sunk into him. He couldn't shake it. It was like the kid had found something good when he looked inside, and then grabbed hold.

Ha!

Lew's throat clogged.

The edge drew nearer. He'd conquered the corner before, spun to the edge and straightened just in time to hug the road and drive on. But this time he'd conquer the pit … and his destiny.

The trees opened to display the road to the left. He sucked in a lungful of air. Would that help him float? He gunned the engine and …

Swoosh!

The back tires sluiced as he made the hard left. His heart pounded his ribcage. He needed to gain control. The rear wheels tasted the edge before they gripped and propelled him forward and down the road. He slammed his brakes, shifted to neutral and pulled his parking brake.

Lew's chest heaved for air, competing for space with his pounding heart. His eyes burned. He gasped for more breaths as he peered around at the trees clapping their leaves in the breeze, like they mocked his failure.

What was he thinking?

Why couldn't he do it?

Coward!

He shook out of the competing voices, shifted into drive, and cranked the stereo. Zepplin played on the classic rock station. He spun the volume control higher to drown out the noise in his head, then drove the rest of the maze of dirt roads until it was time to go home.

Chapter Eleven

Vince pulled up to the ramshackle house. These community projects always energized him—fixing up the home of someone in need. The early July sun beat down on all the Water's Edge Community Church volunteers busy on ladders at the front, or digging in the gardens, or mending the fence.

Times like these he was proudest of his congregation.

Billy Lewis tilted the circular saw up from the lumber he'd cut and waited for the piercing buzz to fade. "Hey Vince."

"Looks like you all got a jump on me. Didn't you say to be here by 10:00 a.m.?"

Billy glanced around. "Oh yeah." Why did he look like he'd been caught with his hand in the till? "I forgot to mention, some of us thought it might be a good idea to get a head start."

Vince scanned the yard filled with workers. "It seems like the whole crew is already here."

Billy grabbed another two-by-four. "Well, you know church folk. Eager to do the Lord's work." His smile seemed a little pained.

Lew lifted a wood board from the stack beside Billy, rolled his eyes and scoffed.

Wait. Lew was here? How did Billy get him to come? Tibo Whitaker, wearing a tool belt filled with real tools, shadowed him wherever he went, and the man didn't even seem to mind.

Vince found his eyes automatically searching for the boy's mother. Was she here? Not anywhere he could see.

Billy jabbed a thumb in his dad's direction. "You've met my pop, right?"

Lew pulled a hammer from Tibo's belt, mussed the kid's

89

hair then pounded a nail through the plank at the frame of the large front window.

"Sure." Vince shoved his hands in his worn jeans pocket. "At The Dock."

"Yep. Lilly-White and I are old friends." Lew spoke through the nails in his teeth as he pounded the wood.

Tibo watched the man as if in awe.

"Lilly-White?" Billy's eyes questioned Vince.

Vince shrugged. "That's what he calls me."

Billy doubled over laughing, almost banging his head into the circular saw. He stomped his foot and pulled in a long breath.

Lew's brow tilted as he eyed his son.

Tibo turned and tilted a brow, too.

Composing himself, Billy straightened his tool belt and slapped an arm around Vince's shoulder. "Well, Lilly-White, let's see what job we can find for you to do."

Billy's brown-eyed gaze trailed the line of the roof where three guys banged shingles into place. His brow furrowed and head shook. Vince was glad he nixed that idea, not being too keen on walking slanted surfaces high off the ground.

"How'd you get your dad here?"

Billy's mustache bent. "Really don't know. I was talking about some of the kids that were coming to volunteer and as I described Tibo, he cut me off and said he was free to help. At first, I didn't connect it, but they seemed to know each other when we got here."

Vince's gaze drifted to the little boy hammering with a plastic tool next to Lew, again wondering about the possible presence of the boy's mom. "They met at The Dock a few nights ago when Mrs. Whitaker was there with her whole family. They seemed to take an immediate liking to each other."

Billy tilted his head. "Why do you always call her Mrs. Whitaker?"

"That's what she wants." Vince toed a rock in the grass.

"Oh."

Vince turned. "So what do you have for me to do?"

Billy narrowed his eyes then led Vince to the side yard where a few parishioners hammered panels into the fence. He began to turn Vince toward the garden.

"Wait." Vince noticed fence panels missing in several other spots. "I can take care of those."

A burst of air exited Billy's mouth.

"Really, Billy. Adam Grant showed me how last time."

The man grimaced.

"You didn't like how it turned out?"

The grimace took over Billy's face. No words.

Vince glared.

Billy swatted his back. "Okay, fine. You take care of those panels over there." Billy's eyes rolled to the heavens as though beseeching God.

"I can do this."

Billy's nod was not convincing. "Right."

Vince would show him. He'd attach the panels better than a pro. Now where was an extra hammer?

He spotted a box full of tools by a patch of garden. Kneeling in the dirt were two teens—a boy and a girl. He took a second look. Cass's girl, wearing short-shorts and a low-cut T that invited the eye whenever she bent over the dirt. And the eyes of the guy next to her had accepted that invitation more than once. Had he been the one to bring them there? Vince scanned again for Cass and figured the guy had. Was Vince disappointed or relieved?

He strode to the gardeners. "Sophie, isn't it? Mrs. Hessing's granddaughter."

She twisted toward him. "Oh hi, Pastor Vince." This is my friend, Sky." Her expression lit as she turned to the kid. "He's been coming to church with us lately and brought Tibo and me here today."

"Yes. I thought I'd seen you all together." Why did Vince's muscles stiffen? He usually loved an opportunity to impact another young life.

The guy never made eye contact. "Well, we better get back

to work." He grabbed the hand shovel Sophie offered, fingers lingering a little too long on hers.

Sophie's smile lengthened as she let go. "Yeah, lots of work weeding this mess."

Vince turned to settle a glare on the boy, but Sky seemed determined not to meet it. He glanced once as though Vince's eyes could scorch.

They could!

What was wrong with Vince? Why did this kid make him feel protective of Cass's daughter? He sucked in a breath, determined to right his home-repair reputation.

After nailing one fence panel into place, Vince inspected it. Crooked. He looked around. How did the other guys do it so well? He blew out an exasperated sigh.

"Here. Let me show you." Lew pried the nails out with a hammer to undo Vince's mess. "Use this board to line the other ones and make them parallel." He gave Vince the nail.

Vince placed it and hit it with the hammer.

"Watch your hands, Pastor," a voice called from the roof. "You don't want to get 'em broke."

Vince smirked at the guy knowing he was referring to one of the many trips to the emergency room he'd had since he became part of the home improvement team. "Ha ha, Jorge. Don't fall from that roof, now."

The guy stood, teetered with a grin, "Whoa, whoa—" until Adam Grant pulled him down, both men chuckling.

Lew's lips tilted. "Well, at least ya try, Lilly-White. I'll give ya that." Lew showed him how to line the panels some more with a patience Billy never gave him. But then again, Billy was all about getting the job done on time.

On occasion, Vince would peek at the teens now planting petunias, Tibo driving a toy truck through the grass beside them.

"Pretty girl, that one." Lew nodded toward Sophie. "Daughter of that woman you were staring at the other night, isn't she?"

Vince met Lew's all-too-knowing gaze. He didn't figure

Lew would appreciate a lie. "Yes."

"I think she's got it bad for the boy."

Vince grunted. He glanced over to see Sky playfully tugging the hem of Sophie's form-fitting T-shirt. His eyes lowered as his smile slid up.

Something burned inside Vince.

"Hey, Lilly-White, relax. They're kids having fun."

Vince knew all about that kind of fun. It didn't make him feel any better. The Sky dude inserted a finger into her belt loop, pulled her closer and whispered in her ear. She giggled as Sky's gaze met Vince's heated stare. Sky let go as if touching hot coals.

"Hey, Vince." Billy's calloused palm waved in front of his face. "I'd like to be finished by the end of the day."

Vince snapped to. "Yeah, sure, right." He stood and picked up a few fence pickets over by the gardeners.

Sky gave him a sideways glance. "So how's the fence going there?" His gaze landed back in the dirt.

"It's doin' fine, Sky." Vince swung the hammer back and forth. "You see," he watched the hammer sway, waiting for Sky to turn his way again, "the trick is …"

Sky looked up at the pause in Vince's words.

"You gotta make sure your hands don't go where they're not supposed to," Vince pointed his eyes to Sophie then back again, "otherwise, your fingers might get broke."

Sky's eyebrows shot up just before he scooted some distance from the girl, and resumed his work.

Vince grinned as he turned. At least he'd accomplished *something* today. He twirled the hammer in the air and—*Ouch!*—dropped it on his toe. Lew shook his head and snickered as Vince picked it from the grass.

~*~

Sophie inspected her nails as Sky revved his car into life. He'd become a little distant after chatting with Pastor Vince. Having faded out when it turned to building stuff, she hadn't heard what they talked about. All she cared about was making the garden beautiful so the family could smile at the lush colors surrounding them.

"How 'bout we go for ice cream cones?" Sky turned his upper body toward her as if to stress the idea.

Oh, ice cream sounded awesome after a long, sweaty day in the sun. "Sure." Good thing Mom had picked Tibo up for a therapy appointment. Sophie wouldn't have felt right getting an ice cream since he couldn't eat any, and she doubted The Ice Cream Stop had non-dairy desserts.

Sky shifted and drove the few blocks to the place. He ordered chocolate on a waffle cone. She ordered mint chip—with extra sprinkles—on a sugar cone. They sat in the car facing each other as they consumed the creamy confection.

Sophie couldn't help but notice the way his tongue traveled the edge of the cone, and his full lips bit into the top. His warm brown eyes lifted to catch hers. A smile grew on his face.

Feeling her cheeks heat, she dropped her attention to her hollowed out cone, and crunched into it. "You're staring at me."

His chuckle sent chills through her arms. "Just returning the favor."

She giggled while finishing the last of her cone. The napkin stuck to her hands when she tried to wipe off the ice cream, so she reached into her purse to find a Wet-one.

"Got one of those for me." Sky plucked bits of napkin off his fingers where they stuck.

"Sure. Give me your hand." Sophie grabbed his left one.

He yanked it back, but she resisted. "Come on, let me clean you up." She smirked at what seemed like a little boy reluctant for a bath then noticed his expression had grown dark.

He tugged harder, bringing attention to his palm, marred on every inch with circular scars. Were those cigarette burns?

Gasping, she released him.

He tucked the hand between his knees.

"What happened, Sky?"

"What?" He stared at his legs.

"You know what I mean. Those scars." She was too upset not to yell.

His gaze was glued to his jeans.

"Sky. What was that?"

"I already told you." He barely moved his jaw to form the words.

"Did your mom do that?" How could someone torture their own child?

His nod was so short she barely saw it. "It's how she punished me when I was bad."

Sophie closed her eyes. Her heart ached for the little boy he used to be. She took his hand in hers, and pressed it between her own. She wanted him to know he was loved ... by Jesus, so she placed the injured palm to her cheek, the harshness against her skin.

His brown eyes lifted to hers searching, longing, receiving what she wanted to give. His other palm closed in on her face.

She shivered.

He pulled her to him. Their lips touched.

Her first kiss. It felt so right, she melted into it.

Something washed over Sophie drawing her closer, deeper into all of who Sky was. The connection intense, like nothing she'd ever known. Was this love?

His hands moved to her hips then slipped into the back of her T-shirt, pulling her into him.

She shivered again. Was this going too far? She didn't know. All she knew was that it felt real good.

A knock fell on the window. "What do you guys recommend?" Pastor Vince's expression was anything but jovial. "Cherry cheesecake flavored ice cream or Rocky Road?"

Sky's jaw grew ridged.

Sophie peeked out the window. How much had the pastor seen? She resisted the urge to palm her flaming cheeks. "I'd, um ..." she cleared the crud from her throat. "I'd get the Rocky Road."

Sky cranked the ignition and revved the engine loud

95

enough Sophie could barely hear the pastor's response. He waved, and entered The Ice Cream Stop as the car jerked into reverse and rolled out of the parking lot.

Chapter Twelve

"You gonna help us out here or what, Perkins?"

Kevin eyed the guy on the ladder, banging a long nail through the gutter. "I need to prep the inside for painting."

The guy scoffed.

"Hey, I got you this job, didn't I?" Kevin strode in through the front door before he could hear any more of the dude's ungrateful remarks. The jerk would be unemployed if it weren't for him.

"How's it going?" Cassandra stepped out of the kitchen.

"Great." He scanned her blouse and slacks. "You look like you need to get somewhere."

She checked her watch. "I have a meeting with some church leaders in McLean Virginia about their special needs program."

"Why don't you go ahead? I've got everything covered here." He forced his friendliest, most trustworthy smile.

"That's okay. My mom should be back with the kids any minute. I'd rather stick around in case you have questions or need something."

Questions. She just didn't trust him. "I think we're good." He gestured to the extra room. "I'm gonna prep the inside to paint."

Cassandra nodded before grabbing a mug and pouring coffee. She sat at the kitchen table, plugged earbuds into her ears, and flipped through her pages of notes.

Now was as good a time as any. The woman lurked over him whenever he was inside the house. At least with the music drowning out sound, he might be able to take a real look around.

Cassandra always seemed protective of her closet. He'd see what he could find there—valuables, bank statements, credit cards—anything that could lead him to her fortune, or be traded for one of its own.

Kevin took one last look at the lady tapping her toe to the beat buzzing from her MP3 player and slipped into the bedroom. Boxes lined the shelves of the walk-in. Plastic drawers were stacked along the floor. He pulled out one after the other, sifted through pages and shook containers, and what did he find? Lots of junk. Pictures, kids' drawings, funky hats, old shoes and a bunch of tangled jewelry. He fisted that and stuffed it in his pockets just in case.

One last set of drawers. He pulled. Jackpot! Financial records. All he needed were a few account numbers and one of his buddies could help him siphon them. He flipped through to find a credit card statement. It only had a five hundred dollar credit limit. No point wasting his time on that. Pushing it aside, he searched for the larger one, or maybe a –Whoa! Here it was.

Kevin's fingers shook as he took in the address of a prominent bank in Philadelphia. He pulled it from the file and scanned the page. Hundreds of thousands of dollars had been moved in and out of the account in this one month—like she'd sold something big, then used the cash for something else. What would it be like to maneuver that kind of dough on a daily basis?

He folded the statement and shoved it in his back pocket, almost giddy at the thought of draining the account somehow. He knew just the guy who could help him.

There was more here. Kevin could feel it. The in-laws— those kids' grandparents—carried a net-worth in the billions. Surely, there was some way to access their wealth as well. But how? Suddenly hundreds-of-thousands sounded like a pittance. The thought of handling millions of dollars made his pulse pound. They'd barely blink at the loss, and Kevin could leave the country and go back to that little town in Mexico he really liked. He'd live like a king there.

What was that sound? Someone was coming. Kevin closed

boxes, shut drawers, stuffed the necklaces deeper into his pockets, and felt to make sure the bank statement didn't stick out.

"What are you doing in here?" Cassandra's head tilted. The earbuds hung from a button, no music pumping out.

He gestured at the dimensions of the space. "I was thinking we should probably make the closet in the addition the same size as the existing rooms. A greater uniformity would add to its resale value." Like he really cared what they sold the place for ten years from now.

His breath halted as he waited for her response. Did she believe him? Green eyes stared straight through him.

Her blink was patronizing. "We already discussed that. I'd rather not add to the expense, and I don't appreciate you continually trying to up-sell this job."

Kevin held up his palms. "That's okay, Mrs. Whitaker. I'm sorry I brought it up."

The steam expelling from her nostrils seemed to cool as the opening of the front door sounded and that little retarded kid darted in and swallowed her in an embrace. She rubbed his back, her features melting into a smile. "Did you have fun, Tibo?"

He peeked up. "Fun."

Her smile grew. She really seemed to love that kid. Even though he was a half-wit. Kevin bet his rich grandparents loved him that much too. The big question was, could that love be measured in dollars and cents?

~*~

Sophie blinked, trying to clear the sleepies out of her eyes as she shuffled through the hallway toward the kitchen. Still exhausted after Grandma dragged her and Tibo around Annapolis yesterday morning, she'd take advantage of the extra hours of rest this summer while she could.

Her next blink came with a knock at the door.

Running a hand through her unruly hair, she twisted the knob to open it, hardly remembering she was still in her pajamas and pink fuzzy slippers. Who'd bang so loud this early in the morning? Okay, maybe ten a.m. wasn't *that* early.

"Sky!" She shut the door in his face.

Mom walked in straightening her business suit. "Who was that?"

"I just slammed the door on Sky." Now, she was mortified.

"Sophie." Mom gave her the are-you-crazy look.

"Can you get it?" She ran into her room. "I need to get dressed."

"Were we expecting him?"

"No!" she called, voice shaking.

Sophie pulled out drawer after drawer. Where was that new top that clung to her shape … and the cute jean shorts with the designs on the pockets? She threw a few items on the floor in the search.

There. She sighed as she pulled off the pajamas, flipped the slippers from her feet, and dressed in record time. Dragging a brush through her long, black hair she checked her reflection. It was the best she could do on such short notice. What was Sky doing here, anyway?

Sophie jogged out the bedroom door, slowing as she approached the living room where she heard Mom chatting with him, and tried to look demure … or something better than crazy, at least. "Oh, hi Sky." Like she hadn't already seen him.

His lips tilted almost flipping her heart. His gaze lowered. "I like that shirt. Is it new?"

She batted her eyelashes—oh my! "Sort of." What in the world did *that* mean? Her brain was definitely on the *air head* setting these days.

His smile stretched. "I was hoping we could go somewhere today."

Sophie deflated. "Grandma's away, and Mom has a meeting with church leaders in Columbia. I have to watch Tibo."

"He can come too. I found this go-cart place that has two-seaters for kids. I thought I'd take you both for some more driving lessons."

He thought of her brother even before he offered to take her out? She closed her mouth when she'd realized it hung open. "You want him to come with us?"

Tibo peeked up from the train set he ran along the track, and smiled.

"Yeah, but I get to drive with Tibo." He grinned at her brother, overheating Sophie's heart. Then smirked mischievously. "Don't want to subject him to women drivers."

"Hey, you said I did a good job the other day."

"Sure, but we're dealing with real human bodies who need to stay safe now. It's a good thing go-carts can take a beating."

Sophie punched his shoulder, and he feigned pain.

Mom came through again, briefcase in hand.

"Mom, can Sky and I take Tibo to ride go-carts?"

She picked lint off the navy skirt, and looked between the two as though it took a while to process the question. "Sure. Just—"

"I know, Mom. Watch him carefully."

As Sky's car headed down the road, Tibo bounced in the back seat. "Kuck," he said as the trucks barreled past. "Fire," he shouted every time a siren blared.

Sophie glanced in the side mirror at the familiar sound of an engine rev. There was that car again. The red one with the tinted windows that raced out of the pool parking lot the other day. It was hard not to notice given the custom painted racing stripes along the sides. Only today, the car changed lanes when Sky did, and matched his every speed. Was it following them?

Sky glanced over. "You okay, Soph?"

Did she dare tell him what was on her mind? No way. He'd think she was paranoid. Why would someone want to follow them? "Sure."

His brows bunched like he didn't believe her, then he peeked in his rear view as if noticing the threat himself. After flipping on his emergency blinkers, he rolled down his window. "I think this guy's trying to pass me."

Sophie scanned the empty lane to the left. "There's plenty

of room." What was that driver *really* trying to do? Her pulse kicked up speed. Would this end in one of those car-jackings she'd seen on the news?

Sky slowed his vehicle, pulled slightly onto the shoulder and waved at the car to go by. The driver seemed to hesitate like he might stop with them. Then it jerked left and squealed past, the smell of burning rubber filling the air.

If only she could see through the dark windows to find out who was on the inside.

Sophie coughed and waved her hand in front of her nose. "What a jerk." She couldn't believe someone would be so rude.

Sky rolled his window up. "Better get used to it. Lots of crazies in this world. Sometimes we have to share the road with them."

"Is that driving lesson number two, oh great teacher?"

"The beginning of it." His dimple twitched.

What did he mean by that? She didn't dare ask.

Sophie blew out a calming breath. "Just glad that car's gone. He was making me nervous."

Sky's lips stretching into a curve made her racing pulse seem a whole lot nicer. She was glad that if she had to face a freaky driver on the road, she'd done it with Sky at the wheel— her protector.

Ten minutes later, he handed cash to the attendant at the window of the go-cart place, and strutted toward the track.

"Come on, Tibo," Sky said conspiratorially. "We're gonna find us a man-car. Fastest one on the lot." He turned, but Tibo was nowhere to be found.

Sophie cursed her negligence. Tibo hadn't drifted off in public in a long time. She'd become sloppy, and now he'd disappeared. She scanned the area.

A loud revving erupted from near the fence. Was that one of the go-carts? Couldn't be. It was too noisy, and sounded like—

There was that car again. Sophie swung around, now frantic to spot her brother, but couldn't see him anywhere.

"Where'd he go?" Sky grimaced. "He was just behind us."

The red car sped out of the parking lot. Sophie began to panic. "Tibo!"

"Car!"

Sophie sagged with the hard sigh that emptied her lungs.

Tibo bounced at the edges of the track watching the vehicle speed away.

"How'd he get over there?"

Sophie headed for her brother. She couldn't answer Sky's question. It was one of those riddles only Tibo had the answer to—and he wasn't talking. She was just glad he was okay.

Sky passed her and swooped her brother in the air. "Hey, dude, don't scare your sister like that." He winked, and Sophie lost another beat of her heart. But an uneasiness settled in her gut. What was that red car doing at the go-cart place? And why did it seem to be following them everywhere they went?

Tibo's belly laugh floated around as Sky swung him. Boy, was he strong.

Sophie tried to put her anxieties out of her mind. After all, Sky didn't seem bothered by the car showing up again. She found a single-seater go-cart, and Sky buckled Tibo into one with two seats. They started the engines, and the two carts went hurtling around the ring at top speed, Tibo screeching with excitement.

Speed. Just what she needed to get her mind off her crazy imagination. Sophie plunged her foot to the floor, pulling the steering wheel to make the curves.

Wham! That side was close.

"Women drivers." Sky shook his head as he and Tibo fled past.

Sophie pulled out and zoomed after him. He threw his head back in a laugh and slapped a high-five with Tibo, then—"

Crash!

He should have watched where he was going. Sophie guffawed as she sluiced by.

Sky's determined expression when he turned from the wall made Sophie's breath catch. Could this car go faster? Her foot already hit the floor, and he was gaining on her again. His smile took on an edge as he pulled up beside her speeding vehicle, then cut in.

Thudd!

"Hey, that's not nice."

Tibo's laugh was delirious, Sky's devilish.

Fine. She'd get them—Whack!

"Are you trying to parallel park, Soph?"

Oh. That was low. Her brows dropped in determination. She'd get him now. Oomph! Whack! Thudd!

… And so it went for the next four rounds. Sky paid for all three of them to go again and again.

When they finally stepped out of the vehicles for the last time—Sophie grateful she wouldn't need a neck brace after so many collisions—all three couldn't stop laughing. Tibo bounced on his toes and clapped.

"How about lunch." Sky opened the back door of his Civic for Tibo and buckled him into the seat.

"We should probably go home to eat. Tibo can only have gluten- and casein-free, remember?"

"Yeah, so I looked up some places online and this deli down the road has gluten-free bread."

"You did that?" Could there be a more perfect specimen of a man? *Sigh!*

"Sure," he said dropping into the driver's seat. "How else was I gonna get you to come out with me today?"

Her heart stopped. She peeked back at her brother, now looking wistfully at the zooming carts they left behind. "Okay. Let's have lunch."

"Do you think you might come to our church again, sometime?" Fear of his rejection made it hard to look at him.

His eyes took her in sideways, a quirk to his cheek. "I don't think your pastor wants me there."

What *were* those negative vibes Pastor Vince seemed to give off around Sky? "We could go to the youth services in another room. I've been checking it out lately, and Ayo, the youth pastor, is really great."

"Ayo?"

"He's from Nigeria."

"He won't stare daggers at me like Pastor Vince, will he?"

Sophie chuckled. "Not likely. He doesn't seem the dagger-staring type." Though neither did Pastor Vince.

"All right, Sophie." His smile sent chills down her arms. "I'll go back. For you."

She raised her eyes to the heavens. It was a start. "And if you like that, maybe you can come to youth night too."

"Sophie." At least he didn't sound dead-set against it.

"Fine. Just promise you'll think about it."

"I'll go to services with you." He placed his hand over hers, warming her entire body. "And if this Ayo dude doesn't give me the evil-eye, I'll *consider* going to youth night. Okay?"

Sophie was falling hard. "Okay."

Chapter Thirteen

Cassandra meandered around the hair salon as Kat took payment from her last customer. Mom had promised to babysit Tibo so she could have a little girl time with the salon owner. A welcome bonus after a long week of juggling Tibo's speech therapy, behavior therapy, and occupational therapy, not to mention the plans for the special needs program. The appointment with a research doctor next week would take a full day's drive to Richmond and back. It was good to have a moment to breathe.

Cassandra ran her fingers along the frames of the pictures on the shop walls. Bible verses and inspirational sayings were alternately hung with scenic pencilings and child-like drawings. She'd learned Kat had a girl away at college. Cassandra pointed to a crayon masterpiece. "Was this your daughter's?"

Kat lifted the large pages of the shop schedule at the front desk as the customer exited, and glanced back. "Oh, no. My Shelby couldn't draw a stick figure. Those were done by a little boy who used to come in here a long time ago."

"You framed them?"

Kat's expression softened as though floating on a memory. "He was such a sweet kid. His mother used to work the sub shop next door, and he hung around the strip while she worked. He landed here one day, and asked to sweep the floor. I'd cut his hair a few times." She shrugged. "He was always so polite, so I let him." Kat shook her head, large loop earrings swinging. "When he started going to school, he did his homework in the waiting area." She smiled sheepishly. "I even helped him with it sometimes. He'd pay me in drawings." Kat strode to the far wall.

"This was his as well."

Cassandra's mouth dropped open in awe at the life-like penciling of a water inlet sheltered by mansion-dotted cliffs. The detail was amazing. "How old was he when he drew that?"

"Around ten. It was the last one he gave me."

"What happened to him?"

Kat's expression grew pained. "One day he stopped coming in." Her eyes glistened. She seemed to hesitate before going on. "I checked at the sub shop and found out his mother quit. I never saw either one of them again."

It was the little kindnesses, sometimes, that meant the most. "I bet he'll remember you forever." More and more Cassandra found herself warming to this woman who possessed such an easy generosity.

Kat straightened the stack of towels on the shelves above the shampoo bowl as though her next question would not unleash a storm. "How long have you and Vince known each other?"

And still it hit Cassandra like a wrecking ball. "What do you mean?" Cassandra had no intention of lying, but needed more time to answer carefully.

Kat moved to the coffee machine. Her bracelets jangled as she tilted the pot and poured a cup. She sat in front of Cassandra on the couch in the waiting area. Her words were soft. "I'm not blind, you know." Her warm smile weakened the alarm that wanted to scream from Cassandra's body. Would telling her relieve the burden?

No way!

Cassandra shifted, then grabbed a magazine from the coffee table.

"There's strong emotion between you two. Either love or hate. I'm guessing both."

"It's not love."

The thin brow above the woman's eye arched as Kat kept her gaze on Cassandra. "What's that line about protesting too much?" The buckles on her boots clanked as she crossed her legs. Her tight smile stretched. "I've known Vince a number of years, and you were not part of them. So, my guess is you knew him during his country-club days."

Cassandra flipped through the magazine in her lap, staring at the blurring images of hairstyles.

"I've heard—from him I might add—I wouldn't have liked him much back then."

Cassandra scoffed.

Kat sighed. "Though I bet he could sweet talk a rhino from charging mid-stride."

Cassandra tossed the magazine on the coffee table. A long silence hung between them, then …

"How old is Sophie?"

Cassandra's eyes darted to Kat.

"She looks an awful lot like Vince."

Cassandra's throat constricted. "She looks an awful lot like a lot of people." Should she leave? Could she even stand on these wobbly legs?

"He has a right to know."

Cassandra's body grew ridged. "You have no idea what you're talking about."

"I know—"

"It's not as simple as you think." Cassandra's breaths struggled to enter her lungs. She heard the long-ago whispers of Tim reminding her to breathe in and out when she had panic attacks with him. It calmed her.

Kat stood, smoothed her jean skirt and filled her cup again. "Vince once told me about this girl." She poured creamer into the coffee. "He said he did something really awful to her that he'd always regret. And though he'd sinned in thousands of other ways, this was the one he couldn't forgive himself."

Cassandra's curiosity peeked beyond control. "Why's that?"

"He told me he'd betrayed her in a very personal way. I happen to think he also cared deeply for her."

Did she want to know the workings of his evil mind? "How'd he betray her?"

"I think he said he led her on as part of a bet."

Cassandra's eyes burned, but she couldn't move to leave. She felt naked, stripped and standing in front of her accusers.

"For some reason, he and his buddies saw her as a challenge because of her religious beliefs."

Kat's gaze probed, but Cassandra couldn't look at her.

"When the girl found out about the bet, his world collapsed."

His world?

Kat sipped her coffee. "Of course that was just before it literally burned to the ground."

Cassandra looked up. "What do you mean?"

"That same night she walked out, never to see him again, his father shot himself in the head and their house caught fire."

Cassandra couldn't breathe. Mr. Steegle's slurred words echoed in her mind as if he were right in front of her. He'd barreled into the bedroom as though he had something important to say, but his expression changed when he caught the two of them in Vince's bed.

"Ah, it seems you won the bet with Drew, huh?" He burped. "Cassandra, The Pure." Then ogled her form covered only by a thin sheet. "Not so pure anymore. Well, I'm not paying for another abortion." The door had slammed before his words even registered in Cassandra's mind.

Kat continued with the nightmare. "The fire marshal believed the bullet hit a lamp on exit, causing it to catch the curtains of his study on fire." The words sounded as though floating through a long, hollow cave. "Vince woke to a haze of smoke and barely made it out alive."

He'd almost died that night? She couldn't grieve him. Then why did this bother her?

"To this day, he feels it was just punishment for the life he'd led. I try to tell him it was only God calling him from that life."

Cassandra's lungs labored for air again. More images of that night stung her vision, tore at her flesh.

Weight on her chest, her body, her limbs. Dried grass and reeds biting into her back and legs. Whiskey-soaked breath clogging the air in front of her. No! Get off! Please don't. Get off!

Her eyes stung, nose burned. Every muscle tensed. Fists balled. Protection. She needed protection.

There was no protection.

"Cassandra, are you all right?"

Breathe!

She wrapped her arms around her ribs and rubbed them till they burned.

Kat's warmth registered beside her. The weight of her palm lay on Cassandra's shoulder. "Do you need some water?"

Breathe in. Breathe out.

In. Out.

In. Out.

"Can I do something for you?"

Cassandra gasped for air. Her heart beat slowed. "It's okay. It's okay. I'm fine." She stood. "I'm sorry, that hasn't happened in a long time."

"What was that?" If worried eyes could pin you to a wall, Kat's did.

Cassandra clutched the edge of a shelf and pulled in three deep breaths. "A panic attack."

"I'm so sorry." Kat's expression registered concern with a tinge of anger. Who was she mad at? "I upset you."

Cassandra swallowed. "No. No. They happen sometimes." She picked up her purse. "I just didn't expect it. It's been a while. I gotta go."

Kat stared after Cassandra as she fled the shop, dropped into the driver-side of her SUV, and sobbed into the steering wheel.

~*~

"Archibald."

Lew turned, the burden of his supervisor's hardened tone

weighing on his shoulders. Did the man always have to use his given name?

The guy thumbed over his shoulder. "You're up for a Breathalyzer."

Lew's shoulders sagged. He cursed. Once. Then twice. Then a few more mutterings as he followed his new boss to his office. The old supervisor had always given him a heads up when Lew'd be picked for the test. This guy was out to get him.

Knowing what the results would be before he even blew through the tube, he took his time down the hall. He calculated his savings. Not hard, since you can't do much with zero. What a way to start a job search. His rent was due and his fridge empty. He had a few dollars in his wallet, but his tongue itched for the burn of a good drink more than a TV dinner.

Lew crossed the threshold and stood in front of the large metal desk. He heard the clank of the door behind him, sending shudders down his back, before his supervisor rounded and pulled the device from a drawer, then shoved it in his face. Lew knew what to do.

Could he pray for a miracle?

The guy glared at Lew's mirthless chuckle. Why not laugh? It was better than the alternative.

~*~

Lew's old friends—Johnny Walker and Jim Beam— clanked together in the paper bag as the boy plowed into him. Again. He couldn't see the kid's face, since it was buried in Lew's T-shirt, arms wrapped tight around him, but between the blond mop of hair on top, and the woman trotting through the strip-mall parking lot calling his name, he knew it was little Tibo.

Cassandra sputtered. "I'm so sorry, Lew. I guess he's really taken a liking to you."

Lew mussed the boy's hair as a burning sensation filled his eyes. The breeze must have blown some dust in there. "That's okay. I like the kid too. We have the same love of loud motors."

111

Tibo peeked up from his embrace. "Wew." Then he backed up into his mom. "Beep, beep, beep."

Grabbing her son, she smirked. "That's him being a truck."

"Figured that." Lew grinned, returning the smile Tibo gave him. "Hey. Ya think he'd like to go to the dirt-track races with me sometime? I could introduce him to some of the drivers. He might like that."

She chuckled. "I think he'd prefer if you introduced him to the cars."

Lew shifted the bag in his hands. The bottles jangled together. "I could do that too."

Cassandra's eyes lifted toward the liquor store sign overhead, then down to the sack in Lew's hands as if drawing in a dotted line from A to B. "Maybe we could meet you there."

He crumpled the sack tighter. Part of him wanted to be angry that she only saw him as a drunk, but something about her gentle smile toward him, and the protective arm she held around her son, made Lew realize he'd do the same thing to protect Tibo from a drunk driver. And that bugged him more. "Of course." His gaze dropped to the cement. "You could do that."

"How about next week?" She reached into her large purse and pulled out a little notebook. Did she really want to hang out at a race track with Lew?

Did he want to hang out with her? "Sure. I'll get some tickets."

She ripped a page from the pad. "Here's my number. Let me know what they cost, and I'll pay you back." She placed a hand on his arm. "Thanks, Lew. Tibo's really going to love this. I'd never thought to take him to a race before."

He dropped his gaze to his latest purchase. "No problem. You don't need to pay me anything." He shrugged. "I get 'em free from my buddy anyhow."

She smiled that gentle smile again. It must be where the kid got his from. "We'll see you then."

Chapter Fourteen

Sophie tapped her jeweled sandal on the concrete sidewalk outside Water's Edge Community Church. Where was Sky? He said he'd be here.

For some reason the verse Amit quoted tonight as she passed him in the back hallways of the church echoed in her mind. His wide smile didn't seem to mesh with the warning tone in his voice. "Above all else, guard yer heart, fo' it is de wellspwing uff life."

Sophie shivered even though the night air had no chill.

She'd watched all the other kids go into the church for youth night over the last half hour. Her stomach growled every time they passed her, opened the door, and let the smell of pizza escape. She straightened the mini skirt she hadn't let her mother see in the changing room when they bought it last week, and pulled up the dangerous neck line of her fitted top. Grandma had given her *the look* when she drove her here, but must have assumed Mom was okay with the new outfit, and didn't want to overstep.

Finally, Sky's car made the loop around the parking lot, and stopped. His eyes scanned her up and down before they met hers, grin lengthening. He strode to the entrance where she waited, lightly touching her bare shoulder with his scarred hand as he neared. She loved the way he no longer hid that part of himself. Were they getting closer?

The warm fizzies sizzled through her at the intensity of his gaze. Oh! My!

"Hey." His eyes smoldered.

"Hey." She attempted to smolder back. "What took you so

long?"

He scratched his jawline. "Wasn't sure it was a good idea to come."

"What do you mean? You're my ride home."

"I don't think your pastor likes me." He grimaced. "He's probably lurking around here ready to banish or shun me or something."

"We're not Amish, Sky." Sophie thought about the looks from the pastor she'd noticed and wondered the same thing. "He wouldn't do that." After all, it didn't make sense given what he preached about loving and forgiving.

"I don't know, Soph. A guy knows *the father* look when he sees it."

"Well, he's not my father." She swatted him. "Now, let's go inside."

They entered the lounge where teens sat around a long table filled with pizza boxes and soda bottles. Coming closer, it was apparent no one else had waited for Sky. Or her. The boxes were empty save scraps of crusty cheese stuck to the bottom.

Sky swiped a hunk of it. "Hungry?"

She speared him with her eyes.

He flinched. "Sorry."

Her stomach growled angrier with the cheese scrap so near. Sky put it in his mouth and chewed. "Mm. Good."

"Oh, you're bad."

His smile made her want to hit him. And kiss him. All at the same time.

Ayo, the youth pastor stepped up. "Don't worry, we ordered more. It should be here within the half hour."

Sophie placed a hand on her rumbling stomach. Hopefully, she could hold out.

Pastor Ayo clapped his hands together. "All right, let's start the activities." Sophie loved the way Ayo's words still held the hint of his native Nigerian. He'd told the group one week his full name was Ayorinde, which means "joy has come." Given his easy-going manner and his wide smile, it fit. He pulled his guitar from its case. "Requests anyone?"

Teens called out song titles. Pastor Ayo played what he knew, the group singing with him, and improvised the rest. Sky gave Sophie a sideways grimace here and there. Clearly this was not his usual idea of fun. But maybe he'd warm up to it. Eventually. For her. She hoped.

Later, Pastor Ayo read the story of Esther, and the group discussed how the events in her life impacted an entire race of people. Sky remained silent, sullen, almost wooden. What was he thinking? Watching him didn't allay her fears, until his fingers reached for hers, trailing the back of her hand, and giving her gooseflesh. His smile slid up on one side, but he didn't turn her way.

Pastor Ayo announced a break before the next activity. Before she could head to the women's room, Sky grasped her hand, pulled her through the door of the lounge, down the hall, and out the back entrance.

"Sky, what are you doing?" she said on a laugh.

His musky scent enveloped her as he spoke into her hair. "Just wanted a little alone time," his hands wrapped around her middle, "so we can talk."

She looked past his lightly whiskered chin to his soulful brown eyes. "What do you wanna talk—"

He pressed his lips to hers and pulled her closer, melding her body to his. She placed her palms on his chest to press him back, but the beat of his heart and the cord of his muscles under her fingers loosened her resolve. His scarred palm slid down her arm, making her ache for his vulnerability. He needed her. And she might just need him too.

His lips trailed her neck, down onto her collar bone as his hands traveled into the back of her shirt and slid upward.

She shivered, but finally pushed away. "Whoa, Sky. We're in the church parking lot." The question was, would she have stopped had they been somewhere else? She no longer knew the answer to that question.

"Right." His sigh held a hint of bitterness. "Pastor Vince

115

might come out and question us on choice of pizza toppings."

~*~

Even though he heard his name, Vince held back. How right that Sky was. With the smell of pizza wafting through the hall, he'd been formulating a question about toppings to use as he separated them. Thank goodness Sophie had pushed the dude away. Vince wasn't sure he could limit the discussion to food choices otherwise.

His heart lodged in his throat, watching this sweet, young girl—Cass's daughter—get swept away by the ragged-jean-wearing Casanova.

Vince stepped into the shadows so he couldn't be seen, but now their voices were muffled. Sophie stared at the concrete, but spoke firmly to the ground. Sky shifted and sneered. He took her hand and pulled her closer, his fingers invading the gap between her skirt waist and shirt. What was she thinking wearing that outfit? Didn't she know what guys like Sky read from that?

Vince did.

Sophie said something else, holding his chest from her. Sky threw up his hands in surrender, spit out one last comment, then left.

She looked so alone watching him leave, staring after him. Good riddance.

Vince backed into the door then headed down the hall. He had a few emails to return and a phone call to make before he went home.

"Hi, Passa Vinss." The enthusiastic lilt to Amit's voice always made Vince smile.

"Are you still here, Amit?"

"Yep. Gonna kween up afta da yoof goop."

"Right." Vince shuffled through the papers on his desk. Did he really want to finish work tonight? Maybe he should just come in early tomorrow.

Amit stood in the doorway, leaning on his industrial

116

broom.

"Is there something I can do for you, Amit?"

"Nope." His eyes sparkled like he was watching bubbles float around the office. "Fo' a man's ways are in full voo uff de Lord, and he examines aw his paths. Das wat I read in da Bible tuh-day."

Vince spied the sermon notes and realized he had too much to do to go home now. "That's nice Amit. So glad you're learning God's word. It'll serve you well."

"Yep." The simple man turned as if studying each wall along the way. "It'll serve you well, Passa Vinss. Das right."

Vince's heart went right out the door with the big guy. Why did God allow someone so sweet to be so afflicted. The workings of God were beyond Vince's understanding, but sometimes he wished God would heed Vince's requests.

Then he thought of the old Vince, and was glad his Creator didn't bow to the likes of him.

After writing up a To Do list for the next day, Vince locked his office door and headed past the sanctuary. He peeked in out of habit—like checking in on God—and found a lone figure in a second-row pew, staring toward the stage.

Sophie.

The loneliness emanated from her as he approached. She barely even registered Vince's presence, then straightened as he sat next to her. "Oh. Hi, Pastor Vince."

"What are you doing in here? Shouldn't you be with the youth group?"

"It's over." Her shoulders rose and fell. "And my ride left me."

"Sky?"

"Yeah."

"Do you need a way home?" Bad question. He couldn't give it to her since he avoided being alone with females so as not to be accused of his former behavior.

"No. I called my mom. She should be here soon."

"What happened with Sky?"

CONNIE ALMONY

She turned. Her eyes held a candor much like her mother's always had. "You should know. You were watching the whole time."

Caught. He fidgeted with the tissue box at the end of the pew. "Not the whole time."

Sophie sighed. "I didn't even get any pizza." She placed her hand on her stomach. "And I'm starving."

Vince stood and held up a finger. "Be right back." He ran to the lounge and found the last box open displaying a lonely triangle dotted with pepperoni. His favorite. He snatched it, grabbed a plate, and ran back to the sanctuary where Sophie sat, a little smile creeping up her face.

"Is this what you want?'

She nodded, smile lengthening.

"Oh, too bad." He held it to his lips. "It's the last one."

Her mouth dropped open. Eyes incredulous.

Vince took just enough of a bite to hook some cheese in his teeth and stretch it for effect. "Mmmm. So good."

"That's just mean."

Vince agreed. "What?" But he feigned innocence instead.

Her voice became brazen for a teen addressing her pastor. "To dangle something you know I want, in front of my face, only to *not* let me have it."

He shook his head. "But pizza's not good for you. I'm doing you a favor not giving it to you."

She planted her fists on her hips. "Then why did you taunt me with it?"

"That's not taunting." The ire in her eyes, so much like Cass, only prompted his mischievous nature. He waved the plate under her nose so she could absorb the aroma. "*This* is taunting."

Oh, her expression so familiar it made him weak. He broke off a crumb of crust. "Here, take this."

She grimaced. "That would only make me hungrier."

"It wouldn't satisfy you?" He put the piece in his mouth.

"No. Tasting it would make me want more."

"Hmmm." He smiled and held the plate out to her. She

118

hesitated before taking it. Probably wondering if he'd jerk it away.

Her chuckle was ornery. "I can't believe you just did that."

"You mean, make you think I was getting you pizza, then not giving it to you."

"Yes."

"I never said I was getting it for you."

"But I … you …" Her brows scrunched together. "It was implied."

"No it wasn't."

She glared.

"You only assumed it from my behavior."

She shrugged. "Right. Exactly."

"Kinda like Sky, tonight."

Her head swiveled. "What?"

"He made assumptions about you based on your behavior."

"What do you mean?" Her defensive tone suggested she knew exactly what he meant.

"You waved a pizza under his nose, so he could see, smell and touch it, but had no plans to let him indulge."

She stared at her nails.

"At least I hope you hadn't planned to." He sat next to her. "You know pizza isn't very nutritious."

Her small chuckle suggested the tension broke a little.

"Careful Sophie. You're a beautiful girl. You don't need to dress like this."

She peeked up at him. His heart hurt for her. He could see she just wanted to be loved.

He nodded to her short skirt. "What you wear, whether you like it or not, sends a message to a guy." He looked into her blue eyes. "Make sure your message is that you deserve his respect. That you want to be loved. Not used."

Sophie nodded, tears gathering. "I don't know why I did it. But somehow …" she picked at the polish on her nails, "wearing this makes me feel powerful, in control."

Vince swallowed hard. "It makes you powerful all right.

But not in control. Kind of like the ring of power in the wrong hands."

Sophie smirked. "Don't tell me you're a *Lord of the Rings* freak like my dad."

Vince warmed at the idea of being like the man she obviously admired. He lifted a shoulder. "A little."

She gave him a placating look. "I get it. This power is dangerous."

He rested his arm along the pew above her shoulders. "Exactly. However, I must say, I love your honesty." He chuckled. "So much like your mom."

Her jerk told him he'd said too much. "Did you know my mom? I mean, before?"

"Get your hands off my daughter!" Cass's voice rang through the sanctuary, echoing like a command from the grave. Sophie bolted upright.

Vince stood. "Cass."

"Sophie, go to the car." Her voice was firm.

"But mom—"

"Sophie," she ground the words through her teeth. "Go to the car. Now!"

Vince braced himself for the onslaught he had no power to defend. Sophie ran out the door, glancing back as if she feared for his safety.

"What were you doing with my daughter?"

"She was upset—"

"And you were comforting her?" The anger in her voice blazed. "How convenient for you."

"What kind of a creep do you think I am?"

Her eyebrows shot high, and her mouth opened to speak.

"Don't answer that. I know full well what kind of creep you think I am." His head swiveled back and forth. "But there is no way I'd hit on that young girl."

"Ha!"

He met her glare and whispered with force. "Is she mine?"

Cassandra blanched.

"Why didn't you ..." He thrust his hands in his pocket. "Never mind."

Cass raised a finger at him like he'd broken his mother's prized vase. "If she had been yours and you had your usual way," her face contorted as though she held back a geyser of emotion, "she'd be dead right now." With those words Cassandra pivoted and strode out the door.

~*~

Cassandra dropped into the driver's seat of her Lincoln Aviator, and started the engine. It gasped and strained and revved before kicking into life. Cassandra could almost hear Sophie's teeth grind next to her.

"What did Vince—" Cassandra glanced over and noticed the skirt that barely covered her daughter. She scanned the rest of Sophie's outfit and air fled her lungs. "What in the world do you think you're doing in those clothes?"

Sophie pulled up the neckline to finally cover the top edges of her lacy pink bra. "I don't need another lecture about my outfit." Her voice cracked. "Pastor Vince gave me the full picture."

"What does that mean?" Cassandra could only imagine what type of picture Vince could draw up.

"He said I was like smelling a pizza without being able to eat it."

"What?" Cassandra almost veered off the road. "He better not have been smelling your pizza."

Sophie sighed emphatically. "No, Mom. You don't get it. He also said it wasn't nutritious."

"What's not nutritious?" Cassandra's muscles seized.

"Pizza, Mom. Aren't you listening?"

Cassandra hoped shaking her head would make the pieces of this conversation fall together right.

Sophie sucked in a big breath, causing her shirt to dip and show her bra again. She turned to face her mother full on. "Pastor Vince suggested I not tempt guys to eat pizza because it's not good for them."

By the pointed look in Sophie's eyes, and the dramatic way she formed the words, Cassandra got the impression Vince imparted a valuable lesson about dressing modestly and saving one's self for marriage without actually using the word "sex." Incredible. Only Vince could talk his way around that one. And for once, she valued that particular gift.

The oncoming headlights whizzed by as Sophie's gaze burned into Cassandra. Her daughter expected something from her, but Cassandra wasn't going to give it.

"Are you ever going to tell me how you know Pastor Vince?"

"No." The headlights were hypnotizing.

Sophie pulled the passenger-side visor down, brushed her black bangs out or her face, and looked hard at her reflection in the little mirror. "Is he—"

At Cassandra's fierce glare, Sophie's mouth shut quick. Now her daughter stared at the headlights too.

The rest of the drive home remained silent except for the occasional rattle of the aging engine and little sniffs from Sophie as she drew the back of her hand under her nose, and knuckled her eyes.

Cassandra's world was unraveling around her. Everyone kept asking the question as though she kept a secret. Little did they know she didn't have the answer herself.

Chapter Fifteen

Sitting at the glass-top table on Billy's waterfront deck, Vince calculated the golf scores of the guys he'd just played with—Billy, John and Ayo. "What did you get on sixteen, again, Billy?"

His friend fished three golf balls out of his cargo shorts, scrunching his fu-man-choo. "Can't remember." He held them up. "But I found three Titlest on that hole, just outside the rough."

"I think it was a twelve." Vince scribbled on the card. "Felt like we were there all day."

Ayo nodded emphatically as he pet Smokey, Billy's German Shepherd, who sniffed the edge of the table.

"Well, yeah. That's a tough hole. Great place to find lost balls though."

John pulled a few from his pocket, and placed them on the table top. "I don't know. I got five on number thirteen. People always hit into the woods to avoid the water there."

Vince sighed at the image of the two men in the trees looking for *other people's* balls rather than their own.

Smokey barked as if he wanted one of those balls himself. Billy dug his hand into the potted plant by the steps, found the ratty rope toy, and tossed it in the lawn. Smokey shot off after it.

"So who won?" Ayo slid into the chair next to Vince.

One of John's pilfered balls hit another, causing a domino rolling effect. He corralled them so they didn't all fall off the table. "I think Billy beat me this time." He looked over at the other man's collection. "That extra Callaway from eighteen put you one over."

"Yeah, but you got a Pro-V and two of mine are Top

Flights." He jabbed a thumb toward Vince. "He'd say yours are more valuable."

Shaking his head, Ayo blew a breath. "I was talking about the score." He turned to Vince, his dreadlocks brushing the shoulder of his striped polo. "Well?"

"You did, my friend."

Ayo's wide smile shone from his dark features. "Two weeks in a row." His eyes probed. "What's with you, man?"

Vince leaned back in his chair. "Got my mind on other things."

"Hmmm." Ayo stood and grabbed a soda can from a cooler.

Vince fished the card into his back pocket.

"That Amit guy seems to be working out, huh?" Billy tugged the rope toy from Smokey's mouth and tossed it again.

"Yeah, the bathrooms have never been cleaner, and I can find things in the supply closet." John sipped from a Dr. Pepper can."

Ayo said, "I think the dude's prophetic."

"How's that?" A breeze brushed over Vince's skin.

"You know how we've all been praying for Neil McLean ever since he told us he planned to propose to Teresa Greenfield?" Ayo glanced around at the concerned nods. "And how we'd all like to tell him she's a shrew, but we're afraid he might get offended?"

"I never said she was a shrew." John, ever the peace-maker.

Ayo's eyes pinned him. "Yeah, but you were thinkin' it."

John's mouth twisted. "Still, we should pray for her."

"Anyway, Neil came up to me last week and said Amit stopped him in the men's room one day and started quoting from Proverbs."

All the men's heads bounced, having been held up by Amit's verses themselves.

"Neil said he quoted Proverbs 27:15-16, *A quarrelsome wife is like a constant dripping on a rainy day, restraining her is like*

124

restraining the wind or grasping oil with the hand."

Billy's mouth dropped open. Vince's muscles tensed, and John stared at Ayo.

Ayo gave them all a knowing look. "Yeah. At first Neil thought it was just the verse he was on that day, but the words kept echoing in his head, until—as he put it—he realized they were true." He tapped his fingers on the glass table. "Neil broke up with Teresa three days ago."

Each man in the group furrowed a muscle on his face. Billy scrunched his mustache. John got mirrored commas on his forehead, as Ayo kept nodding like he knew he hit his mark.

Verses Amit had quoted Vince came back to mind. Like the one that spoke to so many parts of his past, *"Give me neither poverty nor riches, but give me only my daily bread. Otherwise I may have too much and disown you and say 'Who is the Lord?' Or I may become poor and steal and so dishonor the name of God."* Then there was the one he quoted the other day, *"Many are the plans in a man's heart, but it is the Lord's purpose that prevails."* How could Amit know these verses would resonate? Was he telling them something they needed to hear that day? Vince shook his head. "You've been reading too many End Times novels, Ayo."

"Bah." John grimaced.

Billy whapped Ayo on the head. "You had me scared for a minute there."

Now Vince wondered what verses they'd all been quoted.

Needing a break from this conversation, he stood and entered Kat and Billy's house through the sliding-glass door. Kat was washing lettuce in the sink.

"Can I help you with lunch?"

She only shook her head. Something was up. This woman never missed an opportunity to talk.

"I see Lilly-White's here." Lew opened the fridge and took out a beer. "Chasin' little balls into holes?"

"Well some of us were. Others chased them into the rough." Vince smiled at Kat. "Billy still thinks the one with the most balls found wins."

She ripped lettuce as if decapitating it.

Lew's lids lowered to half-mast. "Makes more sense to me. At least the winner has the highest score rather than the lowest." He popped the beer bottle opened with the handle of a drawer. "Don't they teach you boys math in college?" He slid out the back door to the deck before Vince could answer.

"What's Lew doing here?"

Kat arranged the lettuce like she was dressing a reluctant child. "He's moved in." She finally looked up. "Got your old room."

"What? He didn't like Shelby's pink, lacy curtains?"

"She still uses it when she comes to visit." Kat opened the fridge and extracted bags of peppers, onions, and carrots. "He lost his job again."

Vince pushed his hands into his pockets. He knew how helpless Billy and Kat felt when it came to Lew.

"Random testing." She shrugged. "Delivery companies tend to like their drivers sober."

"Is that what's got you in such a foul mood?"

Kat faced him, eyes singeing his.

"Did I do something to make you angry?"

She ripped open the bag of onions, almost sending them up in the air.

"Come on, Kat. You're mad. What's up?"

"What did you *really* do to that girl?"

Where did that come from? "Who? What?"

"Cassandra."

Vince's jaw dropped. His mind couldn't catch up with a way around the truth.

"You said she was furious when she found out about the bet."

Oh boy, she knew too much. "I *never* said it was Cassandra."

Kat eyed him.

"Okay, fine. Yes, it was Cassandra. But you understand why I don't want the rest of the congregation to know about her.

It's not my place to tell."

She pulled a large chopping knife out of the drawer and pointed it at him. "That's not what I'm worried about. I want to know what you did to her."

Toeing one of Smokey's rawhides on the floor, Vince reluctantly said the words again. "I told you. I bet my buddy Drew I could 'de-pure' her, as he called it." Bitterness burned in his chest at the word he now realized stole something precious. "And she found out right after I'd done it."

A heaviness weighed on him. Visions of her pulling herself from his bed after his father had come in, wrapped in his sheets as she sobbed and screamed at him, cut through him, making it hard to speak. She'd tried to dress, while remaining covered, but the movements were awkward and she faltered. Vince wanted to go to her, comfort her, tell her he really did love her, but he could never use that word on her. He'd used it so loosely with all the others, it seemed an empty shell to him. Maybe he could prove what he felt later. Not that night. She wouldn't listen in her state of mind.

He never had the chance.

Kat's hard chopping brought Vince back to the present. "There's more. I know it."

"What do you mean?"

She waved the knife at him again. "That woman is not just mad at you. She's deathly afraid of something."

Could it have to do with Sophie, the teen who happened to be the right age, and didn't seem to have the same coloring as her mother or brother? The thought that the girl could be his, made his stomach churn. "Afraid?"

"I told her about your father and the fire that took your house."

"Why'd you do that, Kat?" He wearied at the thought of her burdened by his life.

"I thought she needed to know." She resumed chopping onions. "While I recounted the story, she seemed to drift away." Kat shook her head, brows crunching together. "And when she came back, she had a panic attack."

Vince straightened. "What?"

"That's what she called it. I thought she was having a seizure or something, but when she could finally breathe right, she said it was a panic attack, and that she hadn't had one in a long time." She put the knife down as if to focus the words. "I think talking about you prompted it."

Chapter Sixteen

Why was Cassandra driving up this meandering road toward the estates that lined the water in the richer neighborhood surrounding Annapolis? She had to see it for herself. The house where Vince used to live, and the water's edge where they spent so much time alone together. That little patch of grass surrounded by the marshy reeds. Private. Intimate.

Dangerous.

Vince would ride his little motor boat to their spot, and pull her out with his strong hands. His chest and back, always tanned, gave his skin a richness that made her want to run her fingers along his muscles, the scent of summer sun surrounding him. They'd sit and talk, the lapping of the waves on the shore framing their words. She felt protected, secure, even loved, as they spoke of their futures.

What a lie.

He told her he'd go to law school and try his hand at politics—make the world a better place. She told him how she wanted to design a mentor program in poor neighborhoods to give hope to kids who hadn't seen much success. Vince had smiled as if he'd approved of her convictions. She'd convinced herself they were speaking of the same goals.

His kisses were always gentle, careful, searching her tentatively. He'd never said the word *love*, she realized, but thought he'd communicated it in so many other ways, like the way he touched her as if she were made of delicate china. Cherished. Valued.

She knew he didn't think much about God, but wondered if that could change. Oh, how she had wished it would. So when he'd asked her to take off the cross she'd always worn around her neck—the one her father had carved from wood, and hung on a leather cord—she told him he could keep it. His lips had trailed her collar bone before the request. She hadn't realized it then, but now knew he couldn't bear to look at it, the intent of his actions weighing on his mind. Cassandra had offered to tie the cross around his neck, but he pushed it into his shorts pocket instead, never to be seen again. When her father died of a brain aneurysm that fall, she felt most at a loss of the prized possession she'd given to the man who couldn't really love. It had been the first of prized possessions she'd given him that night.

Magnolia Estates was carved on the grand sign, lined by flowering trees and lush gardens. Cassandra turned into the subdivision, a red car accelerated past as she left the main road. For some reason the volume of its revving engine made her shiver. Was that the same car she kept seeing around Waters Edge? Why did it seem to be everywhere she was? Like it was stalking her. Probably the bright color and racing stripes just made it stand out.

Cassandra shook her head and continued through the familiar streets, gargantuan houses sprawled up the incline, dangling from cliffs as if clambering to get a better view of the water below. She inched along the road, Vince's old property just ahead, and found a large, but understated building—very unlike the one he had lived in—possessing the property. Her eyes stung as she imagined the young man she used to know, choking on smoke, trying to find his way out to safety, standing before his home watching all that he ever owned crumble to the ground in smoke and ash.

Cassandra jerked at the knock on the window. She rolled it down.

"Can I help you with something?" The woman spoke as if Cassandra's stationary vehicle had blocked her power walk.

"I was just wondering about the family who lived in the house that used to be here." Cassandra didn't know how else to explain her presence.

"You mean the one destroyed by the fire?" The woman's skin hardly moved when she spoke, like it had been injected with too much botox.

"Yes. Did you know them?"

"Of course. They were our neighbors." Was she offended?

Curiosity peaked at the relationship with Vince's family. "Do you know what happened to them?"

Her face registered some form of concern. Whether it was from feigning the expression or the overuse of plastic surgery, it didn't go very far. "After the house burned down with the father inside, the young man discovered his father had lost everything in some bad investments. He stayed with us for a few weeks, but we prompted him to leave. Good thing, because it turns out he later began to deal drugs as a form of employment." She huffed. "Imagine what would have happened had he brought that kind of trouble to my children." She sighed as if her family had escaped a close one. No thought to the young man who'd lost everything and had nowhere to go.

"Thank you." Cassandra shifted and punched the gas before her lungs constricted any more. She couldn't feel sorry for Vince. It was his fault she suffered. His fault all her goals had been destroyed. His fault she once again had nightmares that left her gasping for breaths and searching for safety within her own mind. She wouldn't feel sorry for him. She needed to hate him instead.

The trees hung over the drive as she maneuvered the curves down the hill and into a main road, back to the smaller houses surrounding Water's Edge Community Church. Vince's current neighborhood. She'd drop off her completed report and recommendations for the special needs program at his house, figuring it would be safe to do that while he was at work. She pulled into the drive of the split-level home, grabbed the envelope and walked up the front sidewalk. After opening the storm door, she placed the manila envelope at the bottom, near the hinge.

Just as it swung shut, she heard a loud creak, a man's yell, and a thud. Without thinking she ran to the backyard. Vince lay prostrate on the ground below the skeleton of a deck, wood planks littered around him as if fallen or thrown.

"Vince!" She ran to his body, her heart pounding in her throat. "Vince!" Her voice squeaked as if she might care.

His worn T-shirt clad chest expanded, then his mouth released a breath. When his eyes lit open, Cassandra felt caught by them. "Are you all right?"

His hand covered the one she'd placed on his arm. She pulled it away.

His lids lowered again as if in agony. "Yeah."

She sat back on her heels, hoping her heart would settle.

Grimacing, he pushed to sitting.

"You're in pain, let me help you." Cassandra reached out a hand.

Vince shook his head. "I'm okay."

She waved the hand to emphasize the offer. He grasped it, hands more calloused than she'd remembered. Vince leaned heavily as she tried to pull him to standing. Crying out, he fell back and pulled her to his chest. His blue eyes stung hers as they met. Ten beats of her heart passed, his breath warming her face. He turned away, swallowed, and let go of her hand. It was as though he'd released the lock he had on her—on purpose. Unsettled, she removed herself from him.

He cleared his throat. "Sorry."

Cassandra knelt into the grass. "What hurts?"

"I think I pulled something in my knee."

"Maybe I should take you to the hospital."

He chuckled and shook his head.

"Really Vince. Clearly it's serious. You should have it looked at."

"I know, but give me a minute. It's throbbing right now, and I need to catch a breath."

Cassandra sat beside him where he lay staring at the cloudless sky as though speaking with his eyes to someone above. His chest rose and fell over and over again. She was about to say something when she noticed, just where his T-shirt lifted slightly from his shorts waist, a large scar in the shape of a ragged cross. It drew her in. She hadn't realized she lifted the hem of his shirt to get a better look until he jerked and grasped her fingers. His eyes bore into hers.

"What is that, Vince?" She knew it hadn't been there when they were young.

"That's how my drug supplier let me know he wasn't too happy with me selling to his own personal clients." The words seemed to weary him further. His eyes closed, and only then did she realize it was because her fingers had been tracing the scar.

It was ugly and deep. "He could have killed you."

Vince peered into the sky again. "Almost did."

"Were you selling to his clients?"

His chuckle was humorless. "No. He was a crackhead. Paranoid. The longer I worked for him, the more he accused me of." He took in labored air. "Eventually, I got arrested. He'd set me up. Little did he realize the cops working the arrest wanted him more than me, so they talked me into turning states evidence against him. I got a reduced sentence."

Cassandra's head swiveled back and forth as she watched him stare anywhere but at her.

"Didn't improve much after you left, did I?"

She ached at the despondency in his expression. Somehow the life he'd lived seemed more empty than filled with evil, as she'd once thought.

"How long were you in jail?"

"Six months." A small smile tickled his lips. "The day I stepped out of my cell for the last time, I wondered how I'd support myself. Didn't even know where I'd live." He glanced at her. "My mother hadn't contacted us since she left when I was five. I had no family who cared." He looked to the sky again as if it housed someone dear. "The mechanized door clanked open and there stood Billy Lewis, my mechanic, whose life I'd entangled in drugs. But he'd finished his third try at rehab, and started going to church while I was locked up." Vince's Adam's apple bobbed as he swallowed."He and Kat took me in. He got me a job selling used cars through a guy he knew." He smirked at Cassandra.

133

"That's right, I was a used car salesmen. And good at it too, I might add."

How fitting. Cassandra almost burst out laughing at the thought.

"I went to church with them. Pastor John took me under his wing, like a son, and I eventually decided to finish college—of course no longer at an ivy league school—and become a pastor, like him. John said I had a gift with words." He smirked, his eyes catching hers as if to say he knew what she was thinking about that gift.

Cassandra smiled in spite of herself. "You've led a full and varied life, Vince Steegle, that's for sure."

He groaned as he pushed to sit. "I guess we better try this standing thing again."

Cassandra flinched, having forgotten why they were there. She braced herself as he put his arm around her. Stepping forward, she pushed up as he leaned on his uninjured leg. They stood together, Vince gasping, face mottled.

"You okay?"

"Yeah."

Cassandra waited as he seemed to breathe for composure, leaning against the lower portion of the structure wanting to be a deck.

He turned pleading eyes to her. "Would you mind getting me a clean shirt from inside the house? I don't want to be stinking up the emergency room."

"You'll be all right if I leave you here?"

"Yep."

Cassandra entered his front door, picking up the envelope she'd placed there, and leaving it on an end table by the couch. Looking around, she noticed the sparse furnishings, so unlike the opulence in which he'd grown up. A few pictures here and there, featuring faces she recognized from church. Vince and Pastor John with golf clubs. Vince and Billy holding hammers. There was even one picture of Vince on Billy's custom-painted Harley, looking awkwardly preppie astride the hog. Cassandra chuckled and placed the picture back on the shelf. She entered his bedroom, found the dresser, and opened the third drawer down, as he'd instructed, to retrieve a polo shirt. Scanning the choices, she found a royal blue one and ran her hand over it. This would go perfectly with his eyes. Cassandra gasped at the thought. She can't think of him that way ever again. After yanking out the brown shirt, she exited the house.

Vince pulled the sweaty T-shirt from his back as he saw her coming, wiped his forehead with it, received the polo, and put it on. Cassandra tried not to notice, but her eyes pulled in that direction as if by magnetic draw.

~*~

Vince glanced toward Cass as she drove him to the hospital. If only he could read her thoughts. Why? He didn't need to know any more than he already did about how much she hated him. But fear him? Kat's words, and the look in her face the other night, played in his mind like a haunting tune. What had he done to cause Cass panic attacks. Could he hate himself anymore? He peered up to the heavens. *I know I'm forgiven, Lord. But somehow I can't wash this guilt away. As long as she suffers, I should too.*

Her features remained stern as she maneuvered toward the emergency room entrance and stopped. Cass rounded the car. Vince opened the door, and she lent her shoulder for him to lean on as he hopped into the waiting area.

"Pastor Vince." Cheryl sat behind the desk today. "Where've you been? We haven't seen you in almost two weeks."

Cass turned a questioning look his way.

"I'm kind of a klutz."

"Only when handling tools," the cheery voice added from the desk. She winked.

Cassandra's brow rose. He knew what she was thinking. How he'd always sweet talked the ladies. It was that ability that made him feel impervious to Cass in the first place, and take the bet Drew had offered. Little did Vince know at the time, she'd be the one to entrance him. Her, and that God of hers. Somehow his Creator spoke to him through her even when Vince had refused to listen.

Cass helped Vince to a hard plastic seat, and walked to the desk. "Do you have forms for him to fill out?"

Cheryl waved a file she pulled from a rack in front of her. "Already done." She smirked. "We keep them ready for him when he comes. Just have him sign the bottom, here and here." She indicated the lines. "And we're good to go."

Cassandra's gaze swiveled to meet Vince. He shrugged and smiled. She handed him the forms.

Then he realized … "What were you doing at my house anyway?"

Cass sat next to him. "I was dropping off my recommendations for the special needs program."

He signed the forms in his lap. "Why didn't you just take them to the church?"

She didn't even move.

"Oh." Dumb question. "You thought I'd be there."

Her continued silence confirmed it.

He whispered, "I'm not going to hurt you, Cass."

She stared at the wall in front of her. "I'd have to care for it to hurt this time." She turned her hardened eyes toward him. "Why weren't you at work?"

"Took the afternoon off to add to the deck."

She almost smiled. "You gonna build it all by yourself?"

"Mostly."

"Why don't you get some help?"

Vince's knee seized. He shifted to relieve the pain. "I need to do it on my own."

"Ah. Some male-ego, test of courage thing, huh?"

"Something like that." It felt so comfortable, talking with Cass this way. Like a lifetime of hurt hadn't separated them. "So, while we're waiting, why don't you tell me about your program?"

She leaned her head against the wall, closed her eyes, and sighed hard. "I may have had some delusions of grandeur."

He'd loved that about her, her idealistic visions. "You always did."

She leered at him.

"But in a good way."

Her eyebrows jumped. "*Good* delusions of grandeur?"

"Why don't you tell me, and we'll see if we can make your idea work."

Cassandra shifted her body to face Vince. "It's like this. Some programs have separate classrooms for special needs children, and others have buddies who assist the disabled in a regular classroom."

Vince smiled at the familiar way she spoke as much with her hands as she did her lips. "Which is best?"

"Neither. It depends on the child." She pulled her hair behind her ears, and sat straighter. "Some kids, like Tibo, enjoy a lot of social interaction with all kinds of kids. In fact, I think it's good for non-affected students to spend time with them, so they become familiar. Not something to fear or be separate from."

"Okay. So what's the problem?"

"Well, there are other kids, like Isabella's son, who might become over stimulated in a normal classroom, and might act out because of it."

"Did you speak to Isabella?"

Cassandra's nod was solemn.

"Would she come back if there were a classroom for Sean?"

"She swears she won't, but I think we need to be ready for the next family like hers, so we don't lose them too … And they lose us."

Vince warmed at Cass including herself as part of the church—*his* church. "I agree. So what do you recommend?"

Her eyes were timid, hesitant. "Both."

"You mean a separate classroom *and* a buddy system?"

"Yup."

"That would take a lot of manpower."

She grimaced. "That's the problem. Most churches I visited

barely had enough volunteers willing to help their programs at all. And those that did, usually relied on other parents with special needs.

"That's awful." Vince rubbed his throbbing knee. "The point is to relieve the parents, not burden them more." He shook his head. "And I can't help but wonder if we're losing their other gifts, as well. You know, the ones they bury in the overwhelming care of their child."

Cass's gaze shot to his. "Have you ever heard Isabella sing?"

"No."

"I heard her through the window when I went to interview her at her home." Cass's eyes glistened. "I think it's how she keeps Sean calm. He turns into a pussy cat when he hears it."

Vince sat straighter. "We need to get this program going." His resolve strengthened with each passing day. "I want you to come to the church office next week and order whatever supplies you'll need for the new classroom."

"But—"

"Let me handle the volunteers." He winked.

She jolted and turned away.

Two hours later, his knee no longer throbbed, but the doctor sent him with crutches just in case. Vince knew it would be better by the next morning having had the same kind of strain a few months back. A little rest and Advil would do the trick. Still, he couldn't help thanking his God for the chance to spend time with Cass, if even for a little bit.

Then he thought of the pizza crumb he'd offered Sophie, and how she said it would only make her want more. He looked to Cass, now pulling her car into his driveway, and realized how much he could relate.

Chapter Seventeen

"So good to be in church together."

Cassandra pulled Sophie close. "Mm-hm." She was glad to worship with her kids again too. So why did the air seem to vibrate with anxiety? Was she really going to sit through a painted-on sermon delivered by that silver-tongued charmer who'd ruined her life?

Vince strode up the aisle shaking hands with parishioners at the ends of the pews. His gaze caught with the ones in the middle as he waved a greeting then locked on Cassandra. Her heart dropped as his large smile faltered then rallied as if to reassure her.

He'd asked her to come today. It was important for the special needs program that its creator be present. She sucked in a wad of air, and squeezed Tibo's delicate fingers. He held gently back.

Vince returned to the front pew as the worship band started playing. The music and lyrics reminded her of a God in charge, bringing relief to the pounding of her heart.

Finally, the lights brightened and Vince took the pulpit. "Open your Bibles to First Corinthians, chapter twelve."

Vince read the entire chapter, focusing on spiritual gifts, many different parts, and the body of Christ. As he enunciated certain words, like *gift* and *different*, Cassandra's mind wandered to that moment in the emergency room when he'd said, "And I can't help but wonder if we're losing their other gifts, as well. You know, the ones they bury in the overwhelming care of their child."

Those words had stunned her. To think Vince could be so

deep as to look beyond someone's outward appearance, and consider hidden talents. She checked herself. Vince had seemed deep before, but that was a ruse to get what he wanted. He could always find a person's vulnerability, only it wasn't to help, but to exploit.

Still, it showed he had a keen sense to see beyond the surface. What he could do with that sense if he'd only use it for God.

"So the body is meant to work together. Where this one is weak, the other uses his strength to assist him, allowing that one to use his or her gift for another." His blue eyes moved in Cassandra's direction for one meaningful second. "We," he stretched out his hands to the congregation, "work as a body. A whole. Together."

She shivered. He *was* using it for God.

No, no, no. Not Vince. That's what he wanted everyone to think. He couldn't have changed that much.

"Some of you are gifted in administration." He grinned. "Oh, do I value you. We need you to keep us running. Some are gifted at building." He grimaced, and a rumbling erupted from the congregation. He held his hands up. "And some of us are not." He gestured to the piano and drums still behind him. "Some in music and some at teaching. When one assists the other, the other is freed to unleash his or her gifts for our pleasure," Vince's gaze rose to the ceiling, "and His glory."

He scanned the audience, resting his attention on individuals here and there. They nodded toward him as he did. "Many parts. One body." He interlocked his fingers. "Its beauty is how it works together. Its function is how each part fills the gap of the other, meets the need of the weaker member." His eyes became intense. "And what of that weaker member?" At this, he smiled toward Amit. Then, he brushed his gaze past Tibo before it landed on Cassandra. She swallowed at the way his crooked smile took her to memories she wished she could hate. "What does the Bible say about them?" He paused as if waiting for a word from God Himself. "They are indispensable."

"Preach it." A voice called from the congregation. A few echoes followed.

"What does this mean for Water's Edge Community Church?"

Cassandra dropped her attention to her hands folded in her lap as Vince outlined, in detail, the program Cassandra had designed. She didn't dare look around, now, for fear she'd see a negative reaction in the eyes of the people nearby.

Vince outlined the whys and the wherefores as if he'd studied her document from every angle, pointing out not only how the parishioners could use their gifts to help, but how it would in turn bring more members to the church freeing them up to use *their* gifts.

The room was silent. Cassandra, enthralled by the power this man had with words, with emotion, and the passion of his delivery, swallowed the lump in her throat, almost believing he cared.

"We need you all to make this happen. The ushers will be handing out cards. If you can volunteer in any way, please take one and fill it out."

The ushers stopped at the end of each pew, and handed the cards down the rows. Cassandra dared peek to see if anyone did as she hoped. Some passed the cards, some pocketed them, but many filled them out.

Cassandra's eyes burned as her attention rose to the man at the pulpit. His wink froze her. He did it. Just like he said he would. He took care of the volunteers.

A tear finally fell. She brushed at it, but then another rolled down her other cheek. Her throat clogged. She slipped in front of Tibo, then her mother in the pew. Catching Vince's concerned expression before she turned, she strode out of the sanctuary, barely able to control the tremors, bolted to the bathroom, and sobbed in a stall until her tear ducts had no more to give.

~*~

Vince watched Cass flee like being chased by the devil himself. What had he done wrong? People were signing up, volunteering for her program, and she raced out as if she were angry.

Dejected, he stepped aside as Pastor John rose to do the altar call. Vince stayed up front in case anyone came to receive Jesus as their personal Savior. The parishioners bowed their heads for prayer, and closed their eyes as John had instructed. All but young Tibo in the second row and Amit standing in the back. Vince mouthed the words *close your eyes* to Amit. He smiled big and exaggerated a hard blink as if to obey. Vince blinked back, only to feel the soft gaze of the little boy beside Mrs. Hessing. His expression somehow communicating a peaceful quality that calmed the nerves that had ratcheted at the vision of Cass running from the room. Vince finally closed his eyes too, receiving Pastor John's words about a Savior who washed away his sins.

The music ended. One woman had come forward to pray with John. Vince headed up the aisle and out to take his place at the front door. Cass exited the bathroom.

"What happened to you?" Mrs. Hessing said to her daughter.

It was apparent by the red swollen eyes. "Had something in my eye. Needed to get it out." Evidently she'd noticed as well. Tibo grasped her hand, and took in his mother's face as if studying every cell of her skin. She dropped a kiss on his head and her shoulders seemed to relax at the contact.

Vince greeted the line of people, but barely heard their words. "Thank you. Thank you." He said at their accolades of his sermon. A few had twisted expressions and he wondered if he'd answered them correctly.

"Wasn't that a great sermon?" He heard Mrs. Hessing's voice.

Cassandra nodded, a pained smile on her face.

Her mother patted her hand as she tugged her toward the door. "Let's go thank the Pastor. You're going to have plenty of help with your program, now." Her tug met with resistance as

Cass pointed to her eye, pulled free, and exited out the far door. Mrs. Hessing grimaced after her retreating daughter, then pointed a confounded expression right back at Vince.

~*~

Kevin clapped the dust off his hands as he entered the living room. Cassandra Whitaker sat in a chair, furiously scribbling in a notebook as she flipped through a catalog. Probably from some high-priced furniture store.

He hovered over her. "Looks like we're done here. Would you like to take a final walk-through to see if it meets your expectations?" She'd probably find some flaw to complain about.

She glanced up as if in a fog. "Oh. Uh. Sure. Where are your other guys?"

"I sent them home." Didn't she trust the job was done?

She flopped the catalog onto the coffee table. School supplies? Must be for her retarded kid. "Show me your work." Cassandra straightened from the chair, smoothed her hair from her face, and followed Kevin to the new room.

Kevin led her through the hall and into the first addition. She scanned the ceiling, the walls, and the carpet. "Looks good."

Of course it did. Kevin got the best guys he knew to do the job. He wanted to make sure she trusted him completely, while he'd taken every opportunity to look through her possessions. Unfortunately, the only thing of interest he'd found so far was a bank statement with a balance currently down to the minimum. Must be an old one she didn't use anymore. She probably kept the information from the meatier accounts—and he knew she had some—in another location.

Cassandra followed him into the next room, barely looking at the care he'd taken to edge the paint, and ensure the molding was straight and flush to the wall. "You guys did a great job. What do I owe you?"

She wouldn't get rid of him that easily. He had more searching he needed to do. "Why don't you let me move the furniture into the rooms before I go?" He could take out drawers and rifle through them when she wasn't looking.

Already halfway down the hallway, she called back, "Oh, that's not necessary."

He stepped to follow her. "No. I never consider a job done till everything is right where it belongs."

She met him midpoint, checkbook in hand. "That's very nice of you, but your men are gone. I can handle it from here."

Kevin's gaze hit the checkbook then scanned the empty house. Where was her mother and her kids? How long would they be gone? His attention landed on the lonely woman in front of him, the one who'd grown from the girl who'd never looked his way in high school. The curls escaping her ponytail screamed a vulnerability that made him want to prove his strength.

She tilted her head, brows crinkling.

Kevin shook from his thoughts. Back on track. He had bigger fish to fry. He'd like a look at that book in her hand, and figure a way to drain the account. "You can't move it all by yourself. Let me help."

"Actually, I don't have furniture for those rooms yet, so there's nothing to move.

Cursing to himself, he set his mind on overdrive. He needed something. Time was up. "How 'bout the stuff we moved to open up the wall?"

"Oh yeah. I guess you could help with that. It's a long dresser, and a bit heavy for my mom." She replaced the checkbook on the coffee table. "We can put it in Sophie's room."

Sophie. That cute young thing. He'd been learning a lot about the developing teen over the weeks he'd worked this idea. She was the one who always seemed to be watching the little boy—the kid who couldn't talk. The idea kept flashing in his mind till the checking account no longer interested him. Cassandra Whitaker's weakest point—her kids. Now that was an idea that finally gelled, and if he used it, not only could he get his hands on Cassandra's vast wealth, she'd be the one to hand it to him.

Chapter Eighteen

Lew held the tray of drinks as he slid onto the bench-seat in the stands at the Hagerstown raceway. The sound of roaring motors soothed him like ocean waves did to others.

Tibo pulled his mom to follow.

Lew shook his head at the way Cassandra stepped carefully over trash in those dainty little sandals.

They settled into his favorite spot—close to the track, but high enough to see all the action. People around them stared at the unlikely trio—Tibo, Cassandra, and him—like they wondered how long the prissy-looking chick would stay married to the ragged old coot. Lew laughed at the thought as he checked out the woman next to him brushing track dust from her tidy white shorts. Like he'd marry a Lilly-White. He preferred women with spice.

Cassandra scowled at his chuckle. "What are you laughing at?"

He nodded toward the mud stain on the neatly folded cuff of her designer pants. "I guess I shoulda warned ya 'bout the dirt."

"You'd think I might have figured it out … since it *is* a *dirt*-track race."

"Yep."

Her smile caught him off guard. "But it was worth it, watching Tibo meet the drivers, and see the cars up close."

"Yeah, it was definitely worth it." Lew felt his lip curl higher up than it usually did.

After grabbing two sodas from the drink tray, she handed one to her son. "Thanks, Lew."

He dropped his gaze to his dusty boots, but felt her eyes bore into him.

"Really, Lew. No one has ever taken the time to get to know Tibo like you have. And *no one* shares his passion for cars like you do." She wrapped an arm around the boy, and he giggled. "This means a lot to both of us."

The kid stuck his forefingers in both ears as some engines roared below.

Uh-oh. "He's not gonna freak out with the noise or anything, is he?"

Cassandra looked at her son, whose fingers were pulsing in and out of his ears now. She shook her head. "Oh, no. He's not trying to stop the noise. He's making it more interesting."

Lew grimaced. "But I thought autistic kids—" He cursed. "I mean, *kids with autism*," —he stressed the phrase Kat had told him to use—"hate loud noises."

Cassandra's grin took over her face.

"What?"

She lifted a shoulder. "It's just funny seeing you be so PC. Didn't know you had it in you, Lew."

He grumbled. That's what he got for trying.

"You're right. Most kids with autism are very sensitive to loud noises. Tibo is like that with a few things. Sometimes it's the acoustics of certain buildings—particularly ones that echo. But with most things, he's a sensory *seeker*, not a sensory *avoider*. That's why he loves the engines, and tries to make the noise have more impact by moving his fingers in and out."

Louder roaring sounded from the track. Tibo palmed his ears this time, his smile uncontained.

Lew nodded. "Sorry 'bout the word."

Her brows drew together. "You mean labeling him *autistic* rather than saying he *has autism?*" She smirked. "Or are you talking about the colorful word in between?"

"Well, I guess" —he glanced at the boy who often repeated the last word of a sentence—"both."

She turned her body to look right at him. "Lew, lots of

people use all the right politically correct language, and never once try to engage my son. They give me all kinds of recommendations they've learned from their friends and family members about what to do for kids with autism, and never try to enter our world." A weight seemed to bare down on the woman's expression, but she gave him a small half-grin. "You've done both." She faced forward, swallowed hard, and touched the corner of her eye. "Your actions have more meaning than those words ever will. You treat him as what those *correct* phrases are meant to convey."

He straightened his back, but for some reason couldn't look at the lady next to him. Maybe it had something to do with how hot his face felt right now.

She took a long draw of her soda then pointed the straw his way. "I never realized you were such a great driver."

He chuckled. He liked this prissy woman. But did the guys really have to tell her all the old stories?

"That one racer, Jeremy Holt, said you were his idol when he was a kid. He wanted to drive just like you."

Lew kicked at a beer bottle cap on the board below his feet. "Yeah, well …" He didn't know what else to say. He missed those days, and wished somehow he could do them over, but not mess them up so much.

Bouncing, Tibo's gaze followed the cars taking pre-race laps.

"Why'd you stop?"

Did he have to relive that part too? "Started losing." He ground his bottom lip between his teeth, wishing he had some chewing tobacco. But he quit that stuff long time ago—it was bad for him.

Cassandra shifted her gaze below as the green flag waved, and the race began. Tibo squealed with excitement, setting Lew's heart to pound a happy gong. He never knew he could enjoy watching a kid bounce up and down on a seat. Poor boy's back-side would likely kill him by the end of the day.

Cassandra laughed and nodded to her son. "He's like a

fun-button in our house."

"A fun-button?"

"Yeah, he turns the most mundane activities into a lot of fun." She mussed the kid's hair.

"Are you calling racing mundane?" Lew tried the offended look.

She shook her head. "Of course not. You know what I mean."

He turned to the kid. *Bounce, bounce, bounce.* "I think I do."

They sat in silence, and watched the vehicles hurtle around the track. Lew didn't even know which car was leading. He'd kept his eyes on Tibo throughout the race, his heart swelling with the kid's joy. He might just have to do this again.

Cars crashed. They rolled. Some sped out of the track and into trees that lined the raceway. Round and round they went. Long moments later, the checkered flag waved, and Tibo clapped.

Lew shook his head and grinned. Something warm settled over him and into his chest—weird.

Cassandra grabbed his hand and jumped from the seat. "That's Jeremy's car! Jeremy won!" She turned to Lew. "Your protege."

~*~

When Lew yanked his fingers from Cassandra's, she knew she'd said something that bothered him. She didn't mean to, but sometimes people took her the wrong way. Maybe because she was the kind of girl who wore expensive, white shorts to a dirt track race. Little did they know she didn't have the money to buy *cheap* shorts right now, especially with her children's growing clothing needs. So she had to settle for the things her husband had purchased when he was alive, with the allowance his parents had given him for the family's "proper attire."

Cassandra tried to communicate an apology with her eyes, since she didn't have words for an offense she didn't understand.

"It was the drinking."

She read his lips more than heard him. Was he even speaking to her?

Tibo squealed as more cars drove onto the track.

Cassandra didn't watch this time. She lowered herself to the bench next to Lew and waited, expecting him to elaborate, but as the silence stretched, unsure he would.

Lew turned toward her. He shrugged. "Couldn't stop."

Cassandra placed a hand over his.

"Same reason you wouldn't let the boy drive with me here."

She pulled her hand away, and shook her head. What could she say?

"I don't blame you. I wouldn't trust me with him either."

She shifted her body to face him on the bench. "Lew, it's not just you. I don't trust him alone with anybody. Especially since he can't tell me things."

Lew seemed to consider the grains of wood in the stands before swiveling to meet her gaze. "I bet you'd trust the church folk." There was a challenge in those dark eyes.

Oh, if he only knew … "Not unless I know them really really *really* well."

"*Really* well?" Was he mocking her?

"Yes, *really* well."

"Not your religious friends?"

"Not alone with my son—no." She hesitated wondering if she should disclose the reason for her fears.

"Why not? Do you suspect they aren't as good as they pretend to be?" There was that challenge again.

She'd meet it. "Only the ones pretending to be good." Cassandra drew in a breath as the roaring of another race began in earnest. "Lew, just because a person goes to church, doesn't mean they are a Christian. And even if they are, they're still sinners."

His brows crunched.

"People go to church for lots of reasons—some to follow Jesus, and some to look like they do."

"Why would a person waste an hour on Sunday only to

look like they follow Jesus?"

Cassandra couldn't keep the darkness from her laugh. "Satan loves to use the church for his purposes whenever there is an opening. And unfortunately there are too many in the pews who are open."

"Satan?" Lew's eyelids lowered. " You mean the guy with the pointy tail and pitchfork?"

"No. He's more clever than to appear a *cartoon* of evil."

"I thought you were educated." His sardonic tone told her what he thought of her education.

Cassandra hated when people treated her beliefs like a silly myth. "The more I live, and the more I see people explaining away bad things as if they weren't really bad, and the more I see authority figures abusing power for their own gain, the more I believe there is evil in the world. It's not a great stretch to imagine some *being* is behind it. Someone tempting us to do what we know is wrong, and someone setting out to destroy us, while making us believe we are doing something good."

She waited for Lew to laugh. But he didn't.

A yellow flag waved over the track, and the cars slowed. Tibo's bouncing settled.

"Satan loves to use the church. He accomplishes more than one goal in doing so. First, he tempts the abuser. Next, he traumatizes the victim. And lastly, he covers the church with deceit, leaving non-believers to think we are all hypocrites."

"Abuser?"

She had to use that word, didn't she? "Yes."

He just looked at her—waiting for her to elaborate.

"I had a friend when I was a teenager who had been sexually assaulted by one of the youth leaders."

Lew pointed at her. "I knew it. Dirty secrets."

"It was only a secret until the girl finally told her parents. As soon as the elders were informed, the leader was dismissed from ministry, and charges were filed."

"See? Church folk *are* a bunch of hypocrites."

Cassandra tensed. "That's not fair, Lew. You're letting

Satan win."

"Pfffft."

Heat fumed into her cheeks. "Just because a person claims to be a Christian and doesn't act on that faith, doesn't mean the rest of us are hypocrites."

He opened his mouth …

She raised her voice. "And just because some of us have a bad day, and give in to weakness on occasion, doesn't mean we're hypocrites." Her hands became tense fists.

"But—"

"And just because we have sin in our pasts, and want to live a better life now that we know better, doesn't mean we're hypocrites."

Lew held up his finger, and glanced around at the spectators who'd quieted and turned their way.

She sucked in a breath. "And …"

He arched a brow.

"I'm … I'm done."

He grimaced. "Is bitterness your particular weakness?"

She smirked and Lew joined her in a laugh. "Maybe a little."

Cassandra loved the way his chuckle seemed to reach inside him right now. She'd never heard that from him before.

"Anyway … *that's* why I'm super-protective of my son."

Chapter Nineteen

Cassandra had flipped through an innumerable amount of catalogs displaying the supplies needed for a special needs classroom to teach children about Jesus as their Savior: videos, books, music. She'd have to ask Vince—Pastor Vince, she needed to call him—if they had anything in the budget to purchase things that could help calm a restless child with sensory issues, like weighted vests, balance balls, or textured mats.

She'd considered faxing or emailing the list, but knew it was time to face the man as her boss, be professional, and leave the dwindling animosity at the door.

Was it dwindling?

Her heart pounded as she crossed the threshold to the church offices, Yolanda sitting sentry at the front desk. "Cassandra, right?" Was that a question, confirmation, or accusation? Of course it was only the second time they'd met in the weeks since she'd interviewed for the position.

"Yes. I've come to drop off a list of supplies the special needs classroom will need." She glanced around. "Is Vin—Pastor Vince, here?"

Yolanda's eyebrows jumped at Cassandra's slip. "He stepped out."

Cassandra held up the pages in her hand. "Can I drop this on his desk?"

"Be my guest." Yolanda jabbed a thumb to the open door.

Cassandra hesitated, peering around at the burgundy walls and shelves filled with books: theology, apologetics, Bible studies, devotions, a concordance, a couple of Dickens novels, and … George MacDonald? She'd told him long ago how much she'd loved the author's writings. Had he remembered, or were they the recommendation of a divinity professor?

The scent of him saturated the space like a warning not to enter. She wanted to drink it in, fill her mind with the strength of the young man who'd held her in his arms, and the smiles that seemed to single her out from every other woman in the world. But she knew that drink was poison and shook her mind from the lies.

Wanting him to see the list immediately, she dropped it on the blotter in front of his computer keyboard. She needed to write a note to ask about the sensory items. Finding a message pad, she ripped off a pink page, and searched for a pen. His desk held piles of documents here and there, a docking station for electronics, file holders, and a paper clip tray seemingly made by a Sunday school student, but no pens. She peered around the shelves—nothing.

Cassandra opened the flat drawer of his desk and smiled at the fun-sized Heath bars littered throughout. She'd forgotten about his obsession for chocolate-covered toffee. Some things never changed. In fact, that's what she feared the most. Or did she fear they had. With her mind playing through all of what she'd learned about him over the past several weeks, she no longer knew what she felt regarding Vince at all.

Resisting the urge to snatch a chocolate bar, she dug into the pencil tray instead, only to find the shape of something so familiar she knew it the moment her skin made contact—the cross her father had made for her. The one she'd given to Vince the night he'd—

"I see you've found Pastor Vince's talisman." Yolanda's voice startled her.

Cassandra sank into the leather chair and caressed the divots and jagged spots her father had left to resemble the rough-hewn character of the true cross. "Talisman?"

"Yeah, every now and then I catch him touchin' that thing." Yolanda's expression was curious. "Kinda like you're doin' now."

Cassandra dropped it on the desk.

"Usually, after a tough day or when he's worried about someone." She chuckled. "It must be pretty powerful if people keep feeling the need to rub it all the time."

After wrapping the leather cord around her first two fingers, Cassandra fisted the trinket.

"Seems to give him peace too." Yolanda's voice began to fade as the past took the forefront of Cassandra's mind. "I'm guessing it has some memories attached to it. Maybe something he got in prison."

Cassandra bolted up, crossed the room and rammed past the secretary in the doorway.

"Hey!"

Trudging down the corridor, Cassandra barely processed the woman's words.

"You can't take that. It's not yours."

Out the door, down the cement front steps, Cassandra moved as if on autopilot toward her car. She cranked the engine, cross still clutched in her fist. She knew where she needed to take it.

~*~

"Pastor Vince."

He strode to his office, the smell of a flame-broiled burger wafting from the bag in his hand. After the long morning, crunching numbers to find the funds for the special needs classroom, he couldn't wait to sink his teeth into the doughy bread encasing the salty beef. He dropped into his chair and dug into the bag. A list sat on the blotter next to it.

"She took the cross." Yolanda stood at the door.

He stopped the bag excavation. "She, who? And what cross?" He knew the answers but hoped he was wrong.

Yolanda's eyes bugged. "That Whitaker woman and YOUR cross."

The drawer squealed opened, his fingers feeling the crevices even before he took note of his actions. He dug through every inch. Took out every pen, pencil, rubber band, stamp, Heath bar. She couldn't have it. Yolanda was mistaken. "How did she find it?"

Yolanda's dark brows bunched. "Were you hiding it?"

"Where'd she go?"

Her eyes moved restlessly in their sockets. "High-tailed it right out that door and haven't seen her since."

"How long ago?"

"Just before you got here."

Vince pushed back the chair. Burger forgotten.

"Look Pastor, I didn't know she'd leave with it. Can't you get another one? It couldn't be that expensive. Although, it's kind of creepy she'd up and take something that wasn't hers."

The words trailed him as he headed toward his car. He had to try to find her, and he had a suspicion he knew where she'd go.

~*~

The wheels crunched as Cassandra pulled her SUV next to the vacant lot. Time to face this place.

Oh God, help me.

She finally opened the palm that gripped the small cross her father had formed out of driftwood when she was a little girl. A gift she'd cherished, but had given away—she'd thought—for a good cause.

Why had Vince kept it all these years? Yolanda said it brought him peace.

No. Cassandra could not believe in this man again. She needed to remember what he'd done to her. The lies he told for his own gain. Drew, Vince's old best friend, said he owed Vince one hundred dollars because she'd been taken in by his upturned lips and searching, blue eyes. Drew didn't mind throwing that in her face when …

She couldn't breathe. The wind whipped through the tall grass and reeds that surrounded the shoreline Vince used to motor to in his little boat. All that air moving around her, making her dizzy, but none seemed to want to enter her lungs.

Dropping to the edge of the property where the water lapped the land, face to the ground, she prayed for guidance. Her throat clogged and nose burned, but her breathing slowed.

"I hate him, God," she whispered into the grass. "I know I shouldn't, but I do. He opened the door and stole from me ..." The crack of her voice tore through her throat, "and he never secured the lock." Tears dripped into the mud as thunder rolled in the background. "Why did I let him? I knew better. Why?"

The rumbles of thunder felt more like murmurs of comfort than rebuke.

"I can't forgive him. I won't lie to you, Lord. It's too hard."

My yoke is easy ...

She swallowed hard at the thought, but steeled herself from surrender. The thunder rolled across the sky as though a warrior angel prepared to battle for her.

She lifted the cross from the grass, and pulled back to chuck it in the water.

A hand stopped her wrist.

~*~

Vince couldn't let her do it. He didn't know why. Was it because her father had made the cross, and she'd regret the loss of it at her own hand? Or was it that Vince needed it more than she did?

"Don't." He said when her eyes met his as she stood and turned, his hand still gripping her wrist.

Cassandra's expression went from surprise to entreaty as she gestured with her head for him to let go.

He did.

She lowered her hand.

"Please don't throw that away." He broke eye contact for fear she'd read more than he thought appropriate to say right now.

156

"Why did you keep it?" Her gaze remained on him.

He only shrugged.

Cassandra's fingers unfolded to reveal the trinket—or talisman as Yolanda called it. "Tell me." Her voice a whisper, evidencing emotion he'd remembered from long ago.

"It was yours." Seeing she still held it out to him, he took it from her opened hand. "You gave it to me, I know, with the hope I'd one day turn to God."

Her expression hardened as if she'd figured out the real reason he'd asked her to remove it.

"I couldn't look at it on your neck every time I attempted to seduce you, knowing—or believing—my actions were a lie."

She closed her eyes at what must be confirmation of what she already knew.

"After you left my bedroom in such a rage, it felt as if all the oxygen had gone with you."

She bit her lip and stared at the grass. Vince wanted to touch her but sensed any connection would cause her pain.

"I knew, though I'd pursued you as part of a bet, the more time I spent with you, the more I fell in love with you."

Her green eyes flashed to his with a sense of anger and hurt.

"I knew you wouldn't believe me if I told you, but I vowed to win you back somehow. Prove I cared."

"How?" The word pierced like a knife in his gut.

"I hadn't gotten that far." He closed his fingers around the cross, and reveled in the peace it always gave him. "I tied it around my neck before I slept. The next morning, as I watched all my possessions die in flames, I felt it there and realized it was the only thing I cared to keep."

Cassandra's hardened glare chilled him as a mist fell from the air. "I don't believe you?"

Vince shook his head. "I didn't think you would." He turned from her. "Through the years I realized it wasn't meant to be a reminder of you, but of God. I'd forgotten that until I'd found it in the boxes I brought to Billy's house. Suddenly, the whole story—God's story for me—came together." He rubbed the wood between thumb and forefinger. "I kept it as a reminder of how long God has been pursuing me, and how He has a purpose in that pursuit."

Her lips parted at that. Did she think this a lie too? For some reason he figured not. She looked more surprised than wary.

He stretched it out to her.

She rubbed furiously at her upper arms. "You keep it."

"Your father made it for you."

She shook her head.

"I almost sent it to you when he died that fall."

"How did you know about that?"

"The same way I knew you'd already married."

The green of her eyes speared him.

"Your old manager from the country club kept me up to date those first few months, before I fell out of favor with that crowd."

The light rain pattered in the water beside them.

"Why'd you get married so soon?" Were his suspicions correct?

Her quick intake of air whistled through her teeth. "I'd known Tim for two years at college. He was always a good friend."

"You weren't in love with him."

Her features hardened. "He was the best man I've ever known." Surely in contrast to the one in front of her.

"You weren't in love with him." He repeated the words, daring her to deny it.

"What do you know about love?"

Vince stood his ground. "Though you believe I was only toying with your emotions, I am certain you would never have toyed with mine. There is no way you would have shared a bed with me, then one month later discovered you really loved someone else"

A war waged in Cass's expression. "You know nothing."

He needed to find out. "You never answered my question about Sophie."

Her rage wilted to the point he almost felt the need to catch her. Her breathing picked up speed.

"Please tell me. I promise I won't say anything to her. I just want to hear the words, the confirmation of what I already know."

Cassandra's voice cracked as she placed a hand to her chest. Was she okay? "I can't tell you what you want to hear, Vince Steegle, because I don't know the answer myself."

Lightning flashed through the sky. Did he hear right? How could she not know? Had she jumped in bed with Tim on return to her college dorm? That, he couldn't believe. Anyone could see Sophie didn't resemble the man at all. He'd made note of that from the picture Sophie had shown him that Sunday after church.

Vince stared, pleading for answers with his eyes.

She pulled air into her lungs, a sob escaped. "That night … when I left …" each word was a struggle, "I realized I'd left my Bible here." She closed her eyes as her shoulders seemed to heft air in and out. "I walked the path to get it." A tear rolled down her cheek. "I heard a noise behind me." She grimaced as if in pain. "A part of me wished it was you."

Suddenly, so did Vince.

"But it wasn't you. You never came after me to apologize or explain." She labored for more air through her sobs. "Instead, I got Drew, your best friend." She sneered. "Your *brother*, you used to call him, because he looked so much like you."

Vince's heart stalled. He didn't want to hear anymore, but knew he must.

"He went by your house, and your father told him you won the bet and he owed you a hundred dollars."

Vince remembered telling his father he wasn't up to visitors when Drew showed up that night.

"Drew said …" She seemed to struggle with more than speaking the words. "… he said …" Should he try to calm her? She might get more upset if he did. "… he said it was *his* turn, and that I owed him."

159

Every muscle rigid, Vince could barely control his rage enough to let her continue.

More tears chased the first she'd spent. "He said he wouldn't have to worry about pregnancy because you'd take care of that … or at least your father would." She dropped to the grass and panted, leaning against a large tree. What had looked like sobs, turned into something else. Cassandra seized as she wheezed for breath, and Vince was once again the cause.

He sat beside her and reached for her hand. She jerked away still gasping air. Helpless. Having no idea what to do, he prayed. Words floated to his mind, Bible verses. Psalm 18. Cass's favorite.

He whispered, "The Lord is my rock, my fortress and my deliverer; my God is my rock in whom I take refuge." He muttered low as each word came to him, one by one. "He is my shield and the horn of my salvation, my stronghold." These were the first he'd memorized when he'd begun to study the Bible. "I call to the Lord who is worthy of praise and I am saved from my enemies." Words that steadied him when things got tough. He looked to Cass and saw they steadied her too, so he continued to whisper them till the Psalm was done.

~*~

Her breathing slowed and deepened at the resonance of his voice, speaking words of God Cassandra knew were true. It didn't matter they came from a liar. She peered sideways at him. Yes, it mattered they came from Vince. It was clear he'd remembered her favorite Psalm after all these years. He'd memorized it knowing she was long married and not expected to come back.

Why?

"I'm so sorry." His voice cracked with emotion. "No wonder you hate me so much."

Cassandra focused each breath in and out, each beat of her heart to steady and calm.

160

"I lied to you, led you on, took from you." Vince ground his teeth. "And left you vulnerable to that …" He dropped his head in his hands. "I should have gone after you. At least you would have been safe from *him*."

The rain stopped. Cassandra realized how damp they both were, but didn't care. "Sophie's been asking questions." She shivered and Vince put his arm around her as though the clock had receded sixteen years. This time she didn't jolt at his tentative touch. In fact, it seemed best to nestle into his warmth. "I don't know what to tell her."

He seemed uncertain by her proximity. "I have a feeling, only the truth will satisfy her."

Cassandra's mind drew up the vision of the two of them chatting together in the pew, and what Sophie had revealed about his fatherly advice.

Vince ran his hand up and down her bare arm at the next shiver. It warmed her.

She didn't dare move. "I don't know the truth, and I can't tell her all of it … that she could be the product of such violence."

Vince's arms tightened around her. She felt secure there. "I think we need to find out the truth."

She bolted up and searched his expression.

"If it's me, you can confirm what she already believes." Was he ready for that?

"And if it's not?"

Cassandra felt the swallow at his throat. "Let's just hope she's mine."

Hope? His?

Did he really want to be Sophie's dad? Did Cassandra want that too?

Too overwhelmed by the possibilities, she settled into his chest again. Was this a dream? It must be, because next she said, "Yes, let's hope."

Chapter Twenty

Sophie opened the door at the knock.

Sky gave her a penitent grin from the other side.

"What do you want?" Her voice wasn't exactly inviting.

He eyed the inside of the house, both hands shoved into his worn jeans pockets. "Can I come in?"

Sophie widened the door on a harrumph, letting the jerk inside. He hadn't called or come by ever since that night at the youth group. It was clear she wasn't his type. And if *that* is all he wanted, she no longer wanted to be.

Tibo bolted up from driving a toy truck on the floor, and ran over.

"High-five?" Sky held up his hand.

Tibo slapped it then grinned big.

"Gotta talk to your sister and see if she'll forgive me." His smile almost loosened her resolve. Tibo tilted his head and narrowed his eyes at Sky then jogged back to his truck.

"Oh hi, Sky." Mom appraised him from the kitchen as she lifted the dishes out of the washer then looked to Sophie.

Sophie shrugged a response to the question in her mother's eyes. "We're gonna go out back and talk."

"Sure, hon."

Sophie slid open the screen door. Sky stepped out and took a seat at the edge of an Adirondack chair. Sophie sat across from him.

"I wanted to apologize for treating you," he lifted a shoulder, "the way I did."

She didn't know how to answer him, just searched his face to see if it would reveal the truth. It was then she noticed the smudge of purple above his cheek bone. "What happened to your eye?"

He touched the spot. "Accident skateboarding a week ago. So, you gonna forgive me or what?" His tone held the hint of an edge before he softened it. "Please?"

Oh, he was especially hot sorry, but she wasn't sure she should trust his words. Didn't Mom always warn her that guys would say anything to get what they want?

"Look, I know you don't believe me, but maybe you'll let me come to church with you again. We don't have to be alone or anything. I just want to spend time with you."

She could relate. "You want to come to my church again?"

His grin went lopsided, his eyes sparked. Oh what that did to her insides. She'd forgotten his effect on her. "Yeah, I like the youth group."

"But you don't like Pastor Vince."

"I'll tolerate the dude as long as you let me come with you." He raised his brow in question. "Will you?"

What could it hurt? "I guess."

~*~

Cassandra put the last capsule in Tibo's weekly pill minder when her mother entered, arms lined with grocery-filled plastic bags. Shaking the almost-empty enzyme bottle, Cassandra wearied at the hit her checking account would take at the next order for Tibo's abundance of supplements.

"I got three boxes of that cereal you like—the gluten-free stuff." Mom dropped the load on the counter. "It was on a great sale."

Cassandra couldn't crack a smile.

Mom pulled a milk gallon from the sack. "Where's Sophie?"

"Sky came by. They're out on the deck."

"Sky?"

"Yeah. I think he's apologizing for not being around

lately."

"Hmm." Mom stacked cans of crushed tomatoes in the pantry.

"While they're out there, there's something I need to talk to you about."

Mom pulled a bottle of syrup from the bag, and stretched to put it on a shelf above the stove. "Okay, what?"

"Vince."

Her mother turned. "Sometimes, Cassandra, you say his name like you've known him for a good long time."

Cassandra picked at her thumbnail. "I have."

Mom closed the cabinet door, and leaned against the counter, many questions drawing lines on her forehead.

"We dated the summer before I married Tim."

Mom's eyes crinkled around the edges. "You dated? Why don't I remember meeting him?"

Cassandra hated that she'd lied to her parents back then. If only she'd trusted the advice she'd tried to avoid. "He wasn't in my usual circle of friends, and as you now know," she twirled a strand of hair, "not the usual speed I traveled, either."

Mom was silent, almost as if she were mentally calculating possibilities, and coming up with answers she didn't want. She sank into a chair at the table.

"He could be Sophie's father."

"Could be? Did Tim know?"

Cassandra tore the top of her nail clean off. "Yes. It's why he married me. To give her a father."

"Knowing she could be another man's child?"

"Knowing she *was* another man's child."

"But you said—"

"It's not what you think."

"Then what is it?"

Cassandra could barely control the tremble in her lips. Her mother's gaze didn't waver from her, but she would not meet it. "Vince had bet his best friend, Drew, he could … win me over."

It was clear by her hardened jaw, Mom figured out what

164

Cassandra's vague choice of words meant.

Cassandra ventured a glance. "He won the bet."

Mom gasped, placing a hand to her chest. "I …" Her eyes darted back and forth as though trying to reconcile two images before her.

"Drew was angry, so he …" Cassandra forced herself to think of Vince speaking her favorite verse, calming her, reminding her of her Savior-God. Her breaths grew deep again.

"Oh dear." Mom stood and paced. "He raped you?"

Cassandra nodded.

"And Vince Steegle did nothing to protect you?" Her voice grew pained. "I just can't believe … *Pastor Vince* …" his name fell from an anguished breath.

"He didn't know. Not even about the pregnancy. I'd found out he'd paid for abortions in the past so …"

"So Tim took care of you instead." She banged the counter with her fist.

"Yes."

"Did you ever really love Tim?"

"I grew to."

"You had to quit school." Mom's voice came from clenched teeth.

Cassandra nodded.

The woman's jaw jerked. "And you endured those awful in-laws because—"

"I've never regretted marrying Tim, Mom. He was the best man I've ever known. He taught me so much, and he was an extraordinary father."

Mom closed her eyes, for so long Cassandra worried she'd lost consciousness. "Why are you telling me now?"

"We plan to have Vince tested to find out if he's Sophie's father. He wants to know."

"He has no right."

Cassandra bowed her head. "No, he doesn't."

"Then why?"

"Sophie's been asking, and I need to know the truth."

The sliding-glass door rumbled open. Sophie and Sky emerged laughing. "Grandma, look who came by."

She nodded. "Hello." Then grabbed the keys from the counter.

"Where are you going, Mom?"

The woman ground her teeth. "For a nice, long summer drive."

~*~

"Hi, Pastor Vince."

Vince grasped the delicate fingers of his would-be daughter, finding it hard to let go. "Where's your grandmother?" He'd seen her rush out the far door. Not like her.

"She took Tibo to the car." Sophie shrugged. "I don't know why she flew outta here so fast."

Vince wondered too, especially after enduring some hard stares from the woman throughout his sermon. Something was bothering her, and he had a feeling he knew what. "I noticed Sky came today." Though he left awful quick too.

The coy smile bloomed across her face. "He apologized for what happened before."

Vince wondered about all of what happened that night at the youth group, and was on the verge of asking.

"Mom said you two have a meeting about the special needs program."

And other things.

"She's in the sanctuary with Kat."

Well, that answered his next question.

Sophie headed out the door and down the steps. His heart seemed to chase after her. She was his, he knew it. The connection was too deep.

"Pastor Vince."

He turned to greet the line of parishioners, but his thoughts were already gone. One after the other congratulated him on his gift with words. He smiled, he shook hands, but his mind kept drifting to the sanctuary and the woman inside.

"Hey." John slapped him on the shoulder after the last congregant walked away. "Another good one today." His fatherly smile made Vince proud of the accomplishments his mentor had cultivated.

"Thanks, John." Vince strode toward the sanctuary.

"Vince." Ayo passed from the side corridor. "Got some ideas about that picnic you're planning to raise funds for the program." He mimed shooting a basketball, sending his dreads swaying. "Hoops competition. Beat you on that one for sure." His toothy smile gleamed.

"I like it. And I'll like it even better when I crush you." Vince pulled the sanctuary door as Ayo's buoyant laughter echoed behind him.

His breath caught at the vision of Cassandra, looking especially good, auburn curls falling all over her shoulders. She pulled some strands behind her ear as she spoke intently with Kat.

Kat said something, and Cassandra became animated, talking with her hands. Vince couldn't hold back the grin.

Kat spied him. "And there's the man himself. We were just discussing all you've done to make this happen."

Cassandra's shoes must be her favorite since they now took all her attention.

Kat continued. "I love this picnic idea. I was wondering how we were going to pay for the new stuff. And it's a great way to reach out to the community as well."

His insides warmed at the little smile that grew on Cassandra's face. Had she finally forgiven him? He'd settle for her tolerance right now. He smiled back.

"Pastor Vince?" Kat quirked a grin of her own.

"Uh, yeah. John and Ayo have some great ideas too. Can't wait to put them all together." He touched Cassandra's arm. "In fact, we have a few things to discuss now."

Kat's attention dipped to the contact between them before she walked away.

Cassandra followed him into his office, and closed the

167

door.

He peeked through the window at the secretary who'd agreed to chaperon them from the outer office while catching up on her fiction. They needed to get a jump on planning this picnic before too much summer passed, and he didn't want to take any chances their meeting would reflect badly on Cass's reputation. Yolanda sat, dug out a reading device, and propped her feet onto her desk.

There were a few things he and Cassandra needed to clear up in private.

Cass sat in front of Vince's desk, her expression turning serious.

"Your mom knows, doesn't she?"

The weight of his guilt increased with the nod of her head. She looked into her hands. "I figured if we were going to divulge all eventually, I'd need to start somewhere." She picked at a nail. "I thought she'd be the easiest place to begin."

"And?" Did he really want to know?

Cassandra's lips pressed into a thin line.

"What aren't you saying?"

Her green eyes lifted to his. She swallowed. "I guess it's easier for parishioners to forgive your past sins when they don't know they've been directly impacted by them."

"She hates me?" He deserved no less.

"Give her time to reconcile it."

Reconcile? "How about you?"

The green orbs became watery pools. "I forgive you, Vince."

The sigh broke from him as if he'd held it for sixteen years. The clock on the wall slowly ticked out of pace with his thumping heart.

She cleared her throat and glanced toward the woman just outside the office, obviously deep in a novel. "I've looked into paternity tests online."

"Did you order one?"

She shook her head.

Vince didn't ask why. He knew. The results would change their lives. "When you do, let me know what you need from me—blood, hair, whatever—and I'll make sure you get it."

Her nod was barely perceptible.

"How long does it take?"

"The website says three to five days on receipt of the samples."

His throat constricted. This was really going to happen. He could be the father of a beautiful, wonderful teen. Cass's daughter. Exciting and frightening all at the same time.

Or she could be Drew's.

Vince could almost feel the steady stream of her breath across the desk. "You okay, Cass."

She lifted a shoulder, unsure, but she didn't correct the use of her pet name. Her hand shook as she pulled a curl from her face. She placed her palm on the desk as if to bridge the gap between them. He scanned her expression. Her eyes entreated his.

He covered her fingers with his own. "How about we pray?"

~*~

The burning took over her eyes and nose. Cassandra could barely suppress a sob. She'd hated this man for so many years and now they sat, hand-in-hand, praying they shared a child.

His thumb moved along hers in a soft sweep as he petitioned his God—their God—for peace, for discernment, for guidance. Somehow, she knew, no matter what, all would be well.

The next hour was spent planning a picnic that would kick off the new special needs program and provide funds for the supplies and extra staff they'd need.

She couldn't fathom the dramatic turn her life had taken. Was it a good thing? She didn't dare ask that question out loud for fear it would shatter the delicate glass that protected her.

Time was up. Plans were made. She needed to go home to her family, and face her mother's solemnity at discovering her icon of spirituality was a real human being. Cassandra never imagined she'd be defending him to her, but that was exactly what she'd done over the last two days.

They stood, Vince on one side of the desk, Cassandra the other. The outer office was empty. Yolanda must have gone to the ladies' rooms.

He crossed the room and opened the door for her. She neared him.

"Cassandra?"

She stopped and met the intensity of his blue gaze. It was the look he always had before he took her deep into his kisses as a youth. Today, his eyes seemed to delve into the pit of her soul, looking for the answer to the question he'd forgotten to ask. Did she want him to?

He cleared his throat and straightened. "Could I take you to dinner some time?"

The lack of certainty in his voice gave her pause. This was not the Vince she once knew. She couldn't speak over the thrumming in her ears then felt his fingers grasping hers.

He held them between his warm palms. "Please."

She pulled back. "Let me think about it." Then she walked away.

Chapter Twenty-One

The SUV rattled as Cassandra pressed the gas to accelerate at the green light. One more paycheck and she might risk having Billy look at the engine. Every time she thought about it the distinct cha-ching of a cash register, signifying the emptying of her wallet, rang in her head.

Would this next paycheck cover the needed repairs? Her thoughts meandered to the man who provided that check and the meeting she'd just had with him. They'd spent several afternoons together over the past two weeks finalizing details for the picnic, and scheduling the festive equipment they'd need to rent. Cassandra couldn't believe he'd agreed to a dunk tank. That had been a joke inspired by a vision she had of being the one to send him into the drink. His expression when she mentioned it seemed to say he was well aware of her current fantasy.

The car sputtered some more and cut out right in the middle of Route 2. She sighed, shifted to park, and cranked the engine into a clunky rhythm. "Just get me home ole girl." She patted the dash.

Vince had asked her out to dinner again tonight. Given her mother's new opinion of the man, she didn't feel the time was right to check out this unusual combination of the new and old. She couldn't get over the man who barely made eye-contact as he formed the words, as if he shielded himself from certain rejection. So unlike the old Vince who would have whispered an invitation into her hair knowing the chills would make it impossible to refuse him. She shivered even now at the long-ago memory of his breath on her ear.

How changed he was, and yet not completely. It was as if

God held to gifts He had bestowed on the man while He burned and refined him into a polished vessel, an empty one, ready to be used for His Will.

If only she could be certain he was truly changed, and that all his new-found goodness wasn't only a means to gain favor for his own selfish desires. Her mind ran back to the conversation by the water where he told her why he'd kept the cross. He could have flattered her and said it was to remind him of her, but instead he'd kept it to remember God. The old Vince would have milked the talisman to sweet talk her into bed, especially after having declared his love. The word he'd never used those many years ago.

Might she be able to love this person? The positive answer shook her and more. She could even spend the rest of her life with such a man.

The grinding and crackling of her engine reminded her of how dysfunctional that idea was. She'd thought Vince held lofty goals before. Yes, they were lofty, but he meant to be the sole recipient of any reward.

The noise continued to drowned out the war raging through her mind. She blew a strand of hair from her face as she pulled to the shoulder and shut it off. Maybe a rest and a prayer would make it go away.

Chuckling, she turned the ignition, not believing God would allow it to be that easy. Still, the plea flew from her lips before she tried the key again. But this time the engine made no sound.

Cassandra scanned the tree-lined road. One car passed along the other side, then darkness. She pulled out her cell to call Kat. Maybe she could get Billy to tow her to his shop. It looked like she had no choice but to take it. Only now, she'd have to pay the tow charge as well.

"Kat?" She said after the beep. "I'm stuck on Route 2, just before Mom's sub-division. I don't have Billy's number, but I need a tow. Call me."

She tossed the phone on the passenger's seat. What else

could go wrong?

She jolted at the knock on the window and sighed at the sight of Kevin Perkins peeking in. "Need some help?"

He backed up as she opened the door and stepped out. "Yeah, it looks like my car stalled. Do you know anything about engines?"

"Sure. Let me take a look." He gestured for her to move aside so he could try the key. It behaved just as badly for him. He popped the hood and fished around the engine while she leaned against the door. He peeked around the hood and stared at her for a minute. His gaze was too intimate, causing her to shudder. He'd never hurt her. Would he?

Kevin's attention traveled the dark and lonely road, the thick tree-lined shoulder, and then it seemed to roam her up and down. She'd never felt so vulnerable in his presence before. What about it bothered her tonight? It must be a residual from the panic attacks that had made a reappearance into her life. Her breathing shallowed and her heart sped.

Kevin dropped the hood, his eyes unwavering as he sauntered closer. "You're not going to start that engine here." He licked his lips, his gaze seeming to ravage her face and fall onto her mouth. "I guess you'll need me to take you home."

A gulp of air sucked into her lungs as if she'd come from the deep.

"Something wrong?" Too close. He was entirely too close.

Headlights took the curve along the road. Billy's truck. It slowed and pulled in front of her car. He'd gotten her voice mail.

Did Kevin just curse?

Cassandra gestured to it. "I left a message with a friend. She must have gotten it." Her smile felt pained.

Lew dropped from the high step of the large vehicle. "So what happened here?"

Kevin squared his shoulders as though preparing for a brawl.

~*~

Lew's attention swung from Cassandra Whitaker to the leering, low-life, Kevin Perkins. Lew balled his fists and firmed his jaw. Why was that guy here … with her?

"So glad you got my message. The car just conked out." She seemed overly chipper at Lew's appearance.

He looked at Kevin who was visibly annoyed. "What message? I was just comin' back from another job." Billy had been keeping him busy with work since the delivery place fired him. A regular paycheck and his son seemed to need the help. He'd forgotten how much he loved to tinker with motors.

Her glance to the sky reminded him of Billy. One of those thank-you-God things the boy always did when life went his way.

"I'll tell you what—" Kevin Perkins was like a tick that needed to be smothered and burned before it let go. "We'll let Lew, here, take your vehicle, and I can drive you home."

"Hold up, Cowboy." Lew nodded to the woman. "We have forms she needs to fill out so we don't get stuck with any liability issues." He didn't even know what that meant, but it sounded important rolling off his tongue. He figured Perkins didn't know either, 'cause he didn't argue. "I'll be takin' her to the shop, and she'll get a ride home from Kat."

Perkins looked between them as if trying to figure another piece of faulty logic to keep the woman, but evidently nothing formed. "Fine." He turned to Cassandra. "See ya later."

"Bye, Kevin. I appreciate your help."

From the look on her face, Lew wasn't sure he believed the woman's words, but it wasn't like he could figure out the sex any other day of the week. Who could?

Her eyes turned his way and registered a relief Lew felt to the core of his being. She placed a hand on his arm. "So glad you found me." She practically sighed the words.

He grunted and nodded for her to climb into the truck. He thought about the expression that creep had as he drove away. Lew was glad he found her too.

Lew tilted the flatbed, hooked and connected, and pulled

the Lincoln Aviator aboard. He'd never buy one of these over-priced SUVs. If he had the money, he'd get a 1969, classic-model Dodge Charger. Something with power. He almost chuckled at the woman driving an automobile with oomph. She'd never know what to do with it.

He climbed beside her in the vehicle and veered onto the road toward Billy's shop.

"I hope I'm not keeping you from anything." Cassandra bounced and jostled in the cab as the tires hit a rough patch of road.

He checked his watch. "That's okay. I got another hour before my meeting at the church." Shoot! He didn't mean to say that.

"The only meetings they have tonight are—"

Lew ignored the 'AA' missing from the end of her sentence.

Her smile was soft and sweet as she watched the headlights coming in the other direction. He could barely hear her next words. "Good for you, Lew."

He was beginning to agree.

Chapter Twenty-Two

Vince jogged down the front steps to the canopy set up in front of the church where Cassandra sold tickets for the day's events. Face framed by the curls that escaped her clasp, she glanced his way as she made out change for Adam Grant and his girlfriend, Tiffany. The couple had been coming to church together for several weeks. Knowing the story that had joined them had confirmed to Vince second-chances were possible.

Cass gave Vince a smile that made him wonder if she'd finally acquiesce to his dinner invitation. He'd asked weeks ago, but she eluded him every time he tried to bring it up. It didn't matter. They'd shared many afternoons planning this thing. So what if there was no candlelight, and Yolanda eyeballed them from outside the office window the whole time. It was a chance for them to get to know each other in a way a fancy dinner couldn't match.

He scanned the section of the parking lot that had been cleared for picnic tables, game booths, Ayo's basketball hoop, a moon bounce, and even a dunk tank. He sighed relief at the knowledge his time on the bench would be at the end of the day. Still, he'd been told his appearance in the tank promised to bring lots of cash to the program.

Amit stopped in front of him, already holding a helium-filled balloon and a cotton-candy-wrapped stick. He had streams of tickets flowing from his shorts pocket, and whiskers painted on his face.

Vince pointed to the tickets. "You better hold onto those. They look like they might fall out."

Amit's head bounced with the wide grin as he shoved

them deeper into his pants. "A man's wiches may wansom his life, but a poor man hears no thweat."

Thinking of what Ayo had said about Amit's prophetic verses, Vince shuddered. Then he realized he wasn't rich anymore and had nothing to ransom. Was Amit talking about his tickets? Vince almost wiped his brow and uttered a large "phew." Boy, planning this picnic with the woman he longed to hold again had him on edge. It was like being a meth addict in a room filled with crystal.

Amit trotted away to the water-gun shoot.

A loud rumble rounded the intersection leading to the church and up the drive. It could only mean one thing—Billy, astride his prized Harley donning mirrored shades and a broad smile that almost straightened the fu-man-chu across his face.

"Hey." He slapped Vince's hand in a greeting. "Place looks busy." His deep voice rolled in appreciation. He checked the watch almost camouflaged by the myriad of tattoos covering his forearm. "At noon, I whoop ya over there." He swept his large hand to the basketball hoop and then to the dunk tank. "There, you go down at four." Billy's eyes sparked as he poofed out his fingers and enunciated the next word. "Splash."

Great. "Right, dude. You just try."

Given Billy's expression, it probably wasn't a good thing to challenge him further.

"Pastor Vince." Sophie jogged up pulling a reluctant Sky. "You remember Sky, don't you?"

The boy nodded. "Sir." For some reason the title felt more aloof than polite.

"You know Mr. Lewis, right?"

"Billy," the man corrected. "Met them both at the Sanchez house project."

"Yeah, that's right," Sky said.

Sophie touched Billy's forearm. "What's this tattoo supposed to be?" She pointed to the big red rectangle. "I bet it has a special meaning."

How she could get that from the one most non-descript,

Vince could not fathom. "Are you looking for a testimony?" He loved her little penchant for collecting stories, even if it had come from the other man whom she had called father.

"You remembered?" Her blue eyes—so much like his own—beamed.

"My testimony?" Billy's eyebrows jumped. "Not sure you're ready for that."

Vince nodded. "I have a feeling she could handle it."

"Pastor Vince has already promised to tell me his."

Billy's eyes went wide. "He did?"

"That's only if your mother okays it." Now, more than ever, he knew she'd hear it one way or another.

Sophie tapped the tattoo again. "So, what does it mean?"

"Hmmm." Billy hesitated, probably wondering how to explain it without saying the words. "That had once been a tattoo of something I used to say a lot in my former life. And when I became a Christian I felt it best not to broadcast it anymore."

"Really?"

He nodded.

"Why didn't you have it removed?"

His black T-shirt broadened with the intake of air. "Cuz I wanted it covered with the blood-a-Jesus, baby." He held a hand up for Vince to slap. "The blood-a-Jesus."

Something about Sky's expression drew Vince from the conversation. The kid was silent, stiff. Almost too observant. It crawled into Vince's spine and held tight. He couldn't shake it. Sophie tugged Sky away to the ticket booth, before Vince could appraise him further.

Billy turned. "Have you seen Pop?"

"Lew's coming?" Vince tried not to sound too incredulous. He was supposed to believe in miracles.

"He promised to give hay rides to the kids."

Vince's mouth dropped open.

Billy's grin took on a new dimension of joy. "Even souped up the tractor engine to make it go faster." He nodded toward Mrs. Hessing and her grandson in line for the moon bounce. "I think he's taken a liking to that Tibo kid. Wanted to do it for him."

Vince understood. Tibo had a way of worming into your heart without a word.

"When I told him the picnic was to raise money for the special needs program, Old Softy cleared his throat and pretended to *begrudgingly* volunteer."

~*~

"Time for a changing of the guard."

Cassandra turned to her mother's voice. "Huh?"

Mom gave her a nudge. "You go have some fun, now. I'll take over here for a while."

A warm hand fell on her shoulder, coupled by the deep voice in her ear. "I couldn't agree with you more, Mrs. Hessing."

The shiver at Vince's touch shut down at the animosity in her mother's eyes. Mom looked away without a word.

"Okay, Mom. But I'll be back in an hour."

Mom narrowed her vision to include only Cassandra. "Take as long as you need." She glanced at the pastor. "And try to make some *new* friends."

Cassandra could feel the heaviness that fell over Vince at his touch on the small of her back as he led her away.

He spoke close enough she felt his breath on her face. "Are you ever going to answer my request?"

Cassandra glanced toward her mother. "Now's not the time."

His sigh was deep as he led her through the parking lot.

"Let me show you around." The pressure of his hand at her back became firm, and a small glint shone from his eyes. "Our creation." His gaze flitted toward Sophie, then swept the church lot filled with members of the community coming out for a day of fun. The fruitfulness seemed to fill the spot Cassandra's mom had taken from him. "I've spoken to a few neighborhood attendees with special needs kids who are considering trying us out this Sunday."

179

"Really?"

His smile grew. "Yes, really." His brow twitched and his voice whispered, "Because of you."

"Vince, this was your idea even before I got here."

"But you made it happen. God put us together to finish it." That stole her breath.

"Mom, guess what?" Sophie bounded up, Sky strolling silently behind. "I just heard Lew's giving hay rides with the tractor. Tibo's gonna love that."

Cassandra gasped, realizing he wasn't with her mother or with Sophie. "Where is Tibo?"

"I thought Grandma had him."

"No, she's at the ticket booth." Her pulse raced as her head swiveled in every direction. Where was he?

They all scanned the parking lot. Mothers and fathers strolled from booth to booth, children in tow, laughing as though they had not a care in the world. No Tibo anywhere.

Could he have wandered into the church building? Cassandra turned that way, with a spark of hope wanting to take hold. Maybe he had gone to the bathroom.

Sky ran to a small hill and searched from a position of height. He looked desperate in his attempt, then excited as his gaze lit on something. He pointed. "There he is."

The relief was fierce as Cassandra turned to where Sky pointed. Lew's tractor, dragging a hay and child-filled trailer, rounded a bend displaying a blond boy sitting in the front with Lew, hands on the steering wheel. Tibo's joy was unmistakable as he bounced on the seat and threw back his head with laughter. Lew wore a grin the biggest Cassandra had ever seen. She almost cried with relief.

~*~

"Thank you, Lew."

Lew pivoted to the voice as he turned off the engine. Tibo's mom.

Her eyes shone. "He really enjoyed that." She looked at the kid. "Come on, Tibo." Then gestured for him to climb down from the seat. He followed her direction.

"Tibo can stay." Didn't she see how much fun he was having?

"I think you've spoiled him enough." She smiled to her son who was still bouncing with excitement.

"Let me take him one more time." Why did he feel so alone suddenly?

Cassandra chuckled. "He's ridden five times around with you since I've been watching. You don't need to babysit him anymore. I still can't believe my mother did that to you."

"She didn't make me. I asked." Did she really think it was that Greta woman's idea?

"Oh." She looked incredulous. "Still, I'm gonna take him around to some other games for a while, but I promise I'll bring him back."

Lew scoffed. What would she do? Have the boy's face painted like a puppy? Couldn't she see all he wanted to do was ride? Lew could relate.

A shrill scream pierced the air. Lew swung his head to find Isabella, from Kat's shop, trying to calm her six-year-old who was flapping his arms and wailing.

Cassandra tugged Tibo toward the two, then knelt eye-level with the boy. "Hi, Sean."

His wails turned to whimpers as he seemed to take her in sideways.

Isabella stood silent. Tears trapped in her eyes—Lew could almost feel them. He studied the way Cassandra handled the boy, using a soft voice, like she tested what might upset him … or interest him.

Hmmm.

"Would you like to go on a hay ride?" Cassandra showed him the big trailer filled with bales.

He turned his head looking from the corners of his eyes. His lips straightened from their downward turn and he bounced, whimpers almost turning into a tune.

Lew decided to join them. "How 'bout he ride with me up front?"

"Oh no." Isabella's Hispanic accent thickened. "He'd never stay still. He'd fall for sure."

"I'll take it real slow, and hold tight to the boy."

Cassandra turned to Lew, a smile growing on her lips. "Let him try, Isabella. You could follow them just in case."

Isabella looked between them.

Lew nodded. "I won't go faster than you can walk, and we'll just keep circling around. I bet he'll like it."

Her shoulders rose and fell. "Okay."

Sean had pulled out of her grip and headed for the tractor before Lew even registered her agreement. "Whoa, little one. Wait for me."

As he cranked the engine, the little boy in his arms shook. Lew feared he was having a seizure until the kid let out a joyous squeal. The other riders piled into the trailer, and Lew took another round through the parking lot. Sean felt stiff in his arms, very different from little Tibo, but Lew knew the grunts the boy made were his version of happiness.

Lew glanced to Isabella as she followed them, her face rigid with fear, softening as they slowed to stop. Sean bounced and patted the steering wheel, his straight lips twitching upward.

"Again?" Lew regretted asking out loud, realizing his mother didn't look too thrilled.

She thrust her fists on her hips and gave a reluctant nod.

He mouthed the next words over Sean's head. "You can stay here. We'll be fine."

Her shoulders tensed as though fighting the answer before she nodded again. Lew smiled. Small victory. Not just for Sean, but for Isabella.

Something about it felt really, *really* good.

~*~

"So what's next?"

Sophie wilted at the playful look in Sky's eyes. "I don't know. What do you want to do?"

With his thumb, he touched the flower painted on her cheek. "The purple makes the blue in your eyes stand out."

Oh boy, those willies could immobilize her. His smile turned serious as he dropped his hand from her face. His hot and cold behavior had made her crazy all day, and she couldn't always blame it on the appearance of Pastor Vince.

She checked her watch. "Pastor Vince won't be in the dunk tank for another twenty minutes."

He looked at his flip-flops. "I don't hate your Pastor, Soph. And I don't think it's a good idea to dunk him if I want to get on his good side."

She laughed at the image. "Then what do you want to do?"

"Let's take a break for a while." He scanned around. "Maybe a little time by ourselves."

She couldn't help the fear that probably reached her eyes. Not so much of him as it was her response to him.

"Sophie, we won't go too far." He held his hands up. "I won't even touch you."

The look in his expression stung her. He must think she didn't trust him anymore since he'd pushed her limits of temptation that night at the youth group.

He tilted his head, his expression somber. "C'mon Soph." He toed a pebble on the asphalt, and nodded toward an isolated hill. "How 'bout you sit over there. I'll get us some sodas, and we can relax."

"Okay." Sophie watched him head to the concessions before she climbed the grass. She found a little place in the shade on the other side of some trees. The quiet, away from the crowds was nice.

Sky appeared with the drinks then handed her one. "Wait." He looked between the two cups. "I think this one's yours."

She laughed. "Aren't they both Colas?"

"Yeah, but I already drank out of one. Don't want you gettin' my spit." His smile made her giggle.

Sophie sucked long and hard through the straw, letting the drink cool her from the inside out. She hadn't realized how sweltering it was until just now. They'd been having so much fun, playing the games, watching Tibo on the tractor, and just laughing together. For some reason, she thought Sky needed something to pull him from darker thoughts. If only she knew what seemed to bug him all day long.

The heat must have gotten to her, because now she felt over-tired. The bright sun had been making her squint, giving her a headache. Maybe, finally having the moment to relax, her body was taking advantage of it.

Sky eyed her. "You okay, Soph?"

"Yeah," she breathed, hardly able to keep her head up leaning against the trunk of a tree.

His brow crunched together. "Let me get you something to eat." He stood. "Be right back."

She waved him away and closed her eyes, feeling as though she floated with the birds in the breeze that wafted through her hair. Then somehow the airy feeling of drifting in the winds turned dark and heavy.

Too heavy to move.

Chapter Twenty-Three

Vince climbed onto the tank bench, ready to face the onslaught that threatened to take him down. Prepared for the attack, he wore his bathing suit, an old T-shirt, a snorkel mask, and flippers. The large group that gathered roared at the costume. Vince smiled and bowed. He knew how to gin up a crowd.

Ayo stepped up first, likely feeling his oats having bested Vince at hoops earlier. So, basketball wasn't Vince's game. Did the youth pastor need to bring him down another notch?

Ayo pitched the ball. It flew past the target.

"Whoa. Gettin' a little tired there ole man?" Vince always knew how to goad the kid who barely looked old enough for his new bride.

Ayo squinted, tossing the ball in one hand, bouncing it off his bicep, and catching it.

"Well, aren't you talented?"

Ayo wound up and missed again.

John lobbed him another ball. "One more makes three."

Ayo pitched just as someone yelled in the distance. It flew off course and that was the end of that.

Vince lifted the snorkel mask. "D'you forget your glasses."

Ayo grabbed another ball from John.

"Hey," Vince called. "You're only allowed three."

Ayo pounded it into the palm of Vince's best friend. Billy's large hands consumed the ball as he grinned so big and mischievously Vince thought he'd melt right off the bench and into the water. "Take it easy on me, Billy. You know I love ya."

Billy gathered two more balls from John and juggled them. The enlarging crowd oohed and ahhhhhedd at his extraordinary display.

"I forgot you were a circus clown once."

The balls halted with a hard glare from the juggler. The crowd moaned. Vince sucked a short breath before the yellow streak hit the cage right near his face.

Vince sighed hard. Placing a palm to his chest, he used his best Shakespearian accent. "For the wrath of man worketh not the righteousness of God. James, chapter one, verse twenty."

Billy's chuckle bounced in his chest as his mustache took on an ominous tilt. He pitched again, barely missing the target. "There's a force field around that thing or something."

"Watch out, Billy." Vince said around the snorkel now firmly in his mouth. "Your Star Trek is showing."

Billy straightened to full height. His gaze narrowed on the target, then Vince. The muscle in his cheek twitched. As his attention moved back to the bull's eye, his hands came together around the ball like a major league baseball player beginning a pitch. He pulled his arm back, stepped into the throw, eyes never leaving his objective. The ball released from his fingers and drove straight into the tank arm.

It didn't budge.

Vince's breath eased back into his lungs as he mouthed a *thank you* to the heavens.

"It's rigged," someone shouted from the crowd.

Cassandra strode over and belted the thing with her fist.

Vince grabbed the chicken wire and stood as the bench dropped, barely missing the fall.

"It works." She shot Vince a sparkling eye, before taking her place in the crowd. "It just needs a little muscle." She scanned the throngs and called, "Who's got the muscle?"

"Let me at 'im!"

"Mom?"

Vince sighed relief at the petite Mrs. Hessing who received the next round of balls from John. Only that look in her eye made him—

Thwat!

Her underhanded pitch, drove the ball into the target, sending Vince plunging to the depths.

John's eyes gleamed when he turned them on a soaking Vince. "Guess you didn't know Greta was the strike-out queen of fast-pitch softball back in the day."

Vince shook the water from his ears.

"They called her Cannon Ball."

Vince blew the water from his face. "No, John. I didn't know that." He landed his rear back on the bench and—

Thwat!

Glug, glug, glug.

Vince pulled the mask and snorkel off his face. They didn't help anyhow. The crowd roared pleasure over Vince's demise.

Mrs. Hessing eyed him with a glare that reeked of vengeance laced with a tinge of a smile. Vince sensed she needed this. He resettled on the bench, eyes locked with his accuser.

A look of satisfaction grew across her features as she tossed the ball up and down in one hand. When was she going to throw that last bomb? Vince's heart raced with anticipation. Her Cheshire grin became even more malicious. She swiveled to bow to her raging fans, holding the final ball high above her head. The noise erupted as they shouted and cheered, banging tables and trash cans in a tribal beat.

Thwat!

Plunge!

Chlorinated water stung his nose and dripped down his throat. Vince hadn't even seen her turn. He spit and spewed as the woman strode to the cage, a serious smile hard on her face. He could barely hear her voice over the chants of "Can-non-Ball, Can-non-Ball." She spoke through the holes, "You are now forgiven, Vince Steegle." Shoulders high, she waltzed away.

~*~

The sight of Vince emerging from the dunk tank dripping wet after that line of people plied their hands at immersing him, flooded memories into Cassandra's mind that almost swept her away. They'd spent most of that summer together in bathing suits, swimming at the club or riding in his little boat.

His smile shone through the dark goatee that changed him from a boy to a man. The new Vince. Born again. Cassandra sighed hard as he closed in, rubbing his raven hair with a small towel.

He scanned the area. "Where's Cannon Ball?"

Cassandra had seen her mother say something into the tank after she'd dunked him and wondered what it was. "She took Tibo home. He was getting a bit overstimulated." Cassandra looked to her sandals. "She told me to ask you for a ride since my car is still in Billy's shop."

He rubbed at his face, a knowing grin astride it, but Cassandra could still hear the drip from his shorts. She didn't think that small towel would do the job.

His eyes searched hers. "Your mom said she forgives me."

Cassandra was glad for Vince, but it was clear there was more to that statement.

He stepped close enough he dripped on her shoes. "There's no reason not to—"

"Have you seen Sophie?" Yes, it was a ruse to stop the upcoming question, but she really was getting a little worried. She'd scanned the crowd at the dunk tank, wanting to share in her mother's triumph, but Sophie was nowhere to be found.

His expression turned. "Last I saw her, she was with Sky."

Cassandra's muscles tensed. "I haven't seen him either."

Kat jogged up and slapped Vince on the shoulder. Sprays of water spewed from the sleeve. She looked at Cassandra. "Wow, your mama still can throw."

Vince chuckled. "Especially with the right incentive."

Kat's head tilted.

"I think the kids after her were inspired."

"Have you seen Sophie, Kat." Something began to niggle at Cassandra's nerves. It wasn't like her to disappear. She'd usually have asked to help with Tibo by now.

"No, but Amit's got Sky pinned to the door inside the church, speaking Proverbs over him."

"Where?" Sky, without Sopie? Something wasn't right.

Kat pointed.

Vince grabbed Cassandra's elbow. Apparently, he felt it too. His face tensed, he walked with force. They reached the church front steps and saw the back of Amit inside the glass doors. He appeared to be speaking to Sky. Sky looking trapped.

"The Lord knows the thoughts of man; He knows that they are futile. That's what it says in Psalm 94. Did you know that Sky?" Amit's innocent voice belied the look in Sky's eyes. *"Blessed is the man you discipline, O Lord, the man you teach from your law; you grant him relief from days of trouble, till a pit is dug for the wicked."* His pronunciation was the clearest Cassandra had ever heard.

Sky put up his hands as if to stop Amit from encroaching farther into his personal space. "Um, okay."

Amit's voice deepened. *"Who will rise up for me against the wicked? Who will take a stand for me against evildoers?"*

Sky shook his head, his eyes pleading with Cassandra to extricate him. She'd need to get him away so she could find out what he knew about Sophie.

"Hey, Amit." Vince's gentle voice got the simple man's attention. "I'd love to hear more Proverbs. Why don't you take a walk with me?"

Amit followed as if chasing a shiny, red balloon floating through the air. Their voices diminished down the corridor as Cassandra pinned Sky herself.

"Where's Sophie? I haven't seen her in an hour?"

His eyes widened. "I was trying to find you to ask the same thing. She bugged out on me."

"What?"

"We were sitting up by the trees, and I sensed Sophie might need something to eat. She looked a little tired. So I went to get her a hot dog, but when I came back, she was gone." He shoved his hands in his pockets. "At first I thought she'd come back, so I waited there. But when she didn't I went looking for her."

"Did you say something to upset her?"

"No ma'am."

"Sorry, I didn't mean to accuse you of anything. It's just not like her." She tapped her fingers on her thigh. "Can you show me where you were?"

"Sure."

Vince strode up. Amit waved goodbye, smiling at his pastor. The man's head bobbed as he disappeared out the door.

"We're going to the trees where Sky last saw her. Vince, can you ask around?"

He nodded.

Sky led the way up the hill and rounded the line of trees. A soda cup sat perched beside a trunk as if waiting for someone to finish it. Cassandra's cell rang.

"Cassandra!" Her heart plunged at the panic in her mother's voice. "Where's Sophie?"

The air grew thick around her. "Why, mom?"

Labored breaths stretched over the phone. "Because someone left a note on our door that said they took her, and we better not call the police or she'll be dead."

Sky pivoted at Cassandra's gasp. "What's wrong?"

She held up her forefinger and turned from him, whispering into the phone. "Are you sure?"

"Of course, I'm sure."

Cassandra's breathing sputtered. She could barely think or speak. "Read it to me."

As her mother recited the awful words, Cassandra felt the heat of Sky nearing behind her. What could they do? She didn't know. But until she had more information, she'd have to be careful who she told what.

"Is she okay?" The boy's voice held concern.

No police. No one can know. Cassandra couldn't think fast enough. "She's fine," she finally said. "Sophie's home with her grandma. You can go now."

His brow crinkled as if he didn't believe her, then he

turned to leave, checking behind him a few times before he reached his car.

~*~

Like tunnel vision, Vince spied Cass at the top of the hill by the trees, staring straight at him—horror in her eyes. His heart banged in his chest. Something was wrong. He needed to get to her.

"Pastor Vince," the voices called after him, but he ignored every one, too focused on the woman in his sites. He climbed the hill.

She hadn't moved, her eyes glassy and hollow. "She's been kidnapped."

He grabbed her arm. "What? Why would you think that? Are you sure she's just not mad at Sky." He searched around. "Maybe she wants him to worry."

"Mom found a note at the house."

His mind stalled. It can't be true. "Maybe it's a prank."

She speared him with her eyes. "Who would do such a thing?"

"I don't know. It's just not possible." He paced the grass as Cass fell against a tree and gasped for breath.

"We have to call the police," he finally blurted. Even as he said the words he knew they'd need to consider the ramifications of telling the wrong people. From his contacts at The Dock, he'd learned to be careful with any information he might possess, even with some members of law enforcement.

"We can't. They said they'd kill her if we did."

He pulled her deeper into the trees to stay out of view of the crowd, blood rushing in his ears. "Who kidnapped her? Why?"

Cass shook her head and blinked several times. "Mom found a note at the house. It said they'll return Sophie if I pay them two million dollars." Her voice cracked at the last words.

Vince tensed. "Do you have two million dollars?" He

wanted his daughter back. He was willing to pay any amount—that he could.

"No." It was more sob than speech. "I barely have enough to buy groceries."

He looked at the large, diamond ring on her finger, and wondered. She wouldn't hold back, would she?

"They said they'll contact us with details tomorrow morning at eight."

His Sophie. He'd only known her a short time, and now someone had taken her away. He couldn't form words, so he pulled Cassandra into him as she cried into his shirt.

"Let's take you home. I want to see this note."

~*~

Scriiiiitch.Scriiiiiitch.

Hands propped Sophie's limp body. Head heavy, lulling this way, then that.

Sleeeeeep. I just want to sleep. Please, let me sleep.

Sticky pressure around her head and over her eyes. Squeezing. Tight. She wanted to pull it away, but her arms felt like noodles. No control. Now they were being pressed together behind her back. Hard metal—like bracelets. But somehow not.

Scriiiiitch.Scriiiiitch. Large fingers around her ankles. More sticky squeezing them together. She couldn't move. Didn't want to. Sleep. That's what she'd do. Sleep till this crazy nightmare disappeared.

Chapter Twenty-Four

Vince had read over that letter a thousand times. Good thing he'd suggested they put it and the envelope in two separate Ziploc bags. It would have been worn through otherwise. He wanted to make sure they preserved the evidence as best they could. That is, in case they decided to go to the police. But he suspected that idea carried even more risk. There were rumors of a cop on the take in the Water's Edge department, who was feeding info to the local drug suppliers. That's how the water channels remained active, and The Dock's business lucrative. It would be very likely the kidnapper had connections there. They couldn't chance it.

"Have you had anyone in the house who might know your comings and goings?" Vince readied a notebook to make lists of possibilities.

"Lots of people." Cassandra sighed. "We had a bunch of men in, building the addition—painting, carpeting, moving." She shook her head. "But that was weeks ago. None of them would have known to find us at the picnic today."

"Unless they followed you."

"Do you really believe the kidnapper hadn't planned way ahead of time exactly where they'd take her?" Cassandra didn't seem to. "The picnic was the perfect place."

He couldn't deny that. "Give me their names anyway." He wrote them as she remembered. "Anyone else?"

"The behavioral therapist," Greta called from the kitchen between grunts as she furiously scrubbed the linoleum from her hands and knees. Obviously her method of burning off angst.

Cassandra tilted her head and squinted. "Could she have

…?" Her face mottled. "I might have told her about the picnic too."

"What's her name?"

Cassandra told him. He scribbled it on the page.

"But she doesn't know I have connections to money. You know, my in-laws." She shifted on the couch. "And she's so sweet. Real good with Tibo."

Vince's gaze dropped to the large diamond on her finger. "I have a feeling more people in this town are aware of your in-laws than you realize." He underlined the therapists name in his notes. "Anyone else?"

She leaned into the plush cushions of the couch. "Lots of church members came by to welcome us when we first moved back. Some I hadn't known when I was a kid." She shrugged. "I can't help but wonder if it's someone from church. Someone who'd planned to take her at the picnic just as we were planning the fun of it."

Vince's heart sank at the idea that one of his flock could do something so evil.

A grunt sounded from the kitchen. Greta appeared in the hall. "Well, I'm gonna try to get some sleep. I've already packed Tibo's stuff to take him to my sister's tomorrow."

Vince hoped that would keep the boy safe, but he still worried.

"Thanks, Mom."

It wasn't until Greta had disappeared behind her bedroom door that Vince finally voiced their other option. "What about that ring on your finger?"

She covered the diamond as if to protect it from his suggestion.

"Maybe they'd take it as payment."

She shook her head, lips trembling. "It's not real. I sold the original stone Tim had given me to pay the debts after his death."

Vince was fed up. How could this so-called husband be so unprepared? "You all talk about your late husband like he was some kind of saint, and yet he left you with debts and nothing to show for it but an over-priced car that doesn't work, and threadbare finery."

She glanced down at her high-end designer shorts. "Don't you speak of my husband that way. He went to great personal risk to make sure I and my baby were cared for, when I felt too ashamed to go to anyone else."

"Well, he sure knew how to make his wife grateful for the scraps he dropped." Vince couldn't relieve the frustration fast enough.

"How dare you."

His teeth ground. "I just don't understand how this man, who worked for his filthy rich family, left his wife and kids without a dime to their name."

She didn't say a word, but stared as if waiting for the pulsing in Vince's ears to quiet so he could hear her whispered words. "You may recall, Sophie was not his."

"Did he—?"

"No. He considered her as much his own as if he'd birthed her himself." Cass closed her eyes. "But his parents never believed it. I can't blame them for that. They were right." Her lids lifted. "But Tim never confirmed it to them. They never truly accepted me or her into the family. And because of me, they took great pains to protect Tim from what they had perceived as a gold-digger."

"How'd they do that?" Did he *really* want to know this story?

She sat up. "When Tim began to work for them, they gave him an entry-level position at very low pay. We didn't care. We were prepared to live frugally. However, they never wanted Tim to be seen as cheap to their friends, so they gifted him houses and cars that they made payments on, and insisted Sophie and Tibo had a high-priced education and wore the finest clothing. Tibo even had a special tutor. It was their way of keeping Tim under their thumb. They didn't like his new bend toward philanthropy since he'd become a Christian, and they saw me as an extension of that."

Vince let his head drop into his hands. He was the reason she'd endured their scorn.

Cass swallowed. "When Tim died, they stopped all payments of the things *they'd* pushed on us, leaving me to foot the bill. I sold the things we owned that were of value, including the diamond, to pay the obligations his parents had created."

"Tim was a good man, but not very wise when it came to his mother and father. He hoped one day they'd come around, but that never happened."

"What about Tibo?"

"They claimed he couldn't be their grandchild either, because of his autism." Cass sagged against the couch back, a tear rolling down her cheek. "I didn't care to prove it because they'd want Sophie tested as well. I couldn't do that to her."

Vince sat beside her and covered her hand with his.

She rolled into his chest. "What are we going to do?"

He gathered her in his arms and rubbed her back. "I don't know." Praying silently, longingly, to the rhythm of Cass's labored breaths, he implored his Creator for this great favor to bring his daughter back. Drawn in by the scent of Cass's hair beneath his chin, he kissed her forehead and squeezed her tighter into himself.

She laced her arms around him and nestled closer.

"I love you." His words fell out as if a natural part of his being.

She stiffened and pulled away.

"I'm sorry. I—"

"This isn't the time. We need to figure out what to do about Sophie."

Did she think he didn't know that? Did she think he didn't care that his daughter was in danger?

He stood. Time to act. "I'll be back in the morning before the call."

"Where are you going?"

"I'm going to find our little girl." He opened the front door. "And don't worry, I won't involve the police."

196

~*~

No police.

Vince thought about Adam Grant, the canine cop from the church who worked at Maryland State University. Vince had helped the guy with an investigation last year when Adam needed information about a drug connection from Vince's past. Maybe Adam could return the favor. Vince shook his head as headlights streamed past from cars going in the other direction. That wouldn't work. He didn't dare be seen in Adam's presence, then Cassandra's, for fear there would be an association between the two. Everybody knew Adam was a cop. He sometimes even wore his uniform to church events when he was rushing in from a long shift at work.

Vince wordlessly beseeched his Creator, suddenly understanding why the Holy Spirit interceded with groans that could not otherwise be expressed.

How could they find Sophie without the police? No access to investigators, informants, tracing technology.

"God ..." His voice came out a cry. "Your power is made perfect in our weakness ..." And he definitely felt inadequate to this task. He wanted to plead more, but instead lay his heart in His Father's hands, and rested there.

It's all he had.

Whoa! Vince almost ran into the car in front of him at the thought that just popped into his head. He had access to those who could help. Had God given him this idea? Would He really tell Vince to use his *criminal* friends? Though they usually worked the wrong side of the law, they might have the tools, and connections he needed to find his little girl. But could he trust them? He wasn't sure, but there was one thing he was certain of— he could trust God.

Vince screeched his Elantra around the two-lane median and headed to the one place he could count on to find just the man he needed—The Dock. He muttered a *thank you* to the heavens as his vehicle sped toward its destination.

The gravel crunched under the wheels of his car as he meandered through the crowded lot to find an opening. Music pulsed through the cracks of the wood-paneled building that sat beside an inlet of the Chesapeake Bay as patrons walked in, and stumbled out. It's a wonder no one had ever drowned off that pier—that he knew of, anyway.

Vince found a spot, parked and strode toward the entrance, a different purpose pounding a beat in his chest. His usual reason for coming here was to preserve someone's eternity. His current goal had a shorter time-line. Tonight he needed to save his daughter's life.

Smoke hazed the atmosphere as he stepped inside and wound his way through the crowds. Eddie usually hung out by the bar.

Eddie turned as Vince neared. "Hey, Vince." He stood and slapped Vince on the back. "Haven't seen you round lately. Where've you been?"

Vince wasn't in the mood for pleasantries, but he didn't know how to form the request.

"Mom said you came to visit her when she had pneumonia." Eddie shook his head. "Even brought her some food. Didn't know you could cook, my man."

"I can't. Yolanda and a few other ladies from the church made the meals."

"That was one mean casserole. You tell Yolanda, next time I have a cold, she can bring one of those to my house." He winked.

"You ate your mother's casserole?"

"Just a taste, dude. I didn't clean out my sickly mother's fridge, if that's what you're thinking." Eddie's face turned serious. "Really, man, Mom appreciated it … a lot. Said you prayed over her too."

"That's what we do in my profession." It's all he'd done since he left Cass's house.

"Well …" Eddie sat and twisted his glass back and forth on the bar top, " … it helped a lot, man. Thanks."

"Anytime, Eddie." Vince sucked in the smoke-filled air. "Listen, I need a favor."

Eddie's brows rose. "Shoulda known you'd collect right away."

A woman lifted from a stool and stumbled into Vince. "Sorry," she slurred as her eyes ran over the length of him. She left and Vince took her seat.

"This is serious."

Eddie halted all movement. Something about it comforted Vince. He knew Eddie would help … if he could.

"I need some information—fast. And I can't go to the police."

"Diet Coke, Vince?" When did that bartender get so close? Vince would have to be more careful what he said.

He shook his head. "Won't be here long."

The bartender turned to another patron.

"What kind of info do you need?" Eddie seemed as intense as Vince now.

"You know that woman you keep razzing me about?"

"Yeah."

Vince scanned the area for any possible listeners. Satisfied there were none, he lowered his voice. "Her daughter's been kidnapped."

"That sweet young thing? What for?"

"They think her mom has a lot of money, but she doesn't. She's been cut off by her late-husband's family. The kidnappers want two million dollars."

Eddie's whistle mirrored the concern in his eyes. "What do you want from me?"

"I don't know what I can pay you." Was this useless? Vince had no choice but to find out.

"You think I'd take those prayed-over dollar bills collected in little baskets? They'd probably sizzle in my pocket."

Vince's facial muscles almost relaxed. "I need to find out who has the girl and figure out how to get her back."

Eddie stared at his fingers as they tapped the bar. He

pulled his lips in and out.

Vince waited, wondering what was going through the guy's brain. "You can't tell anyone, especially about the lack of funds. They'd kill Sophie for sure if they knew."

Eddie's eyes lifted to take Vince in. "You care about that little family, don't you?"

Of course he did. "I care about all families."

Eddie harrumphed, grin tilting. "I think there's more to this one."

Vince allowed the man to peruse him. "Well?"

Eddie stood and threw some bills on the bar. "Got some ideas."

"You'll help me?"

"Course I will."

"Where're you going?"

Eddie dropped a hand on Vince's shoulder. "You let me worry 'bout that. I'll contact you soon as I know anything."

Vince felt the air rush from him.

Eddie's gaze ran straight through him. "Then we'll find a way to get that girl back."

~*~

The voices of Rosco and Boss Hogg echoed down the hall of Kat and Billy's house as the front door opened before Vince.

Kat smirked at the noise. "Lew's watchin' his *Dukes of Hazzard* DVD collection—at full volume." She rolled her eyes.

"Where's Billy?" Vince didn't have time to discuss Lew's viewing habits.

Kat's gaze shot back at the intensity of Vince's question. Her eyes narrowed. "You're lucky he's home at all after you cut outta clean-up duty at the picnic. What gives?"

"Get Billy. I'll tell you everything."

Her head swiveled toward the stairs. "Billy," she called at a level competing with the Dukes.

A muffled voice replied, "What?"

"Vince needs to talk to you." The woman had some strong lungs.

A door squeaked open. A toilet flushed. Billy emerged at the top of the steps still buckling his belt. "S'up, Vince?" He strutted the descent. "Come to make excuses?" His smirk protruded from his facial hair.

"Sophie's been kidnapped."

Kat's head snapped back and Billy's jaw dropped. "Who took her," "What d'ya mean," they said over each other.

"Can we sit down?" Vince's legs felt like rubber.

They entered the living room to distance themselves from the roar of General Lee emanating from Lew's television.

Vince perched on the edge of the couch and filled the two in on the note, and how it said not to involve the police.

"So what are you gonna do?" Vince had never seen Billy so serious.

Kat didn't even speak.

"I've already talked to Eddie at The Dock and he's going to see what he can find out."

Kat rubbed her palms on her thighs. "You sure you can trust him? The man sells stolen goods."

"Who better to get information about criminal activity than someone who associates with them?"

Kat shook her head.

"I've known Eddie a long time. He likes money, but he'd never take it at the risk of someone's life. Besides, what other choice do we have? " He closed his lids for a moment of pilfered peace. "We'll see what he comes up with, and wait to hear from the kidnapper in the morning. I wanted you guys ready in case I need your help. And, of course, to pray."

"Count me in too." Lew's voice caused all heads to turn. "Whatever you need," he nodded, fire in his eyes, "just say the word."

Vince almost broke down right there, but he forced himself to remain strong. He swallowed. "Thanks, Lew. I have a feeling I'm going to take you up on that."

Chapter Twenty-Five

Sophie tried to open her eyes, but something held her lids in place. Her shoulders ached, probably from the awkward position she'd slept in all night.

"Mom?" She wriggled, wondering if she'd twisted her sheets too tight around herself. Boy, was she exhausted. She'd never felt so heavy, even after fitness testing in gym class. All those hours in the sun yesterday must have worn her out. The weird dreams didn't help either.

"Mom?" It sort of reminded Sophie of the time she'd gotten her hand stuck in the railing of her headboard when she was little. She'd panicked in her sleepiness, and screamed bloody-murder that day. She wouldn't do that today. Her mom would come in soon, or she'd wiggle out herself.

If only she could see.

Oh, her head felt woozy.

Sophie wanted to clear whatever it was from her face, but her hands were stuck behind her back—like handcuffs.

"Mom!" Now, she was panicking.

"Quiet." The distorted electronic voice laughed. "So, little girl, you want your mom?"

Her heart sank. Her mom wasn't here. This was not home. "Where am I?"

It laughed again, sending a thousand lightning bolts through Sophie's spine. "You are my guest." The voice was distant, giving the room a depth she hadn't felt before. Like a chasm.

"Who are you?"

"Now, now, my friend, if you learn that, I'd have to kill

you." The voice oozed derision, as though spawned from loathing.

"Why am I here?" Sophie forced herself to calm. How did her mother do it when she had a panic attack? Her father would coach her. "Breathe in through your nose. Out through your mouth."

"You will be here until your mother pays me two million dollars."

"Two million dollars? She doesn't have that kind of money." Sophie gasped at her own slip. The idea her mother can't pay might reduce the value of keeping her alive.

"You don't have to tell me what your family is worth. I already know."

Sophie pressed her lips together for fear she'd give too much away. What was she going to do? She couldn't even move.

"Don't worry, little girl, you will be taken care of. Food will be brought to you shortly. But don't try to escape. There is nowhere for you to go. And …" the voice raised at this, "you will be watched twenty-four hours a day."

Sophie didn't respond. She didn't move. The long silence was broken by the sound of footsteps ascending what must have been a wooden staircase. A door closed. And locked.

"Are you there?" She didn't think so, but needed to ask just the same. What did he mean she'd be watched? He obviously wasn't watching now.

Please, God, tell me what to do.

Her father's voice played in her head. "Sometimes the best moments are when God takes everything from you, and all you have is Him." She could see his smile that reminded her she was one loved little girl. "Then you have no choice but to rely on Him alone."

But hadn't God already taken her father?

Her tears were trapped in the sticky film. Sophie guessed it was duct tape that wrapped around her head and secured her ankles. Handcuffs bound her wrists behind her back.

Control the panic. Give it to God.

Breathe in through the nose. Out through the mouth.

The air was thick with dust, mold, and a dank moisture that coated her lungs with a slimy film. The bedspread under her was worn and rough in spots as bare skin from her legs, shoulders, and cheek rubbed against it.

Sophie wriggled on the mattress, feeling for the edges with her bound feet. She needed to get her bearings. Sitting up would be the best way to do that. She stretched out, then scooted, stretched, scooted, till her heel slipped at the end. She latched the edge, pulling herself to lower her legs, and maneuver to an upright position.

"Where are you going?"

The electronic voice may as well have tazed her, the way it shot through and immobilized her at the same time. Only it was lower and lacked the derision of before. Just business.

"I wanted to sit up so I could breathe easier."

"Lie down."

"Could I just—"

"Lie down." It was like talking to a computer.

She obeyed its command. "What if I have to go to the bathroom?" She really didn't want to know, but needed to.

The release of breath was not electrified, like the voice. Then it said, "Do you need to go?"

Fear ripped through her for where this could lead, but she knew it was inevitable. She whispered, "Yes."

The squeak of a chair was followed by footsteps. Latex-covered hands wrapped around her arm, and pulled her to stand. Sophie sensed a large body. Must be a man. He nudged her forward, prompting her to hop with her bound feet.

He pushed from behind, holding both arms, then stopped, squeezing tighter as he did. The squeak of a door hinge. The smell of urine and bleach. Cold tile under her bare feet.

Her lungs constricted as the rubber hands unfastened the buttons at the front of her shorts. His body heat moved away. A door closed.

Sophie stood, no idea what to do. She inched back till her

legs hit the porcelain, then wriggled and pulled till her shorts topped her knees. When she was done, she didn't worry about hygiene in the face of all the other evils. She now needed to figure out how to put her shorts on again.

Sophie slid off the toilet, landing hard on her knees and fell sideways onto the tile, worked her shorts from the back, pulling and wriggling some more until she was covered.

"What are you doing?" The electronic voice droned from behind the door.

"I'm trying to dress." She couldn't help the screech in her cry.

The door squeaked open. Heat fell over her. Too close. Breathing heavy. Tears formed as she braced herself for her fate.

Hands pulled at the front of her shorts.

"No. No. Please." Wet collected inside the duct tape, drowning her eye sockets. "Please." She couldn't think of anything else to say.

The hands stopped, and Sophie noticed her shorts felt more secure. Latex grasped her arm and pulled her off the ground. Pain lanced through her joints as she staggered to her bound feet and cried out.

She was led back to the bed then pushed hard onto its lumpy springs.

~*~

Cassandra spilled the coffee she poured as the knock on the door jerked her from her lethargy. Her lids hung like sandbags over her eyes. Her nose continued to burn and the lump in her throat refused to go down. She'd showered and readied for the day, feeling the need to be prepared for anything, knowing there was nothing she could do—but pray. Could that be enough?

The next knock shook her from that hope.

Cassandra shuffled across the floor, barely able to lift her feet even after swallowing two burning gulps of coffee. She swung the door open to Vince's haggard expression. His hair stuck out all over, and he wore rumpled clothing that looked like the ones he had on at the picnic yesterday. "You look awful."

He pushed past her. "Slept on the couch. Just woke up." He blew out anguished air. "Sorry I'm late. I was hoping to get here early to prepare for the call."

She pointed to the dining table set with phone, pads, and pencils for the notes she'd take about the ransom demands. "I'm as ready as I can be. What else can I do but go through the motions, and hope God drops a miracle in my lap?"

Vince stuffed his hands in his pockets and stared at the carpet.

She closed the door. "Where were you last night? I tried to call, but you didn't pick up."

His whole body spoke fatigue as his attention seemed weighted to the floor. "Putting things together."

"You didn't call the police?"

"No." Was he hiding something? "I wouldn't do that." He scanned the room. "Where's your mom?"

"She's packing Tibo's stuff to take him to her sister's. I hope he'll be safe ..." The burning filled her nose, " ... until it's ..." She couldn't make herself say the word.

Over.

What would that look like? Another funeral? Her eyes began to well. How would Tibo ever understand another loved one no longer in his life? She could never explain it to her language-less little boy.

Her legs wilted beneath her. The room faded. She was falling and couldn't do anything about it until the strong arms wrapped around her and held her up. Safe ... for the moment. She buried her face in Vince's broad chest, the scent of chlorine from the dunk tank still lingering around him. Was it only last night they celebrated the birth of the special needs program with such fun?

Vince's strong fingers spread over her shoulder blades, warm hands pulled her tighter into him.

She pushed his chest. "I'm sorry."

His blue eyes took in every inch of her face as he caressed her cheek with his thumb. "That's okay."

The phone rang, jolting them apart. They both checked their watches. Eight a.m.

Cassandra ran to the dining room, sat by the phone, and lifted the receiver. "Hello?"

Vince's eyes never left her as he paced the room like a vengeful beast, ready to strike his prey. If only he knew where it was.

"Hello to you."

Cassandra shuttered at the eerie, electronically distorted voice that spoke as if he were her best friend. "Where's Sophie? I want to talk to her." She couldn't take in air until she knew her daughter was alive.

Vince stuffed his hands through his hair, seeming to hold his breath as well.

"Patience, Miz Whitaker. You will talk to your little girl in time." His electrified intake of oxygen chilled her. "You have thirty-six hours to get me what I want. Two million dollars in unmarked bills."

Vince halted his pacing and stared as Cassandra scribbled notes. He strode over to watch what she wrote. His brows drew together as he mouthed, "Thirty-six hours?"

Cassandra's throat burned. She shrugged. It didn't matter how long he gave her. She'd never be able to get that kind of money.

Vince laid his palm on her shaking fingers and whispered, "We'll get her back."

Why did she believe him? She'd done it before, only to find he was a liar.

"Miz Whitaker you still there?"

"Yes, of course."

"I will contact you at eight tomorrow night, and tell you where to bring the cash—alone. Be ready to move fast. You will follow my instructions to the letter or your daughter dies." The voice buzzed his chortle. "Do you understand?"

"Yes, of course. I want to speak to her."

"I will decide what you can do."

"How do I know you even—"

"Shut up!"

"Please." The whimper eeked from her spent lungs.

Silence. Then, a shuffling sounded over the line. "Mom!"

"Sophie!" Cassandra wanted to jump through the phone, squeeze her daughter and never let go. "Are you o—"

"That's enough." The voice gouged a hole in Cassandra's chest where Sophie's spirit resided in her heart. "Thirty-six hours." The line went dead.

Cassandra dropped the receiver on the table and sobbed into her arms.

Vince sat next to her. He took the pad and copied her notes. "He'll call again?"

"He said eight tomorrow night."

Vince folded the page, stuffed it in his pocket, and strode to the door.

"Where are you going?"

"I'll let you know as soon as I find out."

Chapter Twenty-Six

"Where's Pastor Vince?"

Cassandra pivoted from the door that had just closed behind the man, to the mother who had exited her bedroom. Why did it feel Vince took the bones from beneath her skin? "He left."

Mom scowled. "He just got here. I thought he was going to help you get Sophie back. What—?"

"Mom." Cassandra couldn't take any more negativity. "I thought you forgave him."

She sighed. "I did. But that's his daughter out there, and he should be by your side, fighting to get her back."

Cassandra fell into the couch cushions, sinking as if in quicksand. "There's nothing he can do. There's nothing anyone can do. Besides, we don't know he's Sophie's father yet."

"That's no excuse. He should be looking under every rock and into every crevice."

"I'm not sure he isn't." What *was* he doing?

Her mother's voice cracked. "He better be."

Tibo backed into the room, circling his arms like wheels. "Beep, beep, beep."

Cassandra grabbed him around the shoulders from behind and held tight. A tear escaped her eyes as she pressed her lips to the top of his head.

Mom went into the bedroom. She came out rolling a suitcase, and wore a back pack over one shoulder. "Come on, Tibo. Time to go to Great-Aunt Kelley's."

Cassandra turned him to face her. He stared deep into her eyes, as if to discern where the hurt had come from. Cassandra bit her lip to keep it from quivering. She pulled him tight to her, more tears threatening to roll out. "Be good for Grandma."

He tilted his attention toward the older woman. "Gamma."

"Did you pack all his supplements?"

"Yes, Cassandra."

"And the gluten- and casein-free food?"

"Mm-hm."

"His favorite—"

Mom held out a palm. "I've got everything he needs, and can buy more if necessary. They have stores there, too, you know."

Cassandra kissed him on the forehead and released her youngest for Mom to take to safety. Would he really be safe? Would the kidnappers find him and take him too?

"Pway," he said, a look of concern on his face.

"Yes, Tibo." And she would. It was all she had.

The loneliness seeped into every cell of her body as she watched them step out of the house then drive away in the car. The only car they had since hers was in the shop. What could she do now? She picked up her phone to call Kat and borrow hers. Cassandra's mother was right. She should be out looking under every rock and into every crevice until she found her daughter.

Or died trying.

~*~

The jangle of the bell above Eddie's pawn shop door sent eerie shivers through Vince's spine. Eddie appeared through a curtained doorway from the back room.

"Got any information?"

Eddie shook his head wearily. "No, dude. But I might have a plan." By the look on the guy's face, he didn't seem too sure.

"I'll take whatever you got."

Eddie watched his thumbs drumming on the glass display counter. Antique swords were laid out below. "Well, I got this buddy." His eyes shifted back and forth. "He kinda prints money."

"Counterfeit?"

"Yeah. I told him 'bout you, and how you needed cash."

Vince felt exposed. "You didn't mention Soph—"

"Naw, I didn't tell him 'bout the girl." He scowled. "I didn't even use your name. I'm not an idiot."

Relief washed over Vince. The more people who knew what they were doing, the more vulnerable they'd be to the kidnapper getting wind of their plans.

"He said he'd take care of you."

This was gold. Or at least the closest they had to it. Finally, something with hope. But … "What's wrong?"

Eddie grimaced. "It'll cost ya."

Vince's chest constricted. "How much?"

"Well," Eddie's mouth twisted this way and that, "About—"

The door swung open so hard the swoosh nearly drown out the sound of the bell.

Cassandra entered. "This is where you are?" Her hardened eyes looked between the men. She gritted her teeth, and ground the words in a low voice. "I need your help, and you're hanging out with your criminal friends?"

Eddie's brows shot high. "Look, lady, I'm tryin' to—"

Vince held up a palm. "Cass, Eddie's gonna help."

~*~

Cassandra's muscles felt like a loosened bungee cord. She'd driven around in Kat's borrowed car not knowing what she was looking for until she spotted Vince's Elantra in the pawn shop parking lot. She looked at the man whose expression seemed weathered by corruption. This peddler of stolen goods was going to find her daughter? "How?"

Vince studied his shoes. "He knows someone who'll provide counterfeit bills to give to the kidnapper."

Her jaw went slack. She was reduced to consorting with

underworld figures. She glanced at her would-be rescuer then the man who'd betrayed her, and knew she had no other choice. "He'll get us two million?"

"Well, that's what I was tellin' the man here, but there's a price."

"How much?"

"Ten thousand dollars."

Cassandra sagged against the counter.

Vince moved so close she could feel the warmth of his breath. "We'll get the money, Cass. I have some put away."

"But—"

"No buts. It must be done."

"There's more." Eddie's tone did not inspire her. "If your kidnapper has been in the business of rippin' people off, he may know how to spot a fake."

Air fled Cassandra's lungs. She lifted her eyes toward the ceiling. "God, can we get a break here?"

"If we add some packs of real bills to the mix, we could hope,"—Eddie retraced Cassandra's gaze to the ceiling, his voice mocking—"or *pray*, the guy doesn't notice the fake ones."

"That's your plan?" Cassandra regretted the words. This Eddie guy had the only idea to get her daughter back. She couldn't alienate him.

Vince placed his warm palm over her hand. "Cass."

She pushed away. "I know. I know." She looked to Eddie. "I'm sorry."

"No prob. I get it. You're worried 'bout your girl."

"Can you keep asking around? See if anyone knows anything."

"Sure thing, Vince."

The voices faded as Cassandra's anxious mind fogged over like the constant sheen over her eyes since she'd first heard about the note. She couldn't cry anymore. She needed to act. How much money did Vince have? Would they have enough to pay the counterfeiter, let alone the additional bills to hide the fakes?

She turned away from the conversation, her gaze trailing

the line of shelves around the shop. How much of Eddie's merchandise had been brought in by people desperate to pay bills, to buy food? How much of it had been stolen? Jewelry, stereos, TVs, music boxes …

Her eye caught. One music box drew her in. Cassandra's muscles tensed as she neared it, noting the familiar carving of the silver. She lifted it to confirm the words her Grandmother had engraved on the bottom, "Call to me and I will answer you and tell you great and unsearchable things you do not know. Jeremiah 33:3." Her heart pounded so hard she could barely remain standing. The last time she'd seen this box was when she'd placed it deep into her lingerie drawer when she and Sophie painted the bedroom.

Cassandra strode across the shop to the man poised to sell it, and singed her words with fire. "Where did you get this?"

"I, uh—"

"This was stolen from me." She pushed it in his face. "You know that don't you?"

"I didn't know where the guy got it." Eddie held up his hands.

"But you know he stole it."

Eddie looked to Vince as if in support for his deeds. "Cass."

She shot her gaze to him. "This man is selling things that were taken from my home, and you want me to trust him?" Her attention swung to Eddie. "Who gave you this?"

Eddie seemed to search the floor for the answer then his eyes shot wide. "I know who has your daughter."

"Don't change the—" The words registered. "What do you mean?"

"Kevin Perkins. He gave me that."

The shop spun. Gears clicked into place. The looks he'd given her and Sophie. The questions he'd asked. But he'd always made them seem like friendly conversation. "He wouldn't have known where we were that day."

"All I know is Perkins gave me that box. Seemed really

ticked he couldn't get something more valuable. He said 'the woman' watched him like a hawk, like she didn't trust him or something."

I wonder why.

"He was working your house for something big. That's his style." Eddie shook his head, his eyes seeming to trail the dimensions of the room. His gaze lingered on the ceiling as if noticing something up there, then back to Cassandra. "I don't usually display stuff I think is local. I send it to my buddy in Baltimore City. We have a sort of agreement." He lifted a shoulder. "But for some reason I put the box up there. Don't know why."

Vince pointed up. "I do."

Eddie stared at the man. "Well, the good news is the dude's not the brightest lamp in the parking lot. He may not pick out the fake bills."

Vince sighed. "Why do I sense bad news?"

Eddie didn't say anything as he glanced to Cassandra.

"Just say it." She'd worry either way.

"Dude's no Einstein, but he's got a mean streak."

"How do you know?" Did she really need this answer?

"Somehow, some joker at Social Services gave Perkins custody of his nephew. When the boy was little, he always had bruises all over him. Broke a lotta bones too."

This was the man who had her daughter.

"Ex-wife disappeared a while back. A lot of us wondered …" He glanced between Cassandra and Vince. "Never mind."

Vince straightened. "Where does he live?"

"No idea, man, but I'll find out. Give me a few hours. I know just the person to look into it for you."

"We can't include more people," Vince cautioned. "It could get back to Perkins."

Eddie chuckled. "Don't worry. This dude don't tell nobody nuthin'."

Kevin Perkins. The man had always found ways to avoid giving Cassandra his number when he built the addition. "Can't we just look him up in the phone book?"

Eddie's expression grew dark. "He might not be smart, but he's got connections that keep him outta jail." He pointed his gaze to Vince then Cassandra. "Likely someone with the PD."

Cassandra gasped. "The police?"

Eddie nodded. "Y'all let me take care o' him. But while I'm workin' on that, make sure you get the cash."

Chapter Twenty-Seven

Sophie drifted in and out of sleep. Whoever kidnapped her must have drugged her too. Maybe there was something in the water he'd let her sip through the straw earlier.

A vision of her father drifted into her thoughts. As always, he had a smile that brought her peace at just the moment she wanted to panic.

"Remember what the Apostle Paul did when he was imprisoned?" His voice echoed through a long, light-filled tunnel.

"Daddy?" Her whimpers into the mattress made her feel weak and impotent against the terror she faced. If only her father was here to rescue her.

"He wrote to think on whatever is true, noble, right, and pure."

"I can't, Daddy." Her nose ran with the tears welling into the duct tape around her eyes. Hands still bound behind her, she had no way to wipe her face.

Her father's expression had such a mixture of love and contentment it communicated more than any words could. "The God of peace will be with you."

"I love you, Daddy."

"Yes. And that is good."

"I miss you."

His smile melted into the deep crevices of her being. "We always had fun together."

"Yes." She missed him so much she ached.

"What was your favorite time?"

How could she pick one among so many? Still, she knew the event that filled her with the most joy. "The time we went with the church to clean up the streets around the tenements in Philly."

His smile stretched into every feature of his face. "Yes, that was my favorite too. We started a baseball game with the kids who asked us what we were doing."

"Remember that little boy with holes in his sneakers?"

"The one who hit the ball and none of us seemed to be able to pick it up till he got to home plate?"

Now, Sophie was smiling. "Yeah, that one. He was so excited. He felt like a superstar. His friends held him up over their heads." Warmth spread through Sophie at the image. She'd carry that one forever.

"Remember, Sophie, what Jesus said on the cross."

Though Sophie's mind ran a number of phrases, she knew which words he meant. These she said out loud. "Father, forgive them. They know not what they do."

"What are you saying?" The electronic voice froze her, and sent the vision of her father fleeing through the bright tunnel as if from evil itself.

He left her there. Alone.

"What did you just say?" The Voice persisted.

"I was thinking about my father."

The air was so still Sophie could hear breathing across the depth of the room.

Though he didn't ask, she felt compelled to elaborate. "He always reminded me of Jesus' words on the cross." She hesitated in order to gauge his reaction. Would he ask her to explain or tell her to shut up?

Nothing.

"After being nailed to the cross for crimes He didn't commit, He said to God, 'Father, forgive them. They know not what they do.'"

The quiet echoed. Was The Voice still there?

"I brought you some food."

How would she eat with her hands tied behind her back? The thought that he might hand-feed her sent slithers down her spine.

"I'll let you out of the hand cuffs, and sit you at a table. If

217

you try anything, I'll have to ..." It seemed an eternity before he completed the sentence. " ... I'll have to hurt you."

Latex-covered hands were on her again, making her feel like a specimen to be observed. They yanked her off the bed to a standing position.

"I thought you were going to take off the hand cuffs."

No answer. He nudged her to hop forward then stopped. Sophie heard what sounded like chair legs scraping across the floor. The hands pulled at the cuffs, and suddenly she was free. He thrust her back into the seat. She gasped.

Footsteps. Clattering. Then the distorted voice, "You have a sandwich on a napkin in front of you. A paper cup of milk to the right."

Sophie lifted her hands to feel the edge of the table, and crawled them up to find the sandwich. Carefully, she inched farther till her right hand met the drink. She drew the bread to her nose. Peanut butter. Not her favorite, but she wouldn't complain. "Thank you."

Still air replied.

Sophie's eyes began to burn, but not for herself. She bit into the sandwich, and swished the milk in her mouth to keep the peanut butter from sticking to her tongue. It felt good to have her hands in front of her, and not pulled back stretching her shoulders unnaturally.

A loneliness permeated the space, and Sophie couldn't figure out what about it grieved her so much. When sleeping, she had the memories of her father—so warm, so good. But now, eating at the table, The Voice sitting nearby, she sensed an emptiness, an echoing hollowness, that threatened to suck the spirit from inside her.

"Do you have any friends?" Her own question surprised her. What was she thinking? She could really tick this guy off.

Quiet.

Sophie pivoted as if to turn toward him, wherever he was, waiting for his answer. She sensed him to her right.

"Eat your lunch," he finally said.

She took another bite. Was he staring at her? What was running through his mind? Sophie prayed silently for protection, prayed for rescue … and prayed for … The Voice. Not knowing what to say, she left him in God's hands. How does one pray for her abductor?

A car engine sounded from outside. A chair squeaked to her right, and something knocked to the floor.

"Time's up."

Sophie could almost hear the natural tones of a real voice beside the distorted one. It seemed familiar.

Hands gripped hers and yanked them behind her. The cuffs closed around her wrists, and she was nudged to hop back to the bed. She didn't even get to finish her milk. Her teeth felt like smoothed-over peanut butter as she ran her tongue along them to dislodge the pasty bits of bread stuck there. Lying sideways with her hands bound behind her back, she swallowed as best she could.

Footsteps tromped up hard stairs. The door opened and shut. Muted voices filtered below, then stopped. The door opened again, slower steps clomped down.

"Did you like your lunch, little girl?"

Sophie shivered at the slithery quality of the voice. Could this be the same person?

"Well?"

"Yes. Thank you." She'd appease his ego. For now.

"You're welcome."

Sophie no longer felt compelled to pray for this person. It seemed pointless. Could it really be futile to pray for any lost soul? She didn't know, but wished her father was here to tell her. Or maybe Pastor Vince.

"I hope you're enjoying your stay with us."

He said "us." How many people were actually involved?

"Aren't you?" The fierceness of his tone shook her.

"Yes." Her words were small against the mattress. She wished she could bury her face in a pillow at least, but none was provided.

"Only one more day, little girl, and we will no longer need you."

She was afraid to ask. "Will you let me go home?"

"That depends on your mother."

Sophie's mind drew up images of her mom pouring over bank statements and bills knowing she did not have the means to pay the ransom. Her throat clogged at the thought.

She was going to die.

~*~

Was it wrong to finally feel some hope? Cassandra glanced to the man driving the car, the one who'd spent time in jail for dealing drugs. The one who'd lied to her in such a personal way so many years ago. Was it wrong to place her daughter's life in his hands ... and those of his outlaw friends?

Vince had promised to take her home after dropping Kat's car off at the hair salon.

"Can you take me to Billy's shop? I need to get my car back. I'll need it for the money drop. Kevin knows my car, and I suspect if he sees me driving something else, he'll wonder what's up."

"I'm driving you." Vince's jaw jerked with tension.

"He said for me to be alone."

"You're not going by yourself."

"You're not coming with me. We can't take that chance."

His lips pressed together as if holding back a dictionary-full of words. He shook his head and sighed. "I'll take you to Billy's. I need to see him anyway."

They rolled into the parking lot across from three open garage doors. Cassandra scanned each bay and didn't see her car. Hopefully that meant it was out back, already finished.

Billy peeked up from under the hood of a Honda Civic and wiped his hands on an oil-smudged cloth. The direction of his fu-man-chu didn't lift like usual. It was pointed down in strong columns to the rigid line of his chin. He met Vince at the frame of the entrance. "Any news?"

Vince looked around as if for listeners. "We think we know who it is."

"Really?"

"Cass had a guy named Kevin Perkins doing work in her mom's house, and we found a music box of hers at Eddie's."

"That creep?" The words ground from the mechanic.

Cassandra swallowed. "You know him?"

Billy gave Vince an ominous look before nodding to Cassandra. "Yep." He hesitated as if contemplating his next words. "Bad news. Always looking for a way to cash in. A little drugs. A scam here or there. I got to know him when he went through a hot-wiring phase—selling parts. We split ways after my last round at 'the 'hab.'"

Cassandra knew he meant the rehab that also brought him to Jesus.

Vince scratched his goatee. "Eddie's gonna set us up with some fake bills to give the guy."

Cassandra flinched at the word "us." Did he really see this as much his problem as hers?

Billy grimaced. "Why don't you just go find him and get Sophie back?"

"We don't know where he is for sure. Eddie's getting someone to look for him. But we don't want to tip him off with what we know, and put Sophie in danger. So we're going to go through with the money drop, but the counterfeiter wants ten thousand dollars to supply the bills, and we'll need more cash to mix in and make it look legit."

Billy whistled.

His expression crushed the teensy bit of hope Cassandra had held onto. She didn't have that kind of money. This only reminded her of the futility of the only plan they had.

"I've got five thousand. Can you lend me some? I'll pay you back as soon as I can."

Cassandra pivoted to the man. Lend *me*? *He'd* pay Billy back?

Billy shifted and shook his head. "Most my dough's tied up in both Kat's and my shops. I might be able to delay some payments, and put others on the credit card." He tapped his booted toe and squinted. "I'll get ya a couple thou' by morning. Will that work?"

Cassandra's mouth went dry. She wanted to tell the man he didn't need to put his credit at risk for her. She'd find a way to come up with the funds herself. Only she had no other choice, but to rely on the generosity of anyone who'd give it to her. Even the man who'd betrayed her so many years ago.

She glanced at her once betrayer and a warmth ran through her. She had a group of people willing to do anything to help her, and Vince was the one heading the team.

"Thank you, Billy." She eeked out of her broken voice. Cassandra cleared her throat and stood taller. "Where's my car. I'm going to need it today."

"Uh ..." She'd never seen the man so sheepish. What was wrong? "Lew's got it."

"What for?" Panic buzzed through her. What if she didn't get it back in time?

Billy's gaze shifted to Vince and back. "Turns out it needed a little more work than we thought."

More money draining from her. "How much?"

Billy shook his head. "No big deal. It's covered."

"What does that mean?"

Vince shoved his hands in his pockets and looked away.

Billy's lips twisted under the facial hair. "Don't worry. He'll drive it to your house tomorrow, in plenty of time."

Cassandra didn't like this. Her heart couldn't take last minute preparations before meeting with a kidnapper. What if it stalled on the way? How would she contact the kidnapper to say she'd be late? What if it conked out while dropping off the money? She wouldn't be able to escape if he realized it was fake. So many scenarios ran through her head, and none of them saw her daughter safe at home.

"But—"

"Cass." Vince's fingers wrapped around her arm. "Billy and Lew will take care of your car." His eyes spoke something that told her he was telling the truth.

But she knew how that had turned out in the past.

Chapter Twenty-Eight

Groggy, Sophie pulled her lids against the force that held them in place. Oh yeah, duct tape. She squirmed as best she could in her limited ability to stretch out the ache in her joints, and tried to relax against the mattress.

Light seared into her vision. Could this be what happens to someone steeped in utter darkness too long? A warmth followed it, and there he was again.

"Daddy." *It was almost a sigh this time.*

He smiled and ease ebbed into her aching joints. "Hi there, sweetheart."

She searched his features, hoping to take every nuance of his contentment inside of her. "Any words of wisdom for me today?"

She could almost feel the hand that reached for her cheek. "Think on Joseph."

Oh yes, another person from the Bible who'd been imprisoned.

"God had a plan."

"I'm scared."

The melancholy of his expression comforted her. He understood. "I know, honey."

"What should I do?"

"Trust God."

"I don't know how anymore," *she whimpered, wishing he'd remove the bindings and pull her into his arms.*

"He is with you always. Remember Genesis 50:20." *It was the verse her father had made her memorize when kids picked on her at the private school.* "Say the words."

"You intended to harm me, but God intended it for good, to accomplish what is now being done, the saving of many lives."

The snorting jolted her. The light faded and pulled away. "Daddy, don't go."

Clattering sounded, then, "Wake up, you're dreaming again."

From beautiful visions to the distorted voice that plagued her days.

She shivered. "Why can't you let me be?" Her anger mounted. "You imprison me all day. Can't I escape in my dreams at night? What do you want from me?" Her sobs muffled in the comforter.

"Tell me your dream."

Sophie hesitated. For all she knew it could be Freddy Kruger on the other side of the room, set to use her hopes against her. But she suspected the nicer Voice. Should she tell him? "I dreamed my father came to talk to me."

A dripping sound caught her attention. Was it raining outside? If only she could see the sun one last time.

Instead her mind drew up a picture of a boy in a multi-colored coat. "My father reminded me of Joseph in the Bible, who was sold into slavery and wrongly imprisoned so lives could be saved."

"You think that's what's happening here? To you?" The derision in The Voice almost made him sound like the other one, the one who made her skin crawl.

Did she think that? "I know God can turn any evil into good."

The chair squeaked and The Voice sounded higher up. "You believe that, Sophie? Evil into Good?" She hadn't heard this kind of anger from him. And he'd never used her name before. Why did it feel so personal?

"I believe God has the power to make all things good, and in the end, He will do exactly that." Somehow those words seeped into her soul. Did she really know this for sure?

"What if that *end* means your death?" Previously, The Voice had eluded that word, almost as if to give her hope, so she would continue to behave.

And yet now, the word no longer scared her. "Then I'll be with God."

The scoff was not distorted.

"If that is His Will, I accept it."

The rattle of something like a chair falling over sounded, almost as though it had been kicked. "You're crazy."

Now she was confused. "You want me to fight for my life?"

"*Yes.*"

This undistorted word was so low, she barely heard it. In fact, she wasn't sure it was real.

~*~

Vince pulled into Cass's mother's drive, the sun sinking below the trees. It had been a long day, driving around, trying to find out more about this Perkins guy. He and Cass had even gone to Home Depot together to see if he was around. Evidently, he'd taken some vacation days.

Vince had closed his savings account. Every drop of it now resided in a duffel bag in the back seat. He pulled it out and followed Cass to the front steps. His cell buzzed. Cass turned to watch him as he checked the ID and pushed the *talk* button. "Eddie, what ya got?"

"Good stuff, my man." Vince's muscles uncoiled with a faint relief.

Cass neared as she saw his reaction.

"Chen's been stalking your guy all day. It turns out he's got a cabin in some woods out in Western Maryland. Chen trailed the dude and looked around the place. My money says the girl's inside."

"Did he see her?"

Cass's eyes went wide at the words.

If anyone could find out what was in that house, it was Chen. The guy had all kinds of equipment to see into the buildings he cased. He didn't like to take chances breaking into them unless they promised gold, or at least a very expensive wide-screen TV and a state-of-the-art stereo.

"Chen could only get a view of the main floor, but he says Perkins and another guy keep going down into the cellar and spending lots of time there."

"Sophie." Vince nodded to Cass. She released a breath.

"Chen's gonna get a little closer to find points of entry, but says the place is stocked with firearms. Apparently, it's the hunting cabin."

Vince tried to hide his concern from Cass's probing gaze. By the look on her face, it didn't work.

"Hey, Vince."

"Yeah?"

"We're close, man. We're gonna bring that girl home." When did this become Eddie's fight too? "Me and Chen. We got a plan. Meet us at the shop in the morning to work out the details— 10:00 a.m. sharp."

"Right." Vince hit *end* and stuffed the phone in his pocket.

"What did he say?"

"I'll tell you inside." Vince followed Cass into the house and filled her in while she made sandwiches for dinner.

"What kind of plan? Going in with guns blazing, getting my Sophie killed."

Vince shook his head. "That's not Chen's style. He's a *cat burglar*—meaning he steals things from houses when the owners are still inside. His goal is stealth. If anyone could go in and get her out without being noticed, it's him."

Cass sliced the last sandwich and dropped the knife on the counter. "I don't know how much more I can take." She sagged against the cabinets.

Vince neared, wanting to gather her into his arms, but every time he'd gotten close, she'd pushed him away. He wanted to comfort her, but knew somehow his comfort also brought her pain. Would she ever trust him again?

They ate in silence together. Cass turned on the news until she said it was too depressing. She flipped to a movie—too happy.

She shook her head. Vince feared her next words.

"I'm going to bed."

How would she take his suggestion? "How about I sleep on your couch?"

Cass glared. "Why would you do that?"

"I don't like you being alone."

"And your presence makes me safer?"

Vince shifted. "Yes, Cass. It does."

Her gaze softened. She gestured to the furniture. "Suit yourself. I'll get you some blankets."

~*~

Vince opened his eyes to the woman emerging from the bathroom, wearing shorts and a sleeve-less blue top, auburn curls glistening from the recent shower. Cass pulled her fingers through her hair, attention focused on the floor.

Her eyes lifted. "Oh. You're awake."

Vince threw off the blanket and sat up on the couch. "What time is it?"

"Six. I couldn't sleep." She sat in the chair, elbows resting on her knees.

He'd only nodded off a couple of hours ago. "Eddie said to come by the shop at 10:00."

Cass leaned her chin into her hands. "You trust this guy to save Sophie?"

"I do." It wasn't even Eddie as much as the feeling in his gut he believed he got from the Holy Spirit. Was it accurate?

"And the *cat* burglar?" Her gaze locked on his.

He didn't falter. "Yes."

"They make a living stealing from people."

"I made a living drugging them." Vince regretted reminding her. This might not be the best argument in his friends' favor. "I have to believe they have some good in them because it gives me hope for myself."

She didn't speak, only stared at the floor.

Vince folded the blanket and placed it over the couch back.

Cass looked up. "Do you believe all people are redeemable?"

Wishing he could pull up an answer from his divinity studies, he chose to speak from his heart instead. "I've seen people in my life who seemed evil through and through." His mind traveled back to his youth. "And I've known others who just seemed lost." He shook his head. "Only God really knows which is which, so we need to listen when He tells us to avoid some, and be ready for those He gives us to guide."

"What if they lead *us* into evil?"

Was that what she thought he did to her? "God is always there, Cass. Even when we stray."

Her nod was barely perceptible. "Yes, He is."

Vince stood and smoothed out the wrinkles in his shorts. He'd been wearing this outfit three days now. He better head home and take a shower himself before they met at Eddie's shop. Maybe that would help clear his mind. "I believe my friends are lost. I see it in their eyes—the purposelessness. They need a reason to check this God of ours out, and I have no idea what that reason for them will be." He sucked in a breath. "But I know God has it all worked out. He just hasn't let me in on the plan yet."

Cass stood. "I better make us some eggs. I suspect we'll need lots of sustenance to get us through this day. It's gonna be a long one."

Chapter Twenty-Nine

Vince sensed Cass's breaths grow shallow as she entered Eddie's pawn shop. Things were coming to a head, and there was no guarantee of the outcome. He placed a hand at her back, and she startled. Glancing toward her, he hoped to decipher if it was okay. She moved closer, as if for more support. He tightened his hold.

Eddie peeked from the curtained room, and nodded for them to come inside it. Used, and likely stolen, goods littered the floor, shelves, and counters in the small space. Chen sat at one of the tables. Vince and Cassandra took a couple of chairs.

"Cass, this is Chen."

The Asian man gave a curt nod as a smile lifted one side of his lips.

Eddie sat in the chair next to Chen. "Chen says he's only seen two guys at the cabin."

"One older. One maybe in his late teens," Chen confirmed. "The older one comes and goes. The younger one stays in the cellar most of the time."

"How do you know this?" Cass looked so innocent, naive, next to Vince's old friends.

Chen's eyelids lowered as his gaze rolled over every inch of her. "I have cameras that see where I want them to."

Vince felt her shiver more than saw it.

"I have been watching the house for most of a day and part of a night. Whatever is in that cellar must be very important."

"Sophie." The break in Cass's voice rattled Vince. They needed to get Sophie home to her mom.

Eddie leaned back in the chair. "Chen says he can get the

girl, but not knowing what's in the cellar, he wants the older guy gone."

Chen nodded as if to agree but did not speak.

"The best time would be when Perkins goes for the money." Eddie faced Cassandra.

Cassandra scowled. "But what if he leads me to the cabin."

Eddie's expression was confident. "He won't lead you to a place he owns."

"So while I'm giving him the counterfeit money, Chen, here, will be rescuing Sophie?"

"Yes."

Vince tensed. If only it were that easy. "Eddie, we still don't have all the cash."

His expression was placid. "How much ya got?"

"With what Billy gave us, we're up to eight thousand."

The guy stood, strode across the room to a safe, spun the dial and opened it. Stacks of bills filled the inside. He grabbed a few and laid them on the table. "That should cover the counterfeit payment." He pulled out some more. "These'll be decoys."

Vince swallowed the lump in his throat. "I'll pay you back as soon as I can."

Eddie smirked. "On your sermon salary. Don't gotta lifetime to wait on that. Consider it payback for bein' nice to my mom ... and prayin' with her."

"That was no thousand dollar prayer." Vince wasn't sure what to think.

"You haven't seen her lately."

"I'll make sure I visit real soon."

Eddie nodded, and caught Vince's gaze. "You do that."

Things were coming together, but something niggled at Vince. He felt like ants were crawling over his skin. Everyone was risking something ... but him. He knew he couldn't go with Cass. That could put her and Sophie in greater danger. But he couldn't just stand by, either. Something told him he had another role.

He glanced to the ceiling and almost nodded ascent to the Word that spoke in his heart. "Sophie won't go with Chen. She doesn't know him. Why would she trust him?"

"You better hope she learns to trust him, dude. He's all she's got."

Vince's leg bounced. "I'll go with Chen."

"Dude, you'll blow the whole thing. Too many bodies make too much noise."

"She needs to know Chen is safe, so she won't resist."

"But—"

Chen's palm halted Eddie's protests. "He can come." He turned to Vince. "You do as I say if you want to get that girl back."

The fear in Cass's eyes drove through him. "Absolutely. But how do we keep Cass safe at the drop off?"

"He said for me to be alone. I have to go by myself."

"I don't like it." If only some invisible person could go with her. He glanced to the ceiling again. *I know You'll be with her God ... but—*

"We have no other choice. I drop off the money. You bring Sophie home."

Vince knew she was right. This was their only hope.

~*~

"I have to go to the bathroom." It wasn't urgent, but Sophie figured she better do it before the *other* Voice came back. At least she trusted this one not to take advantage. The other, she wasn't so sure about.

Steps came close. She braced herself for the yank, but it was gentler this time. He nudged and turned her. She hopped. They had it down to a science now, having done it many times since the first. She even had a way to finagle her pants off and on better with her hands bound behind her. Too bad maneuvering with bound hands and feet weren't skills she could use once she was free.

If she ever escaped this place.

He pulled her from the tile floor then nudged her back the

way they came—she assumed—until, "Ow!" The natural voice ran through her like a poison that burned every blood vessel. Too familiar. Like someone she trusted, but she couldn't place it.

Or didn't want to.

He left her standing in the middle of the floor. She didn't dare move. "What happened?"

Scooching of furniture. Banging on tables. Clattering. "Just stand there," The Voice finally said. "I'll get you back to the bed in a minute. Don't move."

She listened intently. What was happening? She felt like a naked target. Was he going to hurt her? Fear turned her muscles to Jello. Her head felt woozy. She heard what sounded like the elastic pull of the latex gloves. Why was he taking them off?

Her body swayed. Oh no. All limbs bound, she couldn't catch herself. She teetered and leaned, then strong arms kept her from hitting the ground. A bare hand pulled her to standing again. A bare hand with strange calluses—scars.

"Sky?" The question squeaked from her, tearing out her insides.

He didn't say anything.

A door opened.

"Why are you doing this, Sky?"

"So you know your boyfriend is a bad guy now." This voice came from above. Steps descended from that direction. The voice natural, but held the eerie derision of the "other" one. And yet that voice was also known.

That Kevin guy.

"Oh, so smart little girl. Too bad it will cost you your life."

The form of the person beside her stiffened. Would Sky let her die?

Suddenly, she didn't feel as brave as she had only hours before. She had more life she wanted to live. She wanted to see her mother again, her brother, her grandma. She wanted to make new friends at church.

Hands yanked her closer, and led her across the floor. She was nudged to the bed. "You said we'd leave the country. It

233

doesn't matter what she knows."

"We'll see, Sky. Maybe we can take her with us. I'm sure you could make use of her."

Sophie balled up on the bed as if to protect herself with her bound legs. Every part of her ached. "I can't believe you'd do this to me." She hiccupped. "I thought …"

Laughter erupted from the derisive one as his voice and footsteps ascended the stairs then stopped at the sound of a shutting door.

The continual dripping noise reminded her of a Chinese water torture. With each drop, her despair grew. How could she have been so wrong about Sky?

"So, Sophie," She'd never heard Sky's voice so hardened. "Do you still think God can make evil good?" His tone challenged. She wasn't sure where his anger was directed—her, the other man, or maybe something else entirely.

She sniffed hard, and swallowed the lump in her throat. If she said it, maybe she'd actually come to believe it. But now, she wasn't so sure. "God can do anything."

Chapter Thirty

"Can you come in?" The thought of being alone right now left Cassandra weak. She pulled the cash-filled duffel from the back seat of Vince's car.

Vince flinched at her words as though they were the last thing he'd expected. She'd pushed him away for fear he'd betray her again, yet since Sophie went missing he'd been working harder than Cassandra had to get her daughter back. She needed to remember, Sophie could be the child he'd barely had time to know.

What would he do if Sophie turned out to be Drew's?

"Sure." He stepped out of the car, and met her on the walk. His steps were solemn, hands in his pockets, attention to the gravel in front of him.

The house seemed bereft of life. No Tibo making vehicle sounds on the carpet. All his little cars were lined up neatly along the wall, piles of lint stuffed into the crevices of the toys as Tibo liked to do. There was no Sophie blaring David Crowder from her ear buds, and no Mom watching her 24-hour news channels.

Cassandra dropped the duffel on the floor. The sound seemed to echo in the space.

She turned to the man beside her. His blue-eyed gaze caressed her face, hands still firmly in his pockets.

She couldn't help it. Her body longed to be in his strong arms, so she slid her hands between his waist and elbows and pressed her face into his chest, breathing in his scent.

Vince seemed to hesitate before pulling his hands from his pockets and wrapping them around her back. The tentative nature of his care reminded her of the new man he'd become. The man she could rely on. She wanted to absorb his strength, and he seemed okay to let her.

"I think I love you too." She said into his shirt, remembering his admission over a day ago. She'd spurned him at the time, but he'd proved himself over and over to her. She needed for him to know now, before either of them set out to do a job wrought with risk.

Vince ran a hand atop her hair and kissed her forehead. "We're even, then."

She nodded and looked up. "Please be careful tonight."

"I was going to tell you the same thing."

Cassandra pulled tighter and his lips touched hers. It felt like a first kiss, and a last. So sweet and yet longing for completion, as though its impact would have to span eternity. The culmination of all they'd been through together—the hurt and the pain, as well as what God had refined in them with His wisdom, and His all-encompassing love. Cassandra wanted more. She didn't want this to be the end.

Would they all survive this terrible night?

The danger they faced had not been lost on her. She'd gotten the message loud and clear from the comments that were cut short or the looks not well hidden. Kevin Perkins was a ruthless man. A man who'd beaten a young boy, and possibly killed his wife. Who knew what his friend was like, the other man who held her daughter. Somehow, that one scared her even more.

Vince pushed away this time. "I need to get back. Chen has a lot to go over with me about the layout of the area and the rooms in the house. He wants to show me how to use his equipment so everything is seamless."

Seamless. Cassandra liked that plan. "Hug Sophie for me when you get her." She needed to be optimistic. He'd get Sophie back. And Sophie would need his love.

Vince smiled. "You bet I will."

She reached her fingers into his goatee and caressed his chin. "Thank you, Vince Steegle."

He kissed her long and gentle, breathing life into her

weary heart. "You're welcome." One more kiss. "Now, I need to go." He placed his palm on her cheek before stepping out the door and driving away. All she could do over the next several hours was wait for Lew to drop off her car, and Perkins to tell her where to drive it. She thought of her son, now safe with his grandma in another state. She knew what he'd say to do—"Pway!"

~*~

The man lived in the boonies. A long forested drive took Vince to the cottage house hidden by more trees. Not only was Chen's business stealth, apparently so was his lifestyle.

Vince pulled up to the front. Chen waited by the door, as though he'd been there an hour or more, hardening in what sunlight actually reached the place. He checked his watch as Vince stepped out of his Elantra, then entered the house, obviously expecting Vince to follow. He did.

Chen disappeared into a room.

Vince turned to get smacked by a stack of clothes. "Hey."

"Put 'em on."

Vince dropped his attention to the pile on the floor. Camouflage. "Are we headed into combat?"

"I usually work in the dark. Wear black. Might not be dark enough tonight, so we'll need to blend with the trees." Chen pulled a jar from a drawer and shoved it into Vince's palm.

Vince opened it. Green paste. "What's this for?"

Chen dug his fingers inside and slathered it on Vince's face.

Vince stared at the man a full head shorter than himself. "You're serious?"

Chen locked his gaze. "You want that girl back?"

Vince nodded.

"Then, I'm serious."

After covering Vince's skin, Chen opened a cabinet, took two backpacks from hooks, opened some more drawers and loaded one. Binoculars, metal containers, and packages with small printing on the labels. He pulled at some other drawers. "These will be your tools." He dumped a gun, a knife, and a saw onto the table.

Vince shuttered at the memory of the blade that almost removed his spleen before he went to jail. "What's the saw for?"

"There's a padlock on the outer cellar door."

"Won't sawing it make too much noise?"

"No." How could he be so certain?

Chen fished through a flat drawer and took out a black case. He opened its tri-fold flaps, revealing tiny metal rods, various shapes at the ends. "Remember how to use these?"

"It's been a while since you to helped me when I locked myself out of the house. I wasn't very good then." And they didn't have time for him to fumble.

Chen nodded, then surveyed Vince from lowered lids. "What's in this for you?"

Vince couldn't maintain Chen's steely-eyed gaze. He dropped his attention to the floor. How could he explain his love for the people in his life to Chen, a man who saw relationships as dangerous entanglements?

Then it hit Vince. "What's in it for *you*?"

Chen shook his head and began loading the second backpack with the tools he'd shown Vince.

"How're we gonna do this?"

"I'll get the kid outta the house. You get the girl."

"How are you going to—?"

"Don't ask. Just do."

~*~

How does one pass the time waiting for hours to hear from a kidnapper? How does one sit around for the moment to rush as fast as she must to save her daughter? No one ever teaches this stuff in school.

Cassandra paced, prayed, flipped on the TV, flipped off the TV, prayed and paced some more. She opened the duffel bag of bills and counted each stack. She compared one stack to another to see if she could spot the phonies. Her heart sank. She didn't know which was which, but there were definitely some differences.

Cassandra threw the bills inside the bag then looked at them in the shadow within. "Lord, please don't let him notice." She rolled them around and looked again. She prayed that wherever they met, the lighting would be dim.

Tears stung her eyes. No, she wouldn't cry again. She had to be strong. She'd go in there, confident as if she didn't have a care in the world.

But she did. Way too many. More lives were at stake than the one they were trying to save.

Her life was on the line, and so was her daughter's. The man had likely killed before, and she did not doubt he was poised to do so again. Even if Chen freed Sophie, there was no guarantee the man might not discover the bills and kill Cassandra on the spot, leaving Sophie without a mother to come home to. What if the other man killed Vince? Sophie would lose another father — the one she'd barely known.

Too much time to think. Cassandra was infinitely grateful for the sound of her SUV as it drove up to the house. Lew, wearing a T-shirt and jeans, stepped out and strode the sidewalk. She checked her watch. Boy, he cut it close.

Fifteen minutes till eight o'clock. Cassandra opened the door as Lew lifted his fist to knock. His brow see-sawed. "Ready?"

She twisted her face to stop the burn through her sinus passages, and shook her head.

He held up the collection of keys. "Well, your car is."

Cassandra figured Lew wasn't the warm, fuzzy type who'd hug her and talk her through her emotional depths. She'd have to buck it up and do what needed to be done. Standing straighter, she took the keys from Lew's hand. "Thanks."

He stepped inside and grunted. "This the bag?"

She nodded.

He picked it up and opened it. "D'you count it?"

"About a hundred times."

He dropped it on the couch and paced between the rooms.

Now, Cassandra was getting extra nervous. Why hadn't he left? "Is there something I could get you?"

"Nope. Just waitin'."

"For what?" Did she need to pay him something?

He nodded to the phone on the dining room table. "The call."

She was about to ask why, when it rang. Cassandra's heart thundered inside her chest. Her mind whirled in confusion as she wrung her hands. Lew's eyes narrowed. He gestured for her to pick it up.

Sucking in oxygen, she clicked it on. "Hello?"

"Hello, my friend."

Cassandra almost told him that working on her house did not make him a friend, but then realized she couldn't tip him off to what she knew. She pressed her lips tight.

"Are you ready to take a drive?" The distorted voice was cloying.

"Just tell me where."

"Interstate 70 West. You'll be on it for a while. Bring your cell phone. Leave it on." Click.

That was it? That was all he was going to tell her?

"What'd he say?" Lew broke in to her thoughts.

She shook her head as if to flick out the nightmare. "Interstate 70 West. No more."

"Then we better get moving." Lew was out the door before she could protest.

She ran after him. "You can't come. He said for me to be alone."

Lew only smirked as he opened the passenger-side door. "You'll be alone. Or at least you'll look like it." He pushed the seat back, climbed onto the floor. Cassandra's mouth dropped open as he lifted what looked like a glove compartment from a hinge and folded his wiry build underneath it. His hands reached toward the base of the seat, and using a lever, he clicked it back into place.

"How did you do this?"

"Billy has some old friends who like to hide stuff." He lifted the faux glove compartment and caught her attention. "Don't worry. None of them know what it's for."

After arranging the floor mat, she could barely tell he was there.

Cassandra cranked the engine. It purred. The unfamiliar sound gave her comfort. "Will you be all right in there? I have a feeling this is going to be a long drive."

"Don't worry about me," the muffled voice returned. "You'll need the long drive to get used to the upgrades."

"Upgrades?" How much had the repairs required? "What do you mean?"

"Let's just say, your car has a little more power than it used to."

Chapter Thirty-One

It took a good, long while to control the hitch in Sophie's sobs. She didn't know how long because with bound eyes, she still couldn't see a clock. All she knew was that every inch of her felt raw, like she'd been scrubbed with sandpaper.

The room had been so silent she heard Sky's breathing all the way across it. A rustling sounded, reminding her he was human. Or was he?

She decided to speak. "Now that I know who you are, why can't you take the duct tape off my face?"

"No." The answer was harsh, but at least he didn't use the voice distorter anymore.

"Why not?"

No answer.

"Why?" she screamed. She had nothing left to lose after all.

"Shut up, Sophie."

How could she have ever seen this guy as sweet, thoughtful, caring? Images of his teasing grin when he leaned through the car window encouraging her to try parallel parking again, assaulted her memories. The clap of a high-five with Tibo—whose face had demonstrated his own love for Sky—made her want to empty herself of even more tears.

"I can't believe you'd do this to me."

Movement shuffled some more.

"I thought ..." She couldn't get the words through her closing throat.

"That's why I'm not taking off the tape, Soph. Then I'd get the puppy-dog eyes along with the guilt-trip." Something hit the ground and clattered. "I don't need any more guilt." A harsh squeak sounded. His tone grew louder and sharper. "I am what I am, and that's all there is to it. You won't change me. My mother tried and failed. I don't need your high-and-mighty religious crap to tell me anymore."

Sophie barely had control of her voice. "He's gonna kill me. Is that what you want?"

"See, that's the crap I'm talking about." Something hit hard wood. "You all think the worst. He just wants to scare you. Just shut up, do what you're told, and you'll be home safe with your mommy in no time flat." The scorn in his voice ripped through her, leaving scars that would never heal. Scars were hard. That's what she'd be. This jerk would not hurt her again.

~*~

Vince and Chen tromped through the woods. Chen thrust a pointer finger to Vince's boots. "Quieter."

Vince looked at his feet as if he could inform them of the reprimand and make them behave. As evidenced by Chen's scowled glances, Vince didn't think they'd gotten the message. He watched the man beside him, trying to imitate his moves. Chen was cat-like, smooth, agile. Too bad he didn't work for US Intelligence. Now, if only Vince could mimic him.

Vince wanted to rush ahead, but just as he felt his stride, Chen grabbed him and thrust him into the rooted ground. He pointed to a clearing ahead. A cabin sat in the middle of it.

"Stay here." Chen wove his way through the trees, under branches, through thickets. He peered toward the clearing from each new angle. He waved toward Vince then touched a finger to his lips. Duh. Vince knew he needed to be quiet. The question was how to make the sticks beneath his feet not call out his presence. He stepped, and threaded through foliage, doing his best to slink like a feline predator. Chen's smile only reached half his face. Vince could tell it meant Chen noted his improvement. The two fell on their bellies behind a small mound of dirt.

Chen pulled binoculars out of his pack. "This gets us a

view of the kitchen. Door to the cellar meets right there." He handed the equipment to Vince so he could see as well. "Get to know each piece of furniture in case you find yourself moving through it in the dark."

Vince scanned the canopy of trees above them. It would be another hour before the summer sun set, but the shaded spot could limit light if the electricity got cut. He placed the binoculars to his face again and took in the cabinets, the stove, the fridge, and where they stood from the doors. A rifle-filled rack hung on a wall beside the fridge, and a couple hand guns lay on the counter at the ready. These guys weren't playing.

Chen pulled the spy-glasses from Vince's face. "Over there is the outside cellar door with the padlock. When the one leaves to get the cash, I'll make a diversion over there." He pointed toward a less densely forested area. "Hopefully, the other guy will come out, and you can get in through the back."

Vince released a serrated breath. "Hopefully?"

Chen shrugged. "If not, I'll think of something else. But I have a feeling he'll come out for this."

Vince knew better than to ask. He stared at the cabin, so quiet and lifeless. "What do we do now?"

Chen lay taut, every muscle at the ready as he continued to peer through the binoculars. "We wait."

~*~

Cassandra pulled into the vacant lot. The kidnapper told her to wait here for her last instructions. She'd followed all the others to the letter. Good thing Lew was in the car. He evidently knew the area well. A couple times she couldn't find the road Kevin had told her to take, but she'd describe things to Lew and he'd guide her back to the place she needed to go.

The crickets chirped in the open field in front of her. She took this moment to do the breathing she had forgotten to do on the drive.

"We there yet?" Lew's voice filtered through the vinyl

encasement.

Cassandra didn't dare move her lips for fear she was being watched from somewhere. "He said one more call."

Lew didn't answer. No time for pleasant replies or unnecessary words. Silence and solitude needed to be apparent from anyone who might view them from the outside.

Cassandra adjusted the ear piece then untangled the cord connecting it to her phone. She needed to keep busy somehow. The phone's ring shook her.

"I'm here." Her words barely made it through the clog in her throat.

"Good." The Voice slithered. "Just one more place to go." Its musical quality made Cassandra think of a madman dressed in a clown's suit.

She cranked the engine back to life. "Where to?"

"Get back on the road you came from. Take the first entrance on the left. It's unmarked. No street name. But watch out," he said as if he really cared for her safety. "It's hidden by trees. You wouldn't want to miss it."

Cassandra shivered. No, she wouldn't.

"Bad things could happen if you miss it."

Cassandra wouldn't cry. She'd be strong for Sophie. Vince would get her. Sophie would be safe. Unfortunately Vince had taught her long ago that no matter how many nice words are used, reality doesn't always follow.

"There is a graveled section on the side of the road about a quarter mile in. Pull onto it. Fifty feet into the woods, there will be a tree with a rope tied around it. Drop the bag there."

Cassandra waited for more. It didn't come, but he hadn't hung up either. "That's it?" If only it could be that easy. Drop the money, get her daughter back. "Then you'll release Sophie?"

"If everyone behaves."

But Cassandra already had not. "I want to talk to her."

"No." It felt like a hard metal door had slammed.

"If I don't hear her voice, you don't get your money." Was this a bad move?

He slung out a row of curses. Squeaks and thuds and rustling sounded. "Sophie," Cassandra heard from the depths of the cell phone. "Your mummy wants to talk to you."

More rustling. "Mom." Her voice squealed as if in pain. "They're going to—"

Crack!

Cassandra jolted.

"I'll be at the tree. The money better be waiting."

"Don't you hurt my girl." Cassandra went rigid.

"Now, why would I do that?"

"If you do," her throat closed, making her voice go deep, "I'll hunt you down."

Silence. But no click. Cassandra waited for him to end the call.

"Try and find me."

Cassandra collapsed against the wheel as the dial tone sounded in her ear.

"Where now?" Lew's voice pulled her from despair.

"Hidden entrance to the left," she said with as little movement from her face as possible.

"Good."

She wanted to ask Lew, how in the world a hidden entrance could be a good thing, but knew not to use any unnecessary talk now. She'd have to trust in *good*.

~*~

Lord, how many mosquitoes must I endure before this thing gets going? Vince swatted his cheek, then glanced to the man next to him, ever-present binoculars attached to his face. He jerked and before Vince could ask, Chen slapped a palm to Vince's mouth. The seconds till Chen moved again ate through the only flesh not taken by bugs.

A distant clap of a screen door. A man exited the cabin, got into an old red Corvette, and drove away.

Chen's intense expression shifted to Vince. "You better get

her out of there."

"Wha—?"

"Instructions are to kill her at the next call."

"How do you—?"

"Read lips." Chen reached for his bag. "Deaf as a kid. No time to chat." He gestured toward the pack by Vince. "You know what to do?"

"Saw the lock as soon as the guy comes out."

Chen's nod was quick as he swung the back pack onto his shoulder and slunk away. Vince slid in the other direction, toward a path that would get him to the back door while affording a good view of anyone coming from the front.

Adrenaline pumping relentlessly through every vessel of his limbs, he found his place, and waited some more. This must be what a racehorse feels in the gate. Could he take more pounding in his heart?

He watched the still cabin, wondering what was happening inside. Was Sophie safe? Had she been harmed? He couldn't imagine what horrors she must have gone through.

An explosion rocked the woods. Vince ducked for cover. A cracking sounded as limbs and dirt rained everywhere. The cabin door opened and out came …

Sky?

Chapter Thirty-Two

Cassandra pulled into the gravel shoulder and parked. The summer day had long given way to night. "We're here." She mumbled for Lew.

He grunted back.

She stepped out of the vehicle and peered through the woods. She couldn't see the tree with the rope, but grabbed the duffel from the back seat. Carefully, she scanned the area for human activity and found none. She tread through the woods, the earth and sticks crackling beneath her feet. An owl hooted. She flinched.

"Oh God, please get me through this." Her pounding pulse answered. "Save my Sophie."

Something fluttered through her hair. She screeched as she waved it away. How much more could she bear?

Movement to the right. She swung her head around and focused.

Nothing.

Cassandra maneuvered farther into the thicket. Could she see the rope in this light? She wasn't sure. Her feet moved her forward and her mind seemed to numb the images that threatened her anxious imagination. Why didn't she bring a flashlight?

There! The tree with the rope. She almost took off in a trot, but didn't want to bump into the man who meant her daughter harm. She reached it, pivoted a three-sixty to see who might be with her, and dropped the bag.

Was he there? Was he watching her right now? She saw nothing

Taking a deep breath, Cassandra turned back the way she came. Halfway to the car, she heard the rustling of the bag. "Nice," a voice said.

She turned. "Where's Sophie?"

The hooded figure looked up from his crouch over the duffel with a flashlight. He put something over his mouth. "You'll get her. Get in your car and drive home. I'll call and tell you where to find her."

"How do I know you're telling the truth?"

"You'll have to trust me."

"Trust you?"

"That's all you have. Now, run along." He flicked his fingers. "Or you'll never see her again."

Cassandra swallowed hard, backed some, then swiveled.

"Hey," his natural voice yelled. "These are fake."

Hearing his footsteps closing in, she sprinted to the car. The passenger door flung opened, and Lew waved from the driver's seat. "Get in!"

~*~

Bullets pelted trees as Lew shifted and tore off, wheels spinning in the gravel. They passed a parked '80s model Corvette. Lew saw the hooded figure in his rear-view climbing inside.

"It's ruined. He'll kill Sophie."

Lew glanced again at the headlights now following them. "Not if he's chasing us."

Cassandra swung around to confirm it. She gasped. "What if he calls the other guy to do it?"

"Can't hold a phone and steer where I'm gonna take him." Lew decided to stay close enough to let the guy think he could catch them. That way he wouldn't give up and make the call. Lew wound his way back to the main route and turned west. Only five miles to his favorite road. Lew almost chuckled. This was what Billy would call a "God-Thing"—being exactly where he needed to be right when he needed to be there.

He checked the rear-view. The headlights were fading. Lew eased up on the gas, and the car behind closed in. Gunshots hit the hatchback. Lew cursed. A little too close. This was going to be tricky.

One more mile past the Wawa convenience store and he'd make the turn. The lights behind ebbed and flowed, nearer-farther. Cassandra clutched the dash. Her lips moved continuously. Must be pleading to Billy's God. Lew would take all the help he could get!

The turn. Screech. Rubber burned. He pulled the car through the tree-lined dirt road and slowed enough to make sure the other car followed. It did. Lew wove in and out, left and right. Fish-tailed a few times. The car behind him did the same.

The large Aviator would be no match for the guy's Corvette on a regular day. Lew's smile broadened at the thought ... 'cause after he and the boys from the track souped this puppy up ...

This was no regular day!

The straightaway. The pit.

Should he chance it? An SUV maneuvered differently than the Camaro he usually took on this drive. Not low enough to the ground. He may not be able to keep it steady at the edge. They might roll. But if he could maintain control, he was certain Perkins could not.

Cassandra's murmured prayers seemed to intensify beside him. Lew even threw up a *help me Jesus* of his own. He decided to take a chance.

Gunning the engine, Lew felt one with its roar. The headlights behind stretched, then closed again. Gunshots pinged off the Aviator. "Get down."

Cassandra folded over.

"Here we go. You better hold on."

At the silence of shots, Cassandra peeked up, saw the pit shining in the moonlight, and cried out, "Lew, no!"

"I've got it." He told himself as much as her. Could this car hold the edge like his Camaro?

Not usually.

Her prayers were said at the top of her voice, as Lew spun the wheel, slid to the rim, then turned toward it to gain control. The heavier weight took him closer than he'd ever been before, but the wheels seemed to snag some rocks that halted momentum. The top-heavy car tilted in slow motion. Would they roll to the depths? Lew cursed.

Cassandra's cries to God were less coherent.

A split second later, Lew felt a shift that told him where to turn the wheel. He punched the gas and sped from certain death.

Cassandra sucked in a breath.

Lew peeked behind them. The rear-view showed only darkness. Where were Perkins' headlights? Was this good or bad? Lew didn't know. He wanted the guy to follow, but didn't want to get killed. Had Perkins run off the cliff? Lew was too busy keeping his own control to really notice.

He backed into a treed-over, hidden side path then cut the lights.

"What's wrong?" Cassandra gulped air between words.

"He's not behind us anymore."

Her expression seemed to wobble with anxiety. "That's a good thing, right?"

Lew wasn't sure. What if he was calling his friend? "Yeah, I guess." He decided to take a minute and catch his breath too. He needed to be clear-headed just in case. It wasn't just his life he carried in this car. It was Tibo's mom's. The kid couldn't lose another parent.

"I wonder what's happening with Sophie." Her face twisted.

Lew tried not to think about it. He needed to get Cassandra home safe, and hope to meet her daughter there. "Well, I guess we better—"

Zzzzzoom!

The Corvette flashed by their hidden spot in a streak of red. Where was he going now? What took him so long to pass them? Had Perkins stopped to call his pal? They needed to get to the cabin. Billy'd told him where it was. Lew shifted into drive.

"Where're we going?"

"From being the hunt-*ed* to the hunt-*er*."

~*~

Sky was part of this? It took everything Vince had in him not to rush the boy and break his every last bone. Vince ducked behind a bush and watched as Sky held the gun, pointed, scanning the area. Vince unzipped his back pack and found the saw. He didn't have much time to get Sophie.

Another explosion split the night. Sky ran from view. Vince sawed and sawed, and finally the metal broke open. He flung the doors wide, dropped through the slanted entrance, and closed them again. He didn't want a red flag waving that he'd just entered.

The room was quiet except for the gunshots echoing above. Had Sky found Chen?

"Sophie?"

A noise shuffled in the dark. "Pastor Vince?" Her voice was worn, questioning.

He ran to the bed, where she lay bound and blindfolded with duct tape. "Sophie, I'm here. We're gonna get you out." He pulled her up, extricated the knife from his pack, and split open the tape at her feet.

A rush of air sprung from her at the freedom.

The tape around her head would be tricky. He didn't want to scar her face, but it was too tight for the knife to enter easily. He lifted it in the back where her hair kept it loose, and wheedled the blade to knick one notch at a time. Hunks of her hair fell to the floor. Small casualties. Finally, the tape was completely severed. Vince pulled it from the back.

She flinched and gritted her teeth.

"Sorry."

"Just get it off!"

Vince yanked it from the skin around her face, and winced

at the red swellings the adhesive left behind.

Sophie blinked and squinted and blinked some more. She wiggled the hands in cuffs behind her. "Sky has the key," answering Vince's next question.

Vince thought about the saw in his pack then wondered about the lock-picking tools he didn't know how to use. No time. He yanked her forward. "We'll take care of that later. Let's go."

Sophie staggered on wobbly legs, viewing through continually blinking eyes as Vince pulled her to the nearest exit.

Another explosion. Closer this time. Both flinched at the loud bang. A crackling rent the air, and ended with a wham as the cellar doors bounced.

What was that? He looked to his exit point and feared the worst. Pulling Sophie, he tried the doors. They wouldn't budge. Something must have fallen on them.

Sophie scanned up the wooden steps. "Our only hope."

But if that kid came back, all hope was lost.

~*~

Kevin cursed and floored the Corvette toward the cabin. Where had that Aviator gone? One minute it had cleared a corner in the trees. The next it had just disappeared, and Kevin had almost flown into a quarry.

SUVs just weren't that fast.

He'd finally found his way out of the maze of forest and onto the main road. He looked around. No SUVs in sight. He cursed again.

Now, he'd have to start over. Make new demands. Higher this time. But did they know it was him? They could identify his car. Not good. He'd have to take out witnesses. Maybe work the grandparents instead.

He glanced at the duffel beside him, knowing some of those bills were real. But how many? Did Cassandra really not care about her daughter enough to take such a chance? Figures. She'd rather have her designer shoes than family. Probably bumped off the girl's old man herself.

Kevin chuckled to himself. That's what he'd do.

He pulled onto I-70 East. Only two exits to get to his place. Boy, this road was busy for a late-summer's eve. Headlights neared and passed, and flew across the asphalt. Kevin didn't feel like speeding to his destination. He'd had enough of that for one night. The girl wasn't going anywhere.

The rural route stretched out ahead from the exit. Not as highly traveled. Only one pair of headlights rolled a ways behind, and after a few miles, another came in the other direction. He followed the familiar markings to his hunting cabin. A left here. A right there. He pulled into the dirt path that led to the place, but something was wrong. He slowed, feeling the tires crunch the branches that littered the way. It looked like a windstorm had ripped through and uprooted trees.

He hadn't recalled any wind.

Kevin rolled his Corvette farther down the path, watching the house for any movement inside. A flicker. The front door opened. Two people exited.

That Sophie kid!

A guy in camouflage spied his car, and pulled her around the building. Kevin grabbed his gun from the passenger seat and opened his door. This would not end here. He'd kill the man and find another place to keep the girl till he got what he wanted. Cassandra would not win.

Ever!

He exited the car then sprinted after them down a wide path. Where did they think they were going? He knew these woods better than anyone. Even in the dark of night. He aimed his gun toward the movement and shot. Dirt kicked up in the moonlight. A roaring engine rumbled from the road. A crackling sounded in the trees. Kevin turned to find them and saw Sophie fall. Camo-guy yanked her up.

Kevin narrowed his gaze down the gun, Camo-guy in his site. Squeeze the trig—

Wham!

~*~

It was gruesome even if the man was pure evil. If Cassandra didn't have to witness it, she'd have preferred not to … but she did. Kevin Perkins pinned to a tree by her SUV, eyes wide and vacant before he slumped onto her hood. And yet she knew it was the only way they had to stop him from taking that shot.

Lew didn't seem to mind the spectacle.

Cassandra opened the car door with shaky limbs. Her daughter was only feet away and nearing, Vince holding her so she wouldn't stumble over the brush. Cassandra bolted toward the girl and held her frail body until the feel of her sunk deep into Cassandra's soul.

She brushed at her daughter's bangs. "Where's the other guy?"

Sophie's face had swollen welts surrounding her eyes. "You mean Sky?"

"Sky's involved?"

Sophie's lips quivered. Her voice broken. "Yes."

"Lew, take Sophie out of here." Would this ever be done? "Vince and I will look for Sky."

Vince didn't protest. Just helped to load her daughter into the car. Her hands still bound behind her. Vince took a hack-saw from his pack. "Get her far from here and break her free from the cuffs as soon as you can."

Lew nodded, pulled the vehicle back from the tree, letting the empty shell of Perkin's body fall to the earth, then drove away.

Cassandra shivered at the corpse that had once held the spirit of a man. What would he have been like had he known the Savior? She shivered then turned to Vince who's appearance filled her with strength. He took her hand then led her through the path to the cabin while surveying the area.

"Where's Chen?" Every crackle of leaves set Cassandra's nerves on edge.

Vince shook his head. "I haven't seen him since I entered the house. There were gunshots, but I heard Chen's explosions afterward, so I guess he didn't get hit."

"Explosions?"

"Yeah, he used them as diversions."

A hand flung Vince to the ground.

"Man, you're noisy." Chen glared at Vince in the leaves. "I think that Perkins dude is back," he whispered. "He'll find you guys for sure."

"Perkins is dead." Cassandra said, trying to keep the image of his vacant eyes from coming back.

Chen's brow narrowed. "You sure."

"Yes." Vince stood. "Where's the kid?"

"The blond guy? He's under a tree."

Cassandra sighed so hard she deflated. "He's dead?" It made her sad as well as relieved.

Chen hesitated. "Hope not." He looked between them. "Kid saved my life."

"I heard him shoot at you."

"Naw. He wasn't shooting at me. He shot into the air, trying to threaten me so I'd leave. When I set off the last blast, a tree came down toward me. The kid shoved me out of the way and got hit instead."

"I thought you knew what you were doing." Vince glared.

Chen shrugged. "Never used explosives before. Loud's not my style."

Cassandra started to run. "We better find him."

Calling 911 as they followed Chen's direction, she rounded bushes and jumped over fallen trunks. Finally, they came to the spot where the young man lay, face down. "Sky?"

No answer.

Vince felt for a pulse. "He's still alive."

Chapter Thirty-Three

"Punch Billy's number in for me, Sophie."

The young girl in the passenger seat of Vince's Elantra took his cell and scrolled through the names. The new layered haircut Kat had given her after Vince's knife sliced through it to free her from the duct tape, looked cute.

"I bet he's had the whole crew at the Crenshaw house for an hour already." Vince wanted to be insulted that Billy still had such little faith in Vince's ability to help in the repairs, but since Cass asked him to take both Sophie and Tibo to the event so she could catch up on a few things, he didn't care so much today. It was good to have his daughter safe beside him. And it was good that Cass trusted him to take them. He'd been concerned their truce had turned cold since the rescue. Cass had seemed distracted. A little aloof.

Vince looked at the beautiful girl thumbing through his cell, still sporting traces of the red swellings from the duct tape on her face, and his heart filled with pride. When would those tests come back to confirm it so he and Cass could finally tell her the truth? Would Sophie be glad to know? Or would she hate him for the role he played in her mother's sacrifices?

Sophie pressed on the screen. Ringing.

"Hey."

"How long you been there, Billy?"

"Uh, I don't know." Some shuffling in the background. "You got me on speaker?"

"Yeah, Sophie and Tibo are with me."

"You know I hate speaker."

"Comes from having too many secrets." Vince winked at

Sophie.

She giggled.

"So, did the extra hour put you ahead of schedule?"

"It might've if I hadn't forgotten my tools. We've been sharing all morning."

"I'm on my way. I'll swing by your house and get your box."

"Uh, no, that's okay. We're good."

"You just said—"

"No, no Vince."

"I'll get it. See you in ten." Vince heard the guy sigh before ending the call. What was up with that?

"Are you really that bad with a hammer?" The traces of Cass in Sophie's smile unnerved him.

Vince turned to the windshield. "No. I just need more practice, that's all."

Once in front of the Lewis's house Smokey greeted them.

"Oh, they have a dog? Tibo loves dogs. Is he friendly?"

Vince pointed to the grass. "Yeah. There's his favorite toy. Why don't you and Tibo play with him until I come out." His eyebrows wiggled. "You know how Kat likes to talk. It might be a while."

"Come on, Tibo," Sophie grabbed the ragged tennis ball from the lawn. The dog leapt and barked until she threw it out to the side of the house.

Tibo shrieked in laughter as the dog ran back, dropped it at his feet, and licked his hands.

Kat opened the door before Vince even ascended the stairs. "What are you doing here?"

"I feel so welcome." Vince eyed the woman blocking the entrance. "I came for Billy's tools."

"He sent you?" Why was she so incredulous?

"I offered."

She stood there.

"Are you going to get them, or should I search the garage myself?"

Uncertainty played through her face. She pivoted and strode through the living room. Vince meandered around as he always did there. After all, he'd lived there once too. He'd always appreciate the way they'd given him a home when he had none. But that was who they were.

Kat met Vince in the kitchen. "Here you go." She hefted up the large, multi-drawered box.

He took it from her then noticed a person outside on the deck. "Who's that?"

Kat's eyes turned warily. She played with the pages of a recipe book on the counter. "It's Sky."

Vince's body tensed. "What's he doing here?"

"We took him in." She lifted a shoulder. "At least until after his hearing. He had nowhere else to go."

"You took in a stranger?"

"He's not a stranger. I've known him since he was six. His mother used to work the sub shop next to the salon, and Sky always hung out with me."

Vince's jaw went slack. He didn't know how to respond.

"Besides," she swallowed hard, "I feel a little responsible for him ending up with Kevin."

"How's that?"

"When his mom worked, he'd come and help out at the shop, collecting towels from the stations and sweeping the hair off the floor." Her smile was melancholy. "The industrial broom was twice his size."

She shrugged. "He was always such a good boy. He even drew pictures for me. Those are the ones I framed in the shop."

"He drew those?" Vince never expected that from Sky

"Yes." She grimaced. "One day, when he was about ten, I noticed these awful scars on his hand. I suspected they were cigarette burns and called Social Services. I never saw the boy again, and always wondered if he was okay." Her voice cracked. "Then Billy told me what happened … I can't believe he ended up with that creep."

Vince pointed emphatically. "That boy helped to kidnap

my—uh—Sophie, and you're letting him live here?"

"If you really believe he's so bad, why did you tell the police how he'd saved Chen, and that you believe he'd been coerced?"

"A weak moment on my part."

She leveled her gaze on him. "You know that's not true."

"Still, I don't want him anywhere near Sophie."

~*~

Sophie threw the ball. It rolled into the water. Smokey leapt in after it. Uh-oh, Kat might not want the dog sopped.

Tibo's laugh was infectious as the large animal trotted over then shook so hard her brother was splattered with the smell of wet fur.

"C'mon, Tibo, we need to go inside and save Pastor Vince from conversation." She trotted up the stairs of the large back deck.

Sky's brown eyes met her at the top. Her lungs squeezed with the strange dance of averting and staring at the same time. Her mind played images of the fun they'd shared, interspersed with the evil mask she'd created of him in her tape-bound visions. She'd heard the discussion between Pastor Vince and her mom about what he'd done for Chen, and none of it made sense.

She rubbed at the itch the adhesive had left on her face. "I heard you saved Chen's life."

He lifted a shoulder.

She thought about what her father had taught her in her visions about loving your enemies. Still the words were bitter on her tongue. "I'm glad you're okay. I mean, from the tree."

His attention fell to the drawing on the table in front of him. She narrowed her vision to the detailed sketch of the view from the deck—small boats docked at piers, water rippling around them. She didn't know he could draw like that. Why hadn't he shared that with her before?

Because their friendship was a lie.

"Thanks," he finally said.

Sophie checked behind her to make sure Tibo was coming. He was. She headed for the sliding glass door.

"Soph?"

A shiver erupted at the familiar use of her name, but she couldn't turn back. "What?"

"You talked about forgiveness ... well ...in the ... before." The pause was immeasurable. She couldn't move. Her emotions so jumbled there was no way to make them behave.

His intake of breath was audible. "Do you think some day you could forgive me?"

Her eyelids lowered with the ache in her heart. Her lips could barely form the words. "I forgive you Sky."

"Then—"

"I forgive you, Sky ... but I will never—*ever*—trust you again." She rolled the door open and turned to prompt Tibo inside.

Tibo ran up the stairs giggling, the dog nipping at his heels. His eyes lit when he saw Sky.

"Hey, little man." Sky wheeled from the table and held up his hand.

He's in a wheelchair?

Tibo slapped a high-five, and Sky pointed toward the door. "Your sister's waiting. You better get going."

~*~

Vince watched Sophie help Tibo out of the car. His chest burned for the girl after her run-in with Sky. She didn't want to talk about it and Vince didn't push, not officially having that role in her life ... yet. It probably didn't help that her project with Tibo working in the garden would remind her of Sky even more. Vince would have to check on her intermittently and make sure she was okay.

When would those genetic tests come back? He couldn't wait for the day he could tell her all.

He hefted Billy's toolbox from the trunk and lugged it past Eddie who was edging the lawn. "Eddie, what are you doing here?"

Eddie turned off the weed-wacker. "It's my mom's house. Wasn't gonna let your saints do all the work."

"Couldn't you just pay someone to do the lawn work?"

Eddie's cheek twitched. "That's what I was thinkin', till that Yolanda chick came by to drop off another casserole."

"Uh-oh."

"Gave me an earful about how I should take care of my 'mama' and spend more time with her." His eyes widened. "Man, that woman was cold."

"Sorry about that."

Eddie shrugged. "S'okay." A smile edged up one side of his face. "She had all this fire in her eyes and passion in her voice. It was kinda hot. I think I might ask her out sometime."

Vince hitched up Billy's tool box and turned before Eddie could see his eyes bulge. "Good luck with that one."

He lugged the tool chest to Billy in the side yard and dropped it at his boots.

Billy clapped him on the shoulder with a Cheshire grin. "You found them."

"Yeah, that's not all I found at your house."

Billy released a nervous laugh. "Glad you were lucky, then." He pulled the drill from the box then headed down the walk.

"Hey, what do you want me to do?"

Billy grunted and smirked. "Ask Pop. He's got some ideas."

Vince liked this plan. At least Lew was willing to teach him. Vince caught the man as he walked past, carrying a two-by-four. "Billy says you have a job for me."

A slow grin grew. "Yep." He dropped the wood.

"Is it the fence? I'm getting better at fences."

"Nope." Lew threw an arm around him and led him inside the house. "You know how you made the speech at church about how we're all different parts of the body? You know, different gifts working together?"

"You were there?"

He nodded. "Way in the back ... in case I snored."

Vince gave him the evil eye.

"You sure know how to work an audience, Preacher Boy."

"Thanks, Lew."

"That would definitely be your gift."

"Okaaay."

Lew caught his gaze. "But buildin' stuff ain't."

Vince stilled.

"And frankly, we don't have the manpower to take you to the emergency room today."

Vince gestured to the busy workers all over the house. "So what am I supposed to do here? Stand on a table and give a sermon?"

Lew's heavy-lidded grin sent a chill through Vince. "Nope. Got another project for you." He reached behind to extract something from his back pocket and thrust it in Vince's face.

A toilet brush.

"You want me to scrub the toilet?"

He nodded. "And the sink. The tub. The floor needs a good work over too."

Vince pressed his lips.

"You too country club to scrub toilets?" His eyebrow rose. "Didn't that Jesus of yours wash feet?"

What other sermons had Lew snuck into?

Vince grabbed the brush and headed toward the bathroom.

"I'll come by this week and help you with your deck. Maybe give you some pointers."

"You'd do that?"

It was almost a full smile on the former racer's face. "Yep. Already loaded Emergency on speed dial."

~*~

Cassandra parked near the Crenshaw's house, dropped her head back, and rested her eyes. This news would change everything, and she was unsure she could deliver it to Vince without a shaky voice.

Was he ready to hear the truth? Cassandra had spotted the envelope this morning as she plodded through the stack of mail that had piled up over the last week. Who could care about junk mail and bills when one's daughter had been abducted? Even Tibo's therapies had been delayed. She had forgotten all about the genetic testing until many days passed after Sophie had come home. She'd just wanted to revel in her daughter's presence, but worried this news could take her away again.

When Vince had shown up offering to drive them all to the work-day event, Cassandra had jumped at the opportunity to let him take the kids so she could open the envelope alone. Now, she couldn't put off the inevitable. If she didn't tell him today, she'd never find her voice.

I've got this.

God's reminder filled her soul. Hadn't she learned over the past week His will is perfect. Still, she knew it wasn't always easy … but His will was *always* good.

Entering the house, she looked around. "Is Vince here?"

Some guy chuckled. "Bathroom."

"Oh." She clutched the envelope folded neatly in her shorts pocket.

"He's not using it. He's cleaning it." The guy pointed down the hall.

Cassandra followed the direction. As she stepped past a couple bedrooms she heard the humming. *He Loves Us.* Good song. It came from behind a cracked-open door.

Pushing it wider, she spotted Vince on hands and knees scrubbing the floor as though around the throne of grace, rather than a porcelain one.

He startled. "Cass."

She pulled the envelope from her pocket then thrust it out

to him.

His hands shook as he took it from her and scanned the return address. "What's it say? Is she mine?"

Tears burned her eyes. How she could wish Sophie to be the daughter of Vince Steegle, she did not know. She shook her head.

He stood and wilted at the same time.

"She's not your daughter."

He placed the envelope on the sink. "But I want her to be."

Cassandra sniffed hard. "We don't always get what we want."

Vince's hands were slippery wet when he took both of hers. "You don't understand, Cass." His eyes seared into hers. "I *still* want her to be."

"And how do you plan to make that happen?" Had he grown that attached to a child not his own?

He stepped closer, the scent of pine and musk mingled around her. "I hope to marry her mother."

Could he feel her pulse in his grip at her wrists? "You'd marry me just to be Sophie's dad?"

He wiped a palm on his shorts then pulled a stray curl around her ear as his eyes took in every inch of her face. "For a woman so capable, Cass, you can be really dense."

His smirk infuriated her. "What's that supposed to mean?"

He pulled her into him. "It means I want to be your husband—Tibo and Sophie are gravy." He kissed her forehead, her nose, her mouth.

She closed her eyes and whispered against his lips. "Gravy?"

"Mm-hm." His mouth trailed her jawline up to her ear, his voice low. "I mean, I like gravy and all, but—"

"Whoa! What's hap'nin' in here, *Pastor*?" Billy's eyebrows arced as he glanced between the two.

Cassandra pushed at Vince, but he pulled her closer. "Just askin' a girl to marry me. Is that okay with you, *son*?"

"You two gettin' hitched?" Billy's fu-man-chu stretched

wide at his cheeks.

Cassandra gasped. Did he have to say it so loud? The whole house would hear.

Vince looked into Cassandra's face. "She hasn't answered me, yet."

Billy stepped into the bathroom, eyes wild with anticipation. "Well?"

Cassandra felt like little bubbles tickled up through her as she looked between the two best-buds. Both wore the same lines on their foreheads.

Finally Billy made an emphatic questioning gesture with his hands while Vince seemed to hold his breath.

She tilted her eyes to meet Vince's startling blues. "I think I will."

Vince's body sagged relief while Billy whooped and hollered. "Hey, everyone," he yelled out the bathroom door. "Vince and Cassandra are gettin' married!"

Cheers, whistles and claps followed.

Billy ran down the hall, his voice carrying the announcement in every corner of the house. Eventually, it floated outside to an ebullient crowd.

Ayo's face peeked into the bathroom. "Congratulations, my man."

Sophie pushed past the youth pastor then hugged them together, bouncing up and down. "I'm so happy!"

Tibo trotted behind, stretching his arms to include as much family as he could.

Vince tossled his hair and squeezed them all back. "Me too, Sophie."

Cassandra couldn't resist. "Me three."

Tibo's smile sparkled in his eyes as he looked up. "Four."

They all laughed as one.

Epilogue

Dear Diary,

It's been a while since I've written you, but boy do I need to put some things on paper. Maybe it will help me figure them out.

I now understand the meaning of the dream—the one with the beasts trying to carry me away. God was preparing me for a battle that would use me as its pawn. I was neither loser nor victor—not a soldier for either side. Just a girl in the middle as God made Himself known through those who rescued me.

I am okay with that, because I know the good that came from it. I guess Romans 8:28 is true—"And we know that in all things God works for the good of those who love him, who have been called according to his purpose." God even made use of Pastor Vince's criminal past. How crazy is that?

I met some of his old friends this week in church. They said they were there to meet "the girl who caused all the fuss," but I think it was more. They had that look in their eyes that reminded me of someone tasting a rich dessert for the very first time. Like they'd just discovered they'd been denying themselves the indulgence far too long. I wonder if the tax collectors and sinners of Jesus' day looked the same way.

When I sobbed my account of how Sky deceived and kidnapped me, and the conversations we had in that dark, smelly basement, Mom said she believed the story was not over, and my role had been critical—for Sky.

I don't see it. I don't think I even want to. He is a liar and a thief. And I will never trust him again. I told him I forgave him—because I know God wants me to—but do I really? I don't have the answer to that. I don't know that I ever will. They say we must forgive and forget. One thing is for sure—I will always remember.

I know what my father would do ... he would act as though he forgave until his heart finally caught up. Even now, I taste the bitterness on my tongue thinking about doing such a thing. So ... I will pray about it.

Thoughts of my father prompt another question. Was he really my dad? I mean biologically?

And what about Pastor Vince? Should I even call him that? After all, he's going to marry my mom ... and I suspect ...

I can't even write the words. I don't know what to hope. I'd love for him to be my dad—even my real dad—but would that be a slight to the man who'd raised me? I can't bear the thought of someone replacing him, and at the same time I long for Pastor Vince to fill that void.

Is that wrong?

I don't know, but I do wish he and Mom would finally tell me the truth!

Until then, I'll meditate on the verse Amit quoted to me the other day. Proverbs 10:25, "When the storm has swept by, the wicked are gone, but the righteous stand firm forever."

Sophie

THE END

Dear Reader,

I hope you enjoyed Vince and Cass's story. As you can see, there are still questions that need to be answered, and wisdom that needs to unfold. I hope to discover them soon.

Until then, feel free to check out my author site

www.ConnieAlmony.com and sign up for the newsletter. I offer scenes between novels to newsletter recipients, and will be sending out fun *Shorts* until my next novel is out.

If you haven't tried my other books, check out the following pages to see what else is available now. There is also a list of questions for book clubs to use.

If you like either this or any of my other stories, don't forget to review them on Amazon. This helps me to know what works for you, and helps others find the book as well. A win-win!

Until then, God bless!

Love,

Connie Almony

About the Author

Connie Almony is trained as a mental health therapist and likes to mix a little fun with the serious stuff of life. She was a 2012 semi-finalist in the Genesis Contest for Women's Fiction and was awarded an Honorable Mention in the Winter 2012 WOW Flash Fiction Contest. She is also the author of *One Among Men* and *An Insignificant Life*, about women who run dormitories at a major state university, and *At the Edge of a Dark Forest,* a modern-day re-telling of *Beauty and the Beast* about a war-vet, amputee struggling with PTSD. Watch out for more books in each of these series, as well as a multi-author book anthology coming Summer 2016.

You can find Connie on the web at ConnieAlmony.com, where you can sign up for her newsletter, and hosting the following blogs: InfiniteCharacters.com and IndieChristianFictionSearch.Blogspot.com.

You can also meet her at these social media outlets:

https://twitter.com/ConnieAlmony

https://www.facebook.com/ConnieAlmony

http://www.pinterest.com/conniealmony/

Other Books by Connie Almony

Available NOW!

One Among Men (The Maryland State University Series, Book 1)—December 2014

Samantha Hart's job requires she live with 500, hard-partying, college guys, but it only takes one to lead her to danger. She must avert the pitfalls of a woman in her position running an all-male dorm, as well as the dangerous forces that threaten her life.

Chris Johnson, a rock guitarist, has come back to school as a music major, and finds himself in a business relationship with the ruthless supplier of an on-campus drug ring. He's intrigued by the lady RD who lives and works by her faith, while learning more about his musical gift and the God who gave it to him. Can he manage his two worlds without risking Samantha's life?

An Insignificant Life (The Maryland State University Series, Book 2) —June 2015

She is drawn to those who might bring meaning to her world, only to find her past choices could have destroyed the one man who would truly love her.

Tiffany Lundgren is looking for significance in the world of academia, beyond being a visual distraction for men to ogle. But something stands in her way. When she removes the impediment that threatens her professional career, her world spirals deeper, and she discovers the things she once believed brought her strength, have only hardened her on the outside, leaving her insides empty.

Adam Grant, the K-9 campus police officer, wants to be taken seriously in his profession. But after having been purposely left out of the previous undercover investigation, he wonders if his new relationship with the liaison from the Maryland Drug Task Force Initiative will be an open one. Especially since he once tried to date the man's wife. But as the drug trade heats up in the dorms, and lives are being threatened, Adam resolves to get to the bottom of the problem, even to the point of involving his former-drug-dealing pastor.

Will his deeper commitment endanger the woman he's come to love?

At the Edge of a Dark Forest—February 2014

Cole Harrison, an Iraq war veteran, wears his disfigurement like a barrier to those who might love him, shielding them from the ugliness inside. He agrees to try and potentially invest in, a prototype prosthetic with the goal of saving a hopeless man's dreams.

Carly Rose contracts to live with Cole and train him to use his new limbs, only to discover the darkness that wars against the man he could become.

At the Edge of a Dark Forest is a modern-day retelling of *Beauty and the Beast*. Only it is not *her* love that will make him whole.

(Sample below)

At the Edge of a Dark Forest

Chapter One

Cole hobbled up the snow-covered path, his metal crutch doing the work of his missing left leg. He turned to climb the wooded hill to his favorite perch for one last look. Knowing it would take five times as long as it did when he was a kid—having two arms and two legs back then—he scrambled up the frozen incline, using his right arm stump and dragging the crutch along beside him. He'd been a Marine. He'd do this or die.

In fact, he was counting on the latter.

Cole could never take his own life. Somehow, the thought of his remaining manor staff finding his body didn't set well with him. Most of them had been on the payroll since before he was born and were more family than his own parents had been. No, he wouldn't leave his remains for them. But maybe he could challenge God—or at least the elements—enough to where one or the other would finally do the deed.

Was that what drove him to this climb during a blizzard in freezing temps? He'd told Mrs. Rivera, the housekeeper, he needed to go camping—a necessary means of transitioning from war to civilian life. Regardless of the fact he'd been transitioning for years now, and hadn't bothered to pack any gear.

She knew not to stop him. Not that she couldn't, given his current condition. But had she done that, it would have left him feeling more impotent than he did now. He suspected she knelt by her Baby Jesus statue, at this very moment, rolling beads through her fingers as she mouthed the Hail Mary over and over again.

Lotta good that would do.

Cole's moments "transitioning" only doubled in frequency rather than dwindled. He'd started back when he still wore a prosthetic arm and leg, but after months subjecting them to the cold and rain, night and day, they rubbed against his skin, chafing and burning, making him feel more caged than free. He'd finally chucked them over a precipice one morning, vowing never to wear any fake parts again.

He'd kept that vow. This was who he was. Not just after the

IED, but before. Half a man. He'd always been half a man, scarred and disfigured. Only now his outsides displayed what his insides always suspected. No one knew that better than Beckett. And still Beckett had …

He shook the thought from his mind as he scrambled higher to reach the perch that once made him feel king of the mountain. He could oversee his entire domain—the family's wooded acreage that rose and fell at angles as far as he could see. Now his. Solely his. No one left to share it with—except those he paid.

Today he didn't feel like a king. He made his way up the hill like a slithering beast, rustling through the powdery snow. The thump of the intact limb, then a pulling and dragging of the other through the slush. His body left a trail like a snake. That trail would soon be covered by the precipitation falling unceasingly on this night.

He reached the top and spied the mountain road that meandered far below. A snowplow's headlights traveled its length as it temporarily cleared the ice. No other lights followed. No one dared.

Cole collapsed into the plush snow, face to the emptying black sky. Snowflakes enlarged as they fell from the darkness into his eyes. Maybe his limbs—those left—would go numb before he froze to death. Would it be painful? He didn't know. He'd never experienced these kinds of elements in combat. He'd been more used to the heat—blistering heat. Heat so bad it made his vision blur, waves of air that crinkled ahead of him.

Boom!

He jolted at the vision of the IED bursting into flames. That had been real heat! In one instant Lance Corporal Beckett Forsythe had been beside him. The next—nothing but parts. And Cole had been left missing a few of his own.

Was that sweat dripping down his back in these frigid temps? More droplets formed icicles on his forehead. He struggled to slow his breaths, hoping his heartbeat would do the same. He lay back against the fluffy snow again. It wouldn't take long. The fingers on his left hand were already growing numb. He'd read somewhere people often hallucinated before hypothermia set in. Nothing new.

Crash!

Cole bolted up, wishing the visions weren't so real. But this didn't come with a vision. He looked around, fully aware of the frozen forest beneath his body and the vibration that had emanated with the sound.

He scrambled upright, pulled at his metal crutch, and rose to standing. Down the steep slope of the hill, a gouge in the guardrail opened to a trench through the snow. At the bottom lay a car mangled against a tree—its headlights a beacon to whomever might pass by.

No one would. Not on this night. Many roads had already been closed and only emergency vehicles and snow removal trucks traveled the others.

The only chance the driver had was Cole. Some chance. But Cole would not sit back and do nothing. He had to at least try to help. He couldn't let anyone else die just because he wanted to. Do or die trying. The latter still sounded best, but now he needed the former more.

He slid down the steep hill, using his crutch like a ski pole, guiding his trajectory toward the wreckage. Snow packed in under his jacket, melting into his skin. He shivered out the cold he had previously been inviting.

At the bottom he drove the crutch into the earth and pulled up. Under trees, the snow measured inches rather than feet. He could get to the disabled vehicle and check on the driver.

Flexing the fingers of his left hand, he worked out the numbness and cursed his luck. Why'd this jerk have to come out on *this* night, in *this* storm, on *this* mountain?

He trudged toward the car and peered inside. The driver blinked rapidly, his head swinging around as if coming out of a daze. He banged the deflated airbag at the wheel with his fist.

Cole pulled his wool cap lower against the scars running from his scalp into his face, and knocked on the window. The man jumped and turned, eyes white in their largeness.

"Let me help you."

The man seemed to take long moments to process the words then popped the latch on his door. It squealed and crunched. Cole yanked it open with his good hand against the folded metal at the hinge. It gave.

The man scanned Cole's length, no doubt assessing his missing limbs. His mouth dropped open. "You're …" He slammed his fist against the steering wheel again and released a string of language Cole had only heard on the battlefield.

Yes. Cole was a beast. A slithering, angry beast. Uglier on the inside than on the out.

The man peered into the sky. "Lord! Must you continually remind me of my failings?"

Lord? Did this guy really think God would answer? "You comin' or not?"

The man's jaw jerked. He turned his white-cropped head away from Cole. "Not!"

Was Cole that ugly, that horrifying, the guy would rather die in the cold than trust Cole to bring him to safety?

"Look," Cole almost spit fire, "Your cell won't work up here and nobody'd come for you in this weather if it did." He nodded over his shoulder. "My house is just down a path over there. If we help each other out, we could both get there safely."

The man's brows drew together. Cole could almost feel the guy's gaze travel the length of him again, hovering at the stump below his right elbow and then the left thigh missing everything from what once had been a knee. Was that concern on his face? Cole steeled against the idiot's pity. He turned.

"Wait." The car door creaked as the man pushed it wider. "I'm coming with you."

~*~

Cole poured Irish Cream into his coffee as Mrs. Rivera scurried to prepare hot chocolate and cake for their guest. Henry, the man from the vehicle, sat wordlessly by the fire in the living room, wrapped in a blanket.

Mrs. Rivera eyed Cole's elixir. "You should lay off that poison," she said in her thick Mexican accent that hadn't lessened in the thirty years she'd lived in this country. "It'll keel you."

As if that would discourage him from using it. He took a long draw, the heat of the coffee thawing his body, the burn of the alcohol numbing his mind. He poured more coffee, then topped it off with Irish Cream. Mrs. Rivera tsked.

She rattled ahead of him, tray filled with goodies, to the living room where Henry waited. You'd think Henry was an angel sent by God the way she had attended to him, having made a fire, wrapping him in a blanket and taking out the best china for his impromptu visit to the Mansion.

She placed the tray on a coffee table in front of him and poured hot chocolate from the pitcher. He accepted the cup and glanced to Cole before dropping his gaze to the liquid inside. "Thank you."

"De nada." Did she just curtsey? "Let me know if you need anything else. I will prepare a room for you to stay the night."

Henry nodded and glanced at Cole in the archway between the rooms one more time. Did Henry fear him?

Mrs. Rivera took the coffee from Cole's hand. "Let me get this for you." She placed it on the table in front of Henry as if that were where Cole intended to sit. Hand free now, he grasped the metal crutch and hobbled over. Might as well not be a complete ogre to his uninvited guest—well, begrudgingly invited. Mrs. Rivera disappeared through the hall.

Henry turned to Cole and took him in, unflinchingly this time. His gaze traveled up the lonely leg, took in the right-arm stump, then hit on the scar from his upper lip that carved all the way up his left temple. Cole could almost feel the screech of brakes as the man's eyes halted—no doubt at the ugly etching pooled at the end of the scar on his purposely bald head. "How'd you lose your limbs?" This guy got right to the point.

"Iraq. IED."

Henry drew in a breath. "My younger brother lost his in Nam."

Cole wondered what sort of device did the job, but decided not to ask. "Arm and a leg?"

"Both legs."

"Oh."

Did Henry think they were kindred spirits now? Not! "How old is he?"

"He committed suicide on the five-year anniversary of his return." His brows drew together with a sense of anger and irony. What was he thinking? "I vowed to help others like him." His words were strained. "So they wouldn't feel …"

Cole waited for the rest of his sentence, but it didn't come. In fact, he didn't need it. His own bitterness churned against the lowering censors from the excess alcohol in his coffee. He glared at the man on his chair. "How does one help others like your brother?" His sarcasm grew as did the curl of his lip. "House him. Pamper him. Find jobs he can't do with people willing to make it easier for the

277

crippled guy?"

Henry jolted. Tears hung on the edges of his eyes. "My company developed prosthetic limbs for amputees. At one time, it was the leader in research and development, giving the wounded lives closer to what they'd been before the loss."

Cole sensed more. "And now?"

"I gave control to my two sons when I retired early. They believed it wiser to cut costs than to build lives. They ran the company into the ground, peddling defective products that did more harm than good. They even gave bonuses to prosthetists who pushed inferior products."

Henry shifted, placed his mug on the table, his gaze never rising from it.

"Several months ago, a young veteran died when a seriously defective screw caused him to fall down a steep concrete stairway. Since the news coverage, other complaints have come in which have begun to lead to mass recalls."

Cole's breathing slowed as he took in the guilt that poured from this man's features, his posture, his mind.

Henry stared back. "You must hate people like me who profit from other's loss."

"You profited?"

"My company made me a wealthy man."

"Oh."

"But it will all be lost in the lawsuits, when they find the willful neglect of the higher ups in my company." His laugh was bitter. "My sons." He shook his head. "And I will not fight to keep it."

The story was beginning to come together. "What's your company's name?"

"Rose Prosthetics."

Cole tensed. He'd heard about the accident in the news. The victim was a decorated veteran and the head of a large family. His wife widowed, children orphaned, and all because this man's sons felt it more important to make a larger profit off the backs of the desperate. Bitterness swelled, peaked, then dissipated in one instant at the man's despondency.

Henry eyed Cole. "I can see you know the story."

"I do." Cole finished the coffee, his muscles dragging rather than holding him up. It'd been an exhausting evening, climbing those trails and rescuing Henry. Only now he wasn't so sure if he had been the rescuer? Yes, Cole had brought him to his home, but Henry had lent him his arm most of the trail leading there. He wasn't really sure who'd helped whom more.

Cole stood, leaning heavily on his crutch, wavering with the effects of the drink. "Mrs. Rivera will be down to show you to your room." He turned away.

"Why don't you use prosthetics, Cole?"

Cole stopped. The question stabbed him. The answer was none of this guy's business. Couldn't he see Cole's soul was too ugly to care about? The world should know this now more than ever.

"They could make your life much easier."

"Or kill me." Cole felt the man flinch without even seeing him. He regretted the words.

"Not all products are like what my sons built. We did a lot of good for a lot of people before they destroyed the company." He seemed to search for words. "My daughter is nothing like them. She's developed a new socket design that attaches closer to the bone from the outside. It could dramatically change the maneuverability for amputees who want to remain active. It's simple, but incredibly effective." He sucked in more air. "Only now, no one wants anything to do with the Rose family. She can't get any funding to develop the product. My lack of oversight of what my sons were doing has not only ruined her career, but also the future of a product that could help veterans like yourself."

"That's too bad." Cole couldn't control the self-pity that overtook him. "I'm sure she's as nice as a fairytale princess too." He thumped down the hall to his first-floor apartment and slammed the door.

~*~

Three months later ...

Carly Rose pulled up the long drive to the man's house. The forested lane opened, revealing—

Whoa! That was no house. It was more like a very expensive ski chalet. For hordes of guests. What did one man need with all that space? Carly's family had some money, but this guy must be loaded.

She scanned the circular drive. A young man in jeans and a t-shirt rubbed at the gleaming black limo inside an otherwise empty five-car garage. He leaned back and smiled at the shine he'd elicited.

Carly parked beside the front entrance and tried to blow the stray hair from her face. Soaked from the solid hour she'd just spent in the rain explaining to the roadside-assistance guy how to change her flat tire, the hair wouldn't budge.

Hoping Cole Harrison got the message she'd be late—very late— she glanced in the rearview to find a thick black smudge across her cheek. She rubbed. It held fast to her skin. Well, at least it matched the smears from the tire across her rain coat and blue jeans.

Thank goodness this was only an information session. Cole Harrison had finally agreed to try out her prototype prosthetics. It had taken her father much cajoling of the man over breakfast those many months ago, and repeated phone calls since. Why had Mr. Harrison resisted using prosthetics for so long? And why had he relented now? She shrugged. If he liked them, maybe he'd invest in a new company, giving at least part of the Rose family a chance at redemption.

"Am I okay here?" she called to the guy in the garage as she closed the door to her car.

His head bobbed, swinging his dark hair into his face. "Yup."

She poked the doorbell, straightened the still-damp shirt under her drenched raingear and waited. Her toe tapped with the nervous energy that buzzed through her. She fingered the gold cross at her neck.

A fiftyish woman opened the door. "Come in." She motioned for Carly to take off her coat. The woman called to the young man with a Hispanic lilt to her voice, "Beautiful, Manny. Mr. Cole will be very pleased."

Funny. When talking to her father, Carly got the idea that Cole Harrison was not one to be easily pleased. She'd asked her dad why he thought Mr. Harrison would invest in her designs and he'd answered with a far-away look and said, "I don't know, Carly. What other choices do we have?"

Choices. Was the only choice to start a new company? Did Carly want to run a business? That would mean more time with sales figures and less with clients. She didn't want to end up like her brothers, not caring for the people she served.

"Mr. Harrison will be right with you." The woman never asked Carly's name. He must not get many visitors out here.

Carly's gaze rolled over the expanse of the foyer, down several long halls decorated with gold-framed portraits and ornately carved tables, and into a living room housing couches littered with embroidered throw pillows.

The woman pointed. "Have a seat. Can I get you something to drink?"

Carly might have been soaked on the outside from standing in the rain, but the exertion of changing tires left her parched. "Water."

The woman nodded and hustled away.

Carly took a turn about the living room, running her finger along the mantel above the fireplace, noting the crystal set atop it. Pricey. Her eyes drew up to catch her reflection in the mirror above. Wet, straggly blond hair, wrinkled top, black smudges hither and yon—she looked like a mongrel dog. Or maybe the forest animal the mongrel caught up in his teeth. She chuckled. A step up from the ordinary that usually identified her.

Rhythmic thumping and clanging sounded from behind. It stopped. "You're quite the Beauty."

Carly pivoted to see the source of the sarcasm-laden tone, catching sight of the man missing alternate limbs, leaning on a metal crutch. Dark circles ringed his eyes and a scar split the left side of his closely-shaved head.

His gaze scanned her attire with a smirk. "Your father never mentioned you were so … lovely. A fashion plate."

She stifled a comeback about his own appearance, but chose the higher road. "My father never mentioned you were such a wit."

His eyes widened and his lips almost twisted into something one might call a smile.

"Did you get my message?"

He hobbled closer. "Yes. Something about waiting on roadside assistance to change your tire." His gaze rolled over her. "It appears you didn't wait."

She pulled a packet of papers from her case and sat in an armchair. "How about we get started?"

"Certainly." He dropped into the overstuffed sofa.

"I have a number of questions I need you to answer, forms for you to fill out and I'll need to tour the manor's exercise facilities."

"Of course."

"Once you're fitted with the prosthetics, we'll begin rehab." She organized papers on the coffee table.

"Who'll be doing the fitting?"

"I will."

He stared. Was he looking at her or the wall behind her? His arrogance dripped from him like an oozing sore.

"I assure you, I am skilled both as a prosthetist and a physical therapist. I wanted to know all aspects of my field in order to get my designs right."

"Would you like to see your room?"

Was he even listening to her?

"Yes. As I mentioned, I'd like to tour the manor's exercise rooms. I assume that's where most of the rehab will take place."

"Not for rehab. Your apartment." His eyes were a steely blue, softened only by his thick lashes. It seems those and his eyebrows were the only hair he allowed on his entire head.

"My apartment?" Her heart beat against her chest. What had her father signed her up for? How desperate was he to land this investor?

"Yes, upstairs, where you'll be living for the next several months."

Carly placed the pen atop some papers and fingered her cross necklace.

"Didn't your father mention my expectation that rehab be daily? He said you live two hours away."

Carly thought of the lonely drive up the forested mountain road. She suspected there were few, beyond the wildlife, who actually lived within two hours of this place.

"I won't have you working with me exhausted after a long drive," Cole's eyelids hung as though he were bored, "possibly losing tires along the way."

She took in several cycles of breaths, gauging his expression. Could she trust this man—to live with him—in such a remote location? He was a complete stranger to her. An obviously bitter one. She thought about her father's excitement at the prospect of an interested investor. She knew her father's car hadn't met the tree only because of a storm. He'd gone out looking for death. And this hairless man offered him a chance at life.

Why?

"You'll have several rooms to yourself—a bathroom, kitchenette, patio and office. But I will expect you to eat dinner with me every evening."

Her eyebrows shot up of their own volition. "With my imprisonment here, this is beginning to sound like a dark retelling of a Disney flick."

His blink was heavy. "You mean Beauty and the Beast?"

She shrugged.

His lips curled higher. "I guess that makes me the Beauty."

Insolent man.

His tone grew serious. "I suggested you live here for a number of reasons. First," he ticked off a finger from his intact hand, "you live too far away. Second," he ticked off another finger, "we will need lots of time for rehab sessions. Third," his ring finger joined the others, "I'll want to process how things are going with the product at dinnertime. After all, I may be sinking a load of dough into it eventually."

Carly looked around, wondering how much of that "dough" he'd actually miss.

"And lastly," he placed his hand on the stump of his left leg, "given your family's recent dealings," he hesitated, likely for effect, "you will need to earn my trust."

Her fingers balled. "Earn your trust?" The words came out in force. She almost growled, holding in the names she wanted to heap at him. Maybe she was the beast. But he was right. He had no reason to trust her family and more reason not to. Both as a client and an investor.

She wished she could wash away the stain of what her brothers had done to her father's business. It didn't matter he'd had an impeccable reputation for years. All people would remember is how it ended. She had to change that with something new. Cole Harrison was the means with which to do that.

But would she be safe living under the same roof as him?

He must have read the question on her face. "You may call a locksmith to come and change the locks to all your rooms—my expense."

She speared him with her eyes. Carly never liked people answering the thoughts she hadn't voiced.

"And Mrs. Rivera will be here with you, not to mention the rest of the manor staff."

"Yes, I will." Did Mrs. Rivera appear at his word? She placed a tray with plates of cookies, a soda and a glass of water on the table between them.

She looked harmless enough.

Carly would do anything for her father. Especially after her brothers had destroyed his dream. She needed to rebuild it, even if it meant taking some risks. Someone needed to look out for him. "When do I move in?"

"As soon as you wish."

~*~

Cole liked this woman. She'd taken every inch of him in when she first turned his way, and never flinched. Must be a hazard of the trade—seeing limbless, disfigured wretches on a regular basis.

Not a trace of pity in her eyes. Good. He deserved none. He wasn't the hero.

Carly also had a spark of something else. A hint of spice. Cole liked spice. Too bad spice didn't like him back. Nothing could.

Should he have Jurvis look into her? His man-of-business, who sensed the housing bust months before it happened, had a financial sense none could match. Jurvis could smell a parasite a mile away.

Not necessary. Cole could figure this one out. Either her products worked or they didn't. He'd give her the opportunity to prove herself. Nothing more. Nothing less.

Besides, Carly intrigued him. The only time she'd flinched during their meeting was at the moment he'd mentioned her looks. What had she been thinking? Did it bother her that she was plain? Had her vanity been pierced? He regretted his sarcastic jabs once the totality of them tumbled from his lips. It's what made the men of his Marine unit hate him.

All, but one.

He'd vowed to become more likeable after the IED, but it was too late. His looks had been the only thing that attracted people to him before, especially women. Now his appearance matched what had always been inside—useless flesh.

Acknowledgments

"But seek first his kingdom and his righteousness, and all these things will be given to you as well."—Matthew 6:33 NIV

I call this verse "step one." If you start here, everything else is perfect. So I'll begin by thanking my God. He is the alpha and omega, the beginning and end. The all in all. Without Him, there is nothing good. I like *good,* so I will thank Him for it.

I also want to thank my family, my husband and my kids, who encourage and inspire me as well as put up with all my author idiosyncrasies. I must thank my mom, dad, sisters and their families. This story, in particular, has a lot of loved ones in it. I always say I don't ever want to write Christians doing wonderful things unless I know Christians who've done that wonderful thing. I'm grateful to know many generous people. I cried when I wrote about their extraordinary acts in this novel, knowing the true story of the real generosity.

As always, my critique partners deserve a boatload of thanks as well: Mildred Colvin, Gail Palotta, June Foster, and Vanessa Riley, and my editor, Nadine Brandes. Who knows what kind of gunk I'd be writing if it weren't for the crafting help I get from these skilled wordsmiths. Don't forget to search out all of their novels.

For my last novel, *An Insignificant Life,* I gathered a wonderful Launch Team to help me spread the word about my books: Chris Granville, Noela Nancarrow, Dana Michael, Robin Bunting, Jen Smindak, Susan Snodgrass, Sherry Hoover, Ann Ellison, Rachel Trautmiller, and Cami Pernell (and those who want to remain anonymous). I want to thank you all for your tireless efforts in making these novels known. It has been wonderful getting to know each of you a little better every day.

Thank you to the wonderful young woman who has contributed visual details to the last two covers—Jordan Almony. I hope to see more of your artwork in future covers.

David Crowder was the muse for this one—particularly the CD *Church Music.* Something about this band seemed to encapsulate the feel of a "redneck church" pastored by a former country clubber ...

not to mention the unusual friendship of Vince and Billy, whose joint love for Christ surpassed any other thing that would usually divide them.

Lastly, I want to give a shout out to the Young Life ministry for teens with special needs, called Capernaum. Our local group is led by the awesome duo, Kelly and Kristin Caprarola. This ministry has brought great joy to those often neglected by the rest of the world (and sometimes, even the church). A portion of the current sales of *Flee from Evil* will go to this wonderful ministry.

Reading Group Questions

1. One of the themes in *Flee from Evil* is about forgiveness. I wanted to write about real people who knew what God wanted them to do, and yet struggled with forgiving at the same time. Have you ever had a hard time forgiving someone? What happened that helped you forgive?

2. Another theme in this story is about how God can turn any evil into good (Romans 8:28)—not just what happens *to* you, but even the bad things you've done. Share how God has used bad things for His glory in *your* life.

3. As is mentioned in the Acknowledgments, I never like to show Christians doing extraordinary things unless I *know* Christians who've done those extraordinary things. This rule keeps me from painting Christians in a seemingly unrealistic light—making them out to be better than they really are. However, though the world may ignore these things, Christians are impacting many lives for the good. Share some examples of people in your life who have awed you with their generosity.

4. Vince and Cassandra have a conversation about whether or not all people are redeemable. Vince says the Holy Spirit sometimes tells us to avoid some, and guide those He gives us to guide. Can you think of examples of each of these ideas in your life?

5. What did you think of Vince's friendship with Billy? How do you think two men can be such close friends even though they are so different?

6. When Kat shares her husband's previous struggles with drugs, she says sharing her story of brokenness can help others, because Jesus meets us in our brokenness. What do you think of that statement?

7. Do you know anyone with special needs or a family dealing with disability? Has God revealed their gifting to you? If so, please share.

8. Do you think your church needs to do more for those with special needs and their families.

9.   How has God met *you* in your brokenness?

10.   Sophie wonders if she has really forgiven Sky. What do you think biblical forgiveness *really* looks like?